Organizer Backup

Luella Linley
License
to
Meddle

BOOK 1

MEREDITH RESCE

Organized Backup

Book 1 Luella Linley – License to Meddle

Golden Grain Publishing

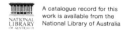

PO Box 880 Unley SA 5061

The National Library of Australia Cataloguing-in-Publication Information:

A catalogue record for this work is available from the National Library of Australia

978-0-6489537-0-8 – Paperback
978-0-6489537-1-5 – eBook

Cover Design: Jessica Resce and David Resce

Regency romance author, Luella Linley, arranges her characters' lives, making sure that they weather all storms and live happily-ever-after. Her characters are putty in her hands, but her 21st Century adult children are not so easily organized. When her daughter, Megan, asks for support with an inappropriate situation at work, Luella decides Megan should get a boyfriend to intimidate her boss. The cop who just pulled Luella over for speeding is a likely candidate.

Cam Fletcher is expecting to be interviewed by a famous author. Instead of sharing insights into his job working in the police force, he is sharing a meal with the famous author and her daughter, Megan. When left alone with Megan, Cam wonders when the interview will begin. The parents' extended absence gives him a clue, which Megan confirms. Luella Linley is playing matchmaker, but is he willing to play the game?

Endorsements

"Get ready for some fun in this story that blends truth and fiction, love and grace-filled faith, with laugh out loud moments and drama that meant I read this in one sitting."

Carolyn Miller, bestselling author of the Regency Brides series

Regency romance author Luella Linley has the best of intentions … and can't understand why her children don't appreciate her talent for matchmaking. A fake engagement, a daughter in trouble, and a handsome policeman playing the hero—what could possibly go wrong? This funny and charming romantic comedy from Meredith Resce, that also touches on the more serious issues of faith and workplace relations, will put a smile on your face and give you food for thought. Highly recommended.

Narelle Atkins, author of 'Solo Tu'

"Readers of Christian fiction, both modern and of the 'bonnet' variety will enjoy Organized Backup. Meredith Resce writes delightful characters, crisp dialogue and enough twists to keep you guessing. Faith is real in her books, and well displayed."

Cecily Anne Paterson writes 'braveheart' fiction for young teen girls and teaches memoir writing at the Red Lounge for Writers.

"If you love fake relationships and strapping Aussie policemen, then check out this book!"

Jessica Kate, author of 'Love and Other Mistakes'

A note for non-Australian readers: Thank you for deciding to read 'Organized Backup'. I have set this novel in Adelaide, South Australia, and wrestled with the idea of whether I should adapt language and measurements to that usually understood by North American readers. In the end, though I have changed the spelling from Australian to US, I have retained the local Australian language. I hope you enjoy the local Aussie flavor. Below is a glossary of terms you may encounter that you may find unfamiliar.

Glossary of terms:

Mobile phone - cell phone

Hyacinth Bucket – a pedantic, pretentious main character from British Comedy *Keeping Up Appearances*. Famous for her candle-light suppers and soirees.

AFL – Australian Football League. A code of football called Aussie Rules.

SAPOL – South Australian Police

Boot of the car – trunk

Tradie – a universal name for brickies (bricklayer), chippies (carpenter), sparkies (electrician) or other people who work in the building and construction industry

Meal times – different states and regions in Australia give meals different names. Tea is often the name given to the evening meal. Sometimes it is called dinner.

Chips – like the British, Australians will eat fish and chips—fries that are thick-cut

Batching – the term applied to single men who fend for themselves domestically

Bins – trash cans. In Australia we have wheelie bins with different colored lids for different types of rubbish (trash).

Units and flats – another name for apartments

Soft drink – soda or coke

Holidays – vacation. We have summer holidays over Christmas and New Year. Workers can take holidays as annual leave at any time of the year.

Tim Tams – Australia's most exportable chocolate biscuit (and by biscuit, I mean cookie).

Safe Work SA - SafeWork SA is responsible for providing work health and safety, public safety and state-based industrial relations services across South Australia.

Ambos – paramedics or EMT workers

A and E – Accident and Emergency or emergency room

Chapter One

"Mum, are you sure this is how you want to start your book?"

Louise stopped typing and glanced over her shoulder at Megan.

"I wish you wouldn't read my work until it's finished." Louise pressed save on her latest Luella Linley Regency romance and closed the laptop. "Now, what is it you want?"

"I just don't think you should start your story with your villain attacking your heroine."

Really? Louise spun her office chair around, forcing her daughter to step back. "Could you give me a chance to establish the story, Megan, before you give your professional advice?"

"I'm not sure I would want to read a story that starts out like that."

"Don't you worry. Our hero was just about to burst onto the scene. Besides, isn't this how life is sometimes?"

Megan sighed and flopped down into the tub chair that was next to her mother's desk.

"You see." Louise pointed at her daughter. "You've got a villain in your life giving you grief."

"Don't remind me, please."

"And at any moment, a hero is likely to burst in and take him to task."

"Mother. There is a significant difference between your romance novels and my real-life stress at work. You do understand the concept of fiction."

Louise stood up and held her hand out to pull her daughter out of the chair. "I understand the difference, but there's nothing wrong with hoping for a romantic solution to my daughter's dramas."

Megan laughed. "Hope away, Mother. I wish you luck."

"Really?"

"No! Of course not. I have a real workplace problem, and I need a professional workplace solution."

"Well, if I can help—"

"You can supply me with tea and cake and a listening ear. That is all I need for the moment."

Perhaps. But there were always possibilities, and Louise was willing to be on the lookout should one happen by.

* * *

Megan's skin crawled as Shane placed his hand on her shoulder. She wanted to duck her shoulder and move away from his touch but didn't. Was she being too sensitive, reading something into his action that wasn't there?

"Have you managed to sort out those outstanding accounts?" Shane asked.

"Yes, and I've got the sales reports ready." Megan sat forward in her chair, and Shane's hand fell away. Thank goodness. He gave her the creeps.

"What about those stock orders? When are they due to be delivered to the warehouse?"

"I was on the phone to the shipping company this morning, and your container has cleared customs. They should be in the warehouse today or tomorrow."

"Can you get—"

"The warehouse staff have all the orders and will get stock delivered to retailers the minute the crates are opened."

He was still standing there. Megan gritted her teeth, half expecting him to put his hand on her shoulder again.

"Since you're up-to-date, what about we go out for lunch?"

Not on your life! "I can't. I've got to sort out the Work Safe procedure notes and organize a meeting for all sales staff."

"Government regulations can wait, Megan. I think we could find better things to do than fuss over safety procedures."

What a sleaze. Or at least, it sounded like sleaze. Megan shuddered.

"I assume you'll be asking Sue and the kids to our staff dinner?" Bring up the wife. Try and distract him.

"Sue has gone to her mother's. I wouldn't count on seeing her anytime soon."

"What? Is everything all right?" Megan spun her chair around to face him.

"Everything's perfect. I can go home and not have to put up with her nagging and stress."

"Shane! Are you and Sue all right? You know, together, as a couple?"

"She's asking for a divorce."

"I'm so sorry." Boy, was she sorry. Sue was her last buffer against Shane, the husband with a wandering eye turned boss with wandering hands.

Shane shrugged and smiled—or was that a leer? Megan shivered as he leaned in and placed his mouth close to her ear.

"My house is all my own at the moment. If you'd like to come by, I'd be happy to take all the sympathy you can give."

Megan stood up, her office chair rolling back and hitting the filing cabinet with a metallic clang. He was crowding her workstation so she pushed past and walked to the small kitchen area. "I won't be coming to your place, Shane, now or ever. I would prefer you didn't ask me again."

Why was he following her? She pasted on her most determined look and turned around to stare him down. He stopped. *Thank you, Lord.* He was still smiling, which was highly inappropriate given he'd just announced his marriage was over. Then he allowed his eyebrows to suggest outrageous things. Why did she have to be polite and look at the man when she was speaking to him?

"If you don't mind, I'm going to make a coffee. I'll bring yours to your office in a moment."

Was he going to back down? Megan reached deep for the courage to maintain her authoritative stance.

"Coffee will be great. Bring yours in with you and we can chat over the break."

Not likely. Megan let out the breath she'd been holding as he returned to his office. She turned on the kettle and took out her mobile phone. She scrolled through favorite contacts and pressed her mother's number. How desperate was she that she needed to call her mother for help? This situation was impossible.

"Megan, are you OK?"

"My boss is being a sleaze again," she said in a low tone, watching Shane through his office window. "Worse than usual."

"Again? Shouldn't you contact someone? Make a complaint?"

"Who? The guidelines suggest a complaint of sexual harassment should be directed to the HR manager."

"Well call the HR manager. Straight away."

"We don't have one. All HR responsibility is part of my portfolio."

"Surely there's someone else you could go to."

"Like the boss of the company?"

"Shane."

"Exactly. He gives me the creeps."

"What you need is a boyfriend to come around and show a bit of strength. Rattle Shane's cage."

"Mum, please. I don't need a boyfriend posturing around the place. I need a job where the boss shows respect, understands boundaries and doesn't think he's God's gift to women."

"Have you been looking?"

"Every. Day. But I can't give my notice here until I find something that pays the same or better."

"You can come back home."

"I just moved out. I'm a new homeowner with a thumping great mortgage, remember? I can't tell Shane to get lost until I have another source of income."

"Well, I can only suggest you get a boyfriend—"

"Mum!"

"Or move back home."

"Neither of those things is an option. We discussed this last week. I need to get a new job."

"You need to make it clear you don't think his actions are appropriate. Threaten him with legal action or something." It sounded so simple when Mum said it in her no-nonsense tone. If only.

"I wish I could. I'm not sure my story would hold any weight if I brought it to a lawyer."

"Why not?"

"It's just innuendo and the occasional touch."

"Megan! You call the cops if he touches you again!"

"And tell them what? He placed his hand on my shoulder? I don't think that's an indictable offense."

"I have an idea. Give me a couple of days and I think we'll be able to sort out your boss and his inappropriate behavior."

"Mum. Please. I just need you to listen. I don't need you to interfere."

"I'm your mother, and this man needs to be dealt with. You just leave it to me."

Megan disconnected the call. What could be worse than having Shane schmoozing all over her? It depended on what her mother had in mind. Given Mum made a living from creating conflicts and resolutions, nothing was out of the realms of possibility—for her. Megan would have to wait and see. In the meantime, she'd be scouring the employment websites.

* * *

Josiah shivered in the cold as he dismounted from his horse and draped the reins over the low-hanging branch of a willow tree. The mist hung over the lake, and the birds were still, following their predawn cacophony, as if they sensed the mounting tension. Lord Osmond was already pacing the area in front of the lake, and the ominous silence added to Josiah's anxiety. Was it too late to back out?

"Are you ready, my lord?"

Josiah's valet stood behind him, holding the wooden case containing the duelling pistols.

"Can we ever be ready for a moment such as this?" Josiah asked. "But what choice do I have?"

"Walk away, my lord. No one will think any the less of you for it."

"I will think the less of me." His honor was at stake. More importantly, Lady Rosalie's reputation was at stake. "After the way Osmond

has treated Lady Rosalie, I would not be able to bear my image in the looking glass again if I did not face him down this morning."

He untied his heavy cape and flung it over his valet's arm. But what were those thundering hooves? And the flashing blue and red lights? A siren. The police.

The police? The police! Louise Brooker checked her dashboard. She was driving way over the speed limit. Josiah's tension leading up to this deadly duel had caught her imagination, and she had got lost in Regency England, forgetting small matters like speed limits and leaving the freeway two exits earlier.

How humiliating, being pulled over to the side of the freeway. Louise pressed the window button and turned her sweetest smile on the officer as he leaned down to face her. Oh, my goodness. He would make a perfect Lord Josiah—a tall strapping fellow who wore his uniform and weaponry with ease. Yes, he would sort the evil Lord Osmond out in no time at all.

"Do you have any reason why you were traveling twenty kilometers per hour over the speed limit?" Constable Perfect asked her.

"I do apologize," Louise said. "There is a matter of two young men about to kill each other and I was rather caught up in how that was going to turn out."

"I beg your pardon?"

Constable Perfect's eyes shifted as he surveyed the back seat of Louise's car.

"Not in real life," she said. "In my imagination."

The policeman frowned and took out his ticket book.

"I need to see your driver's license," he said.

"Oh, of course." Louise leaned over to her purse and fumbled about until she had worked the small plastic card out of the wallet pocket.

"Mrs. Brooker." He took the license from her and began to write some details down. "You do realize that the speed limit along this stretch is a generous one hundred kilometers per hour and you were traveling a hundred and twenty?"

"Goodness! Really? That fast?"

He continued to write. He was left-handed and his ring finger was bare. No wife! *Thank you, Lord.* More perfect by the moment.

"Where are you stationed?" Louise asked.

The constable didn't answer.

"I'd like to contact your superior, if I may."

"Why? You were clearly over the limit."

"Oh, no, nothing like that, Constable Fletcher." She could see his ID badge now. "I would like to contact him on another matter altogether. Are you stationed in the southern areas police station?"

"I am, Mrs. Brooker, but I assure you, this ticket will still have to be paid."

"Of course. What's your first name?"

"Beg yours?"

"Name? What is your name?"

"Senior Constable Cameron Fletcher. If you wish to make a complaint, you should address the senior sergeant on duty."

"Oh no! No complaint. You've done a wonderful job. Thank you so much."

Louise put her finger on the button to put the window up again.

"You'll need to take this ticket, Mrs. Brooker." Constable Fletcher waved the paper at her and she was forced to lower the window again.

"Oh, yes. Of course. I hope to see you soon."

Louise pulled the car back into the flow of freeway traffic. Josiah and Osmond would keep for the moment. Constable Fletcher presented a whole new set of possibilities to be considered.

* * *

It wasn't until the next day, when Cam Fletcher opened his inbox to find an email with a letterhead in fancy calligraphic font, that he remembered the odd encounter. Luella Linley, author. Was this the strange woman he'd pulled over yesterday? He kept reading and the clues clicked into place. Now the line about the two young men about to kill each other made sense.

> *Dear Senior Constable Fletcher,*

> *It was lovely to meet you yesterday. You handled yourself professionally, and I felt quite ashamed of myself for traveling so far over the speed limit. I was caught up thinking about a dramatic plot for my new novel and lost concentration.*

> *I am an author, you see. Having met you yesterday, I was wondering if I might organize an interview with you. I often interview professionals for research for my novels. Please let me know if you would be available to help me with my new project. I would be pleased to have you over for dinner.*

> *Yours sincerely,*

> *Luella Linley*

He'd written a ticket out for Mrs. Brooker and walked away from the encounter feeling like he'd been the one pulled over and interrogated. So this inquisitive driver was Luella Linley. Cam closed the email and opened the search engine just to confirm. Yep. There was a large studio photograph of the woman he'd pulled over for speeding. She apparently wrote under a pen name. He browsed her website and saw she had a plethora of novels on the market, with books available through all the major bookstores.

And she'd asked him to dinner. Was that appropriate? Best ask his boss before getting himself in too deep.

"You into romance novels now?"

Cam was startled by his colleague's question.

"Thanks for reading over my shoulder," Cam replied. "Very professional."

"Sorry." Constable Joel Baker pulled out the chair at the next desk and sat down next to Cam. "I need the name of that psych you were seeing."

"He was a counselor. What do you need a psych for?"

"Just family stuff, you know. Lilly's sister is …"

Cam held up his hand. "You don't need to tell me if it's private." He opened another search tab and typed in the name of his counselor. When it came up, he copied the contact details and pasted them into an email.

When Joel's phone pinged, he opened it. "Thanks, man." He stood up. "So you'd tell me if anything was up, wouldn't you?"

"What makes you think anything's up?"

"Looking up romance writers—it's not your usual style."

"It's completely professional. I gave her a speeding ticket yesterday."

"Right."

Was Joel smirking?

"She's famous, if you must know!" Cam called after Joel's retreating figure.

* * *

Cam was getting used to coming home to the house he'd grown up in. He'd decided to give up his rental when his dad had required palliative care and had stayed on after his father's death. Inhaling the aroma of something cooking, he decided that living with his mum had distinct advantages.

"Mum, have you heard of a writer by the name of Luella Linley?" Cam sat at the kitchen table with a cup of coffee, watching his mother prepare dinner.

"Luella Linley!" His mother put her potato peeler down on the sink and turned to face him. "I have a whole shelf devoted to her titles and have her next book on pre-order."

"Really?"

"She's one of my favorite authors."

"She invited me to dinner."

"How did you meet Luella Linley?" Mum took a seat opposite him at the table, vegetables forgotten.

"I pulled her over for speeding."

"Oh, Cam, you didn't."

"She was doing a hundred and twenty. It's my job."

"Yes, but Luella Linley. She's such a good author, and so popular."

"And she was driving too fast."

"She asked you to dinner? Is she trying to bribe her way out of the ticket?"

"Hardly. I'm not open to bribery and corruption."

"Well, I hope you go. I'll go if you won't. I'd love to talk to her. Her books are amazing." She was as eager as a teenage groupie.

"She says she wants to interview me for a new project."

Mum frowned.

"What? Don't you think my job is interesting enough to supply her with the information she needs?"

"It's not that," she said. "Luella Linley writes romance."

"I guessed that much." Famous or not, romance wasn't his thing.

"Regency romance, to be specific."

"What's Regency romance?"

"Does the name Mr Darcy ring any bells?"

He'd heard the name before but couldn't think where.

"Pride and Prejudice? Jane Austen?"

Aha! His mother's great obsession. BBC period drama series—his cue to go to the gym.

Now *he* frowned. He hadn't ever sat through so much as half an episode, but what he'd seen on screen before he could escape was enough to know. "Why would she want to interview me? I don't think a 21st Century cop is likely to pop up in a British historical drama."

"I'm sure I don't know." Mum went back to peeling her potatoes. "I hope you'll go though. I'll send along my set of her novels. See if you can get her to sign them for me."

Chapter Two

What a day. Dodging Shane and still keeping up her work responsibilities had consumed most of her mental energy, and Megan was glad her mother had invited her to dinner. At least she didn't have to think about what to eat. Megan fumbled with the front door key of her parent's home. She probably should return it since she was pretending to be a financially independent and responsible homeowner. But Shane was breathing down her neck at work—literally—and she needed the reassurance that she could run home to her parents if things became unbearable.

"Hey, Dad." Megan leaned on the door jamb of her father's office, second door off to the left after she entered. Dad pointed to the phone he held against his ear and mouthed 'hello'. He hadn't finished his work day yet. At least he didn't have far to travel after work, since he worked from home.

"Is that you, Megan?" Mum called from the kitchen.

"What're you cooking? It smells divine."

"I'm experimenting," Mum said. "One of those Jamie Oliver easy meals, with a Luella Linley twist."

"Experiment away." Megan came into the kitchen. "I hardly have time to think about cooking now I'm in charge of my own kitchen." She lifted the lid from the casserole dish and inhaled the savory aroma.

"Are Pete and Rianne coming as well?" she asked.

"No. Your brother is off spending as much time as possible with Rianne before she leaves."

"She's still going to Europe, then? I thought she'd stay now they're engaged."

"Don't ask me." Mum raised her hands as if in surrender. "I give up on your brother and his girlfriends."

"He's only had two, Mum. You're being dramatic."

"Yes, well, I would've thought he'd have married one of them by this time, and now Rianne is going off on an extended study exchange."

"Well, you've cooked heaps. Is Chloe coming?"

"No, Chloe's still interstate and won't be back until next week."

"I can't wait for her to get back. I've missed her. That's the last time I'm letting her go away to study."

Mum smiled. "You have that much influence over your sister, do you?"

"It's all very well she wants to further her nursing qualifications, but she could have done that here in one of the Adelaide hospitals, surely."

"I'll let you take that up with her when she gets back." Mum put the casserole dish back in the oven.

"So if Pete's not coming and Chloe's not coming, why have you cooked so much food?"

"I have invited someone else for dinner."

"Who?" Mum busied herself with mixing some sort of gravy. Even from behind, she had that guilty look. "Mum. Who have you invited? You knew I was coming around for dinner tonight."

"No one you need to worry about." Mum clapped the lid back onto the saucepan. "Just someone who's going to help me with an interview for my writing."

A Jane Austen scholar? A history professor? A Regency expert? They were sure to be old and bookish. Her mother's stories appealed to a specific audience, not Megan's demographic.

"Would you mind setting the table in the dining room?" Mum asked. "Just the four of us tonight."

Megan went to the dining room sideboard. If their expected guest was one of the Regency crowd, she'd use the embroidered table-cloth, the silver cutlery and candelabra, and her mother's rosebud formal china. She wasn't the daughter of an avid Regency fanatic for nothing. She knew how the game was played.

The doorbell rang as she finished setting the table in a manner that would have made Hyacinth Bucket proud.

"I'll get it!" Dad called from the study.

"Shouldn't you meet your guest, since they've come for your interview?" Megan filled the water jug from the filter tap.

"No, I think your father will be the best one to welcome Senior Constable Fletcher."

"A policeman? Wow! How are you going to work that into your story?"

Before Mum could answer—not that Megan expected she would—Dad showed the guest into the formal lounge, off the dining room.

"We'd best go and meet him." Mum folded a tea towel and placed it on the cupboard. "Come on."

Megan followed her mother, expecting to meet an ancient academic gentleman.

Oh, my stars! Was this gorgeous man an expert in Regency period literature?

"Megan?"

Someone had said something and she'd missed it. How long had her mouth been hanging open? How embarrassing.

"Nice to meet you." Whatever-his-name-was stepped forward, holding his hand out to shake. Where had her good sense gone? All she could do was shake his hand in return and nod. What a turn of events.

"Why don't you gentlemen take a seat in the dining room? Megan and I will serve dinner and be with you presently." Mum tugged Megan's arm to draw her away.

"Impressed?" Mum asked as they entered the kitchen.

"Good heavens, Mother. I can't see that man knowing anything about the Regency. Didn't you say he was a policeman?"

"Never mind that. Let's get dinner on the table. Then we can talk."

Talk? That didn't seem likely at the moment. But she could sit and bask. Basking was probably more realistic at this point.

* * *

Cam's attention trailed after the attractive young woman as she followed Mrs Brooker back to the kitchen. He'd been surprised to find someone other than the author and her husband at home. Pleasantly surprised.

"So, how long have you been in the police force, Constable Fletcher?" Mr. Brooker's question drew Cam's attention away from the kitchen. He followed his host's example and sat down on one of the lounge chairs. The middle-aged father seemed a quiet sort of person, compared to his vivacious wife.

"I started at the South Australian Police academy when I was nineteen," Cam said. "I've worked my way up to Senior Constable First Class over the last ten years."

Mr. Brooker nodded and hummed but didn't say anything else. Awkward.

"Your wife is quite famous," Cam persisted regardless. "My mother is a huge fan."

"You don't say?"

"She even sent her novels along with me, in the hope I'd be able to get an autograph."

"Louise loves her writing," Mr Brooker said. "Not really my cup of tea, but she makes a living out of it."

"My mother is into all the BBC period drama shows, but I tend to run for the hills when I see they're on."

"You a sporting man?"

Cam nodded. "Basketball, mainly, but I watch a lot of sport on pay-TV."

"We're big into AFL in this house." Mr Brooker sat forward with his elbows on his knees, obviously more comfortable moving the topic of conversation to sport.

"Your wife and daughter as well?"

Mr. Brooker nodded, but didn't say anything else as Mrs. Brooker and her daughter entered, bearing dishes of food.

"Dad, you haven't got onto football already?" Megan placed a casserole dish on the cork tablemat.

"Not yet," he replied.

"Are you interested in football, Constable Fletcher?" Mrs. Brooker asked as she took her seat at the table.

"Call me Cam," he replied. "Yeah, I like watching."

"Did you ever play?" Megan asked.

"Only in high school. I broke my collarbone and did my knee, so I've steered away to a less aggressive sport."

The conversation paused while Mr. Brooker said grace, then continued discussing sport and his job. They were prepared to give stick to Mrs. Brooker over the matter of the speeding ticket. He'd almost forgotten why he'd come when she got up from the table.

"Russell, could you help me in the kitchen, please."

Mr. Brooker let out a huff and dragged himself out of the chair. Cam hid a wry smile. It was obvious he wasn't used to doing kitchen work. They disappeared through the door to the kitchen and Cam was now alone with the daughter. Megan? This was awkward.

"I'm so sorry." Her expression was all different shades of embarrassment.

"Why should you be sorry?" he asked.

"My mother is scheming, and you've just been thrown right in it."

Cam stopped chewing the last of his bread roll. What had he been thrown into?

"I thought I'd come to do an interview for her new novel."

"Do you know what sort of novels my mother writes?" Megan asked.

"Regency romance." *Thank you, Mother, for the heads-up.*

Megan looked surprised. "I'm assuming you know what Regency romance is?"

"Not really. My mother is a huge fan, and even if I'd decided not to come, she would have made me come anyway." He held up the bag of novels. "She's hoping your mum might sign them for her."

Megan smiled. She reached across the table and took the bag from him. "She'll sign them, but that's not why she asked you here."

"Yes, she told me."

"What? That you're here for an interview?"

Cam nodded.

Megan smiled. "That's amusing. I hope you're right, but I can't see how interviewing a SAPOL senior constable is going to help her writing."

"I did wonder about that."

"Yes, well let me give you my version of why she invited you."

Cam glanced toward the closed kitchen door. How long did it take to prepare dessert?

"As I said, I'm very sorry."

"You suspect an ulterior motive."

"I would lay money on it."

"Perhaps you'd better tell me the worst since it appears they're not hurrying back with dessert."

"I guarantee Dad is sat at the kitchen table and has already finished his pudding."

"Go on."

"I've been having trouble at work with my boss …"

"What sort of trouble?"

"The usual. He's a creep, and I'd leave if I didn't need the money."

Cam frowned. He hated hearing about sexual harassment. These guys need a good hit in the head.

"So your mother hopes I'll help you deal with him."

"I guess …"

"Police only get involved if you have a case for sexual assault or stalking, and then you have to come into the station to make a formal complaint."

"I'm not sure that my situation is that drastic."

"Tell me more information about what's happened."

Megan outlined the scenario, but she didn't say the magic words—punch, choke or grope. This wasn't really his department.

"And you've taken this to HR or your union representative?"

"No union and HR is my department."

"So this creep is the boss. No one higher?"

Megan shook her head.

Cam's dinner felt sour in his stomach. He hated hearing about guys who thought they had a right to impose themselves on women. Often it was subtle innuendo and they got away with it.

"I suggest you write down anything that even looks like inappropriate behavior so when you make a complaint, you'll have documented evidence that this was not a one-time 'mistake.'" Cam used the air quotes. He'd heard that excuse from perps more times than he cared to count.

Megan nodded, took a deep breath and bit her top lip. There was something else. Where were her parents?

"Is there something else you need to say?" Cam asked.

"You'll notice the extended absence." She gestured with her head towards the closed kitchen door.

"Perhaps they're baking from scratch."

Megan gave a half-hearted smile.

"My mother is taking a leaf out of Jane Austen's book, and keeping everyone out of the room while you have an opportunity to declare your undying affection."

"What?"

Megan laughed, and he became aware of the look of panic that must be on his face. He forced himself to relax. She was joking, surely.

"Dramatic much?"

"I confess, I am a little lost," Cam said.

"Not a fan of Austen, then?" The look of amusement on her face was gorgeous, and he took a moment to focus and process the question.

Other than a vague recollection that Austen was one of his mother's favorite movie producers, he thought Austen was either a town in Texas or a make of car.

"My mother suggested I get a boyfriend and have him come around to the office and prance around a bit, as if staking territory. I'm guessing she saw an opportunity when you pulled her over. I bet you were wearing a gun."

An icy feeling washed through his stomach, followed by a buzz that traveled right up into his chest.

"That's why I'm sorry," Megan said. "She figures all she needs to do is find the right characters, place them alone in a room for an extended period, and wait for the magic."

Cam laughed, but it was a cover-up for how he was feeling. Shanghaied? Manipulated? Thrown in the way of a golden opportunity?

Wait! What? Golden opportunity?

Megan stood up from her seat at the dining room table. "I'll go fetch them back. Dad has probably finished the leftovers and his dessert, and is eyeing ours as we speak."

"Wait." Megan stopped and turned back to face him. What was he doing? Had he lost his mind? Quite possibly. She had that expectant look on her face. Too late to back out.

"I'll play the game if you want."

* * *

"Well? How did you go?" Mum began stacking the dishwasher now that their guest had gone.

Megan knew exactly what her mother was asking but had no intention of cooperating.

"How did what go?"

"You know …" Mum waggled her eyebrows.

"I should be asking you that question. How did the interview go?"

"Very interesting. I learned a lot about the workings of a Senior Constable First Class. Did you know Constable Fletcher has worked with the drug squad?"

Butter wouldn't melt in her mouth. Her mother was committed to playing this charade right through to completion.

"How exactly will you be working drug crimes and modern law enforcement into your current novel?"

"Don't you worry about that."

"Have you got some time-travel element going on?"

"I have nondisclosure agreements I have to abide by."

When it suited her.

"He seemed like a lovely young man," Mum persisted.

"Very nice." And a good sport, though she had no intention of letting her mother know what they'd worked out to address the 'Shane' problem.

"I hope we see him again sometime," Mum said.

Megan finished wiping the sink, hung up the tea towel and picked up her handbag and keys.

"You never know. If you aren't careful with your driving, you might find he pulls you over and gives you another ticket."

"Unlikely," Mum said. "That was a one-off thing since he isn't in the traffic division."

"Wrong place, right time?" Megan asked.

"That depends on how you look at it."

Indeed. Megan leaned in and kissed her mother on the cheek.

"Thanks for dinner. I best get along home. I've got work in the morning."

"You watch out for that boss of yours. If he gives you any trouble, call Constable Fletcher. I'm sure he would swing by and help you out if you asked."

Megan smiled and opened the front door. If only Mum knew.

Chapter Three

Cam checked his phone calendar. He wanted to drop by Megan's work after he started his afternoon shift, so he had his uniform on. A uniform, especially a uniform with weapons, was intimidating. A statement. This guy needed to back off.

Megan had said she felt safe on Mondays and Fridays—the book-keeper was definitely in the office on those days, even if the sales reps weren't, and Shane usually behaved. That left Cam Tuesday through to Thursday to pop in when he was in the area.

"Why are we stopping here?" Joel asked as they pulled up outside Telford Wholesalers office.

"I'm just following something up," Cam replied. "There's a café across the road. Why don't you run in and get our afternoon coffee?"

Joel shrugged and got out of the car at the same time Cam did. Good. That should appear intimidating to anyone inside who might be looking out.

The office wasn't big. The shopfront had a few electronic items on display and a reception desk. Megan looked up as he walked through the door.

"Hi." Her smile grew ten degrees warmer and he couldn't help but smile back.

Where was the evil Shane? He did a quick scan of the office and saw a frowning, thirty-something man exiting one of the two office doors at the rear of the showroom. The man himself, right on cue.

"Is there a problem?" the man asked.

"Nothing to worry about, Shane," Megan said. "This is my boy-friend, Cam."

That should have led to niceties like, 'nice to meet you' or a hand-shake or something, but Cam had no urge to be polite and barely nodded. Shane responded in kind. No surprise there.

Megan came out from behind her workstation, took Cam by the arm, and led him towards the front of the showroom.

"I'm running a business here," Shane called after her. "This is not a social club."

Megan turned her back on him and aimed a strained smile in Cam's direction.

"Just wanted to see if you're OK," Cam said.

"I'm fine." Her anxious look belied her words.

"Are you free for lunch tomorrow?" Where had that come from? Whether he'd intended to make a lunch date or not, this superficial chitchat wasn't telling him anything, and the tension in the office was unbearable. What was she thinking?

"Sure."

"I want you in the office over the lunch hour," Shane called out again. This guy was insufferable and he had supersonic hearing.

"That's OK, I'll come earlier and call it an early lunch." Cam saw Shane was still listening—and reacting. "It's against the law to deny a worker their lunch break. I'm sure your boss knows that."

"Are you working afternoon shift again tomorrow?" Megan asked.

Cam nodded. "Otherwise I'd come around to your place for dinner."

He should have gone to acting school. This improvisation thing was excellent fun, especially watching Shane's reaction. He was livid—mouth pinched, eyes narrowed, standing upright like a grizzly bear ready to attack. *Bring it on, man.*

Cam felt Megan's hand on his arm again and her touch made him aware his muscles were bunched ready for a round in the ring.

"I'll walk you out," she said.

See you around, Bucko! It would have been wonderful to say those words out loud, but he didn't want to break into a fight on their first meeting.

"When you said intimidate, I didn't think you'd go quite so territorial."

Megan's words were like a sucker punch. He studied her face and saw her eyes shining.

"I'm sorry," he said. "I shouldn't have been so rude to your boss."

"It's not that. It's just that you were sizing each other up like a pair of wild stallions ready to clash. I thought I was going to get caught in between."

"I wouldn't hurt you." Cam was chagrined. Did he just present himself to be as bad as Shane? "I'm sorry, Megan. I just wanted him to back off."

"I want him to back off as well. He's been all over me this morning."

"Has he touched you?" The electric charge jolted through him again and he felt his body tense.

"Hand on the shoulder several times, though I asked him not to, and he keeps saying things—innuendo mostly."

Cam looked back through the shopfront window. Shane was watching them.

"You need to be careful, Megan. I've seen those obsessive sorts before."

"Do you think having you come will make it worse?"

"I think he realizes you have someone to call at a moment's notice. Did you put my number on speed dial?"

She nodded. She looked so sad and vulnerable—not at all like the lively woman he'd met a few nights ago at her mother's place.

"I'll drive by later this afternoon, but if you have any worry that he will hurt you, call straight away. I'll come back."

"Thank you, Cam."

"You still look worried."

"Perhaps I shouldn't have said you were my boyfriend."

"Boyfriend!" Joel spoke from behind them. "Following something up, hey?" His partner stood there with two take-out coffee cups in a cardboard tray.

Cam saw Megan flush red. This was embarrassing for her. And him.

"Thanks for your sensitivity," Cam said to Joel. "This is Megan, and I'm following a line of inquiry if you must know."

"Sure." Joel wore a stupid grin. Cam had some explaining to do.

"I better go," Cam said. "Call me later."

Megan nodded. She still looked vulnerable, but he couldn't stay here all day. He joined his partner as they got in their squad car and drove away.

"Why didn't you kiss her goodbye?" Joel asked, not even trying to hide his mirth.

"I'd better explain."

"What, that you've found a girlfriend at last? I was beginning to despair." Joel thought he was so funny.

"Not a girlfriend. I'm helping her out."

"Could have fooled me—with all that romantic tension between you—it looked pretty girlfriend-like to me."

"Megan is in a sticky situation with her boss—verging on sexual harassment. Probably is sexual harassment, but he hasn't quite crossed a line, and she can't take it to anyone in the company as she is the last port of call."

"So you're trying to rattle his cage?"

"Somewhat."

"By posing as her boyfriend."

Cam nodded.

"You're not convincing enough."

"You just said there was a heap of romantic tension."

"Yeah, because I know you. I can tell you're interested, but if her boss has already marked her, he won't buy the charade. You should have kissed her goodbye."

"I'm trying to deal with an issue of trespass into her personal space. My trespassing isn't going to make the situation better."

Joel just grinned.

"What?"

"You like her."

"I don't know her well enough to say that, but I am already certain I can't stand her boss. He'd better watch his step."

"I take it we're driving by for more coffee later."

"Of course."

Cam started the car and put it in reverse.

"Cam?" What was that serious note in Joel's voice.

"What?" A glance in his direction showed a look of concern.

"Don't let this guy get under your skin."

Cam didn't reply. He hated being reminded of his past. Besides, it was different now. With God and the counselor, he was much less explosive than he'd been five years ago.

* * *

"I don't want him in this office again, Megan. Is that clear?"

Shane had not relaxed. He was still wound up and looking ready for a fight.

"He'll come if I call him," Megan said. She stood to her full height and tilted her chin up, wishing she had the confidence to back her tone and stance.

"If you want to keep your job, you will not be taking personal calls either on the phone or in person. Don't think I won't fire you."

"Is that an official warning?" Megan asked.

"I'm not stupid, Megan. I know you can't afford to lose this job. Not with your new mortgage."

"How do you know about that?" Icy panic twisted in her stomach.

"I have my ways of keeping track of my staff."

Megan pushed past him and went to her workstation. How did he know that she'd just taken out a mortgage? She hadn't told him. How did he know?

She opened the document she'd been working on when Cam had arrived but couldn't focus. Shane was still watching her from only a few feet away. Her phone pinged and she glanced at the message alert. Cam.

Are you OK?

She wanted to answer, but Shane was watching and, given his warning, she decided to pretend it was of no significance. She had to get her mind back on the task at hand.

The last couple of hours at work were unbearable. Shane watched her like a hawk and she didn't dare answer the text message until the second one arrived.

I'm driving by again. Shall I come in? Are you OK?

She picked up the phone.

He's threatened dismissal if I do personal stuff during company time. I'll call you after work.

Only fifteen minutes to go.

Megan did her best to finish everything she had on her to-do list and even worked ten minutes past five. She shut her computer, picked up her phone and bag, and started toward the door.

"I want to see you before you go," Shane said from the doorway. "In my office."

"No, Shane. I have an appointment, and I've already stayed an extra ten minutes."

"You're putting your job at risk, Megan."

"You can't fire me for leaving after my contracted work hours." She took a deep breath and walked out the door.

Her heart was pumping at an elevated rate. She could feel it, along with the tension pushing up in her throat. She blinked back tears as she walked toward the car park on the corner of the block. Surely he wouldn't fire her. He couldn't. She needed the money. As she approached the corner, her phone rang. Cam.

"Are you OK?"

Megan opened her mouth to answer, then found her jaw had frozen up and a lump had formed in her throat. She nodded her head, then shook it, both actions of no use in communicating over a telephone link.

"Where are you?" Cam asked. "I'll drive by."

She managed to get the address out, then stood by her car. She closed her eyes and turned her face towards the late afternoon sun, holding back tears. What was she going to do?

The crunch of tires on gravel alerted her to the approach of the squad car, and she opened her eyes. Joel was driving, and Cam jumped out of the car before it had come to a standstill. Wretched tears chose that moment to break the dam wall.

How ironic that she should walk straight into Cam's strong embrace, accepting the comfort of his soothing touch without hesitation, yet she recoiled and panicked if Shane touched her. Cam was safe. She could feel it as she melted into him.

"Did he hurt you?" Cam said quietly next to her ear.

She shook her head.

"Talk to me."

She stepped back. Joel was standing by the car, concern written all over his face.

"He's taken it up a notch, threatening me with dismissal if I have any personal contact at all during work hours. I can't afford to lose the job without finding something else first."

"Isn't your safety more important?" Cam asked.

How had she got to this stage of feeling so controlled and vulnerable? How was she going to manage the mortgage?

"Your mum and dad seem like the kind of people who would help you out while you sorted something."

Megan nodded. They would. Of course they would. But she had failed her first attempt at adulting and hated to admit it. A twenty-eight-year-old failure as a grown-up. She had to push through this crisis. On her own.

Chapter Four

"I'm going out on my lunch break." Megan didn't pause to see if Shane would react. She needed to get out.

"I want you to work over lunch today. You can eat in my office."

"No, Shane. You can't ask that of me. It's against Fair Work Regulations. I am going earlier, as I told you yesterday. There is nothing I need to do in the office for the next hour."

"Are you meeting up with that copper?"

"That isn't any of your business."

"I don't like him."

Ironic. Cam didn't like Shane either. "You don't need to like him, Shane. It's none of your business."

Megan took her bag and walked out the front door before he could say anything else. Had she made a mistake involving Cam in this situation? It had been bad before, but Shane's controlling behavior had escalated since she'd presented Cam as her boyfriend. On the other hand, Megan was glad to have something to look forward to in meeting up with Cam. Was that just because he gave sensible advice and support? Or was it because he was a ridiculously good-looking and caring man?

Cam was waiting in the carpark when she arrived. He was wearing a casual zip-up jacket over his work uniform—not armed, with a gun at least. His killer looks were another proposition altogether.

"How was your morning?" he asked as she got in his car and fastened her seatbelt.

"Same as usual, with an extra side of tension and suspicion."

"Did you find any new jobs online to apply for last night?"

"There were a couple of jobs, but I'm not sure I have all the required qualifications."

Cam drove his car to a café a couple of streets away, and they went inside. After placing their lunch orders, Cam sat down and sought her eyes.

"I'm sorry to say it, but your boss appears to have a classic case of obsession."

Megan nodded. "I think I'm just beginning to figure that out. Since his wife left him, he's become more and more fixated on me. He's always trying to get me alone."

"You should avoid that at all costs."

Megan nodded again, this time swallowing back the lump that had formed in her throat. "The trouble is, we are often alone in the office. The sales reps come in and out, but are mostly on the road, and the bookkeeper is only in twice a week."

"Are you afraid of him?" Cam asked.

Was she? Mostly she was annoyed, but since Shane met Cam and his demanding and controlling had escalated, her feelings were something beyond annoyed.

"I'm not sure. He's probably harmless. Just thinks he's God's gift."

"Do you mind if I turn up the 'boyfriend' image a few notches?"

"Depends. I'm a bit scared it will end in a fight."

"I'll avoid a fight, but I'm hoping he will see you have your heart set elsewhere and will leave you alone."

"Do you think that would work?" Megan hoped it might, but then what did Cam mean by turning up the 'boyfriend' image?

"If you don't mind, let's give it a go and see how he responds. He will either back down or his behavior will escalate to a point where I can issue him with an official warning."

Megan laughed. "I issue him with warnings every day. It doesn't make any difference."

"Yes, but if, after the warning, he persists, he may be liable for prosecution."

"Really?"

"If his behavior escalates, yes."

The waiter brought their food. Megan waited for him to leave and then noticed Cam was waiting.

"Do you pray before you eat?" she asked.

"Usually. Do you?"

Megan nodded and responded when Cam reached his hand across the table. He thanked God for the meal, and probably prayed something else as well, but Megan missed it all. He was holding her hand, and the warm energy that was flowing straight up her arm to her heart was like a shot of mind-numbing drug. She was supposed to be thanking God in her heart as well—and she was, but not for the food. All she could think of was how her hand was nestled warmly in his.

* * *

It was hard concentrating on being genuinely thankful in prayer when there were some strange currents going back and forth between them, but Cam did his best. Then suddenly she pulled her hand back and put it in her lap. Cam watched fear shape her expression, not to mention the flush that had infused her cheeks. Had he frightened her by holding her hand? He was about to apologize then stopped. She was looking at someone behind him.

"Has Shane followed us here?"

"How did he find us?" she whispered.

A surge of anger went like a shard of molten iron through his system. He wanted to get up and smash Shane's head into the wall. Instead, he took a deep breath and counted slowly to ten. His anger was getting easier to control thanks to his counseling sessions and new-found faith. Once the urge towards violence subsided, Cam returned his focus to Megan. She was terrified. He reached out his hand again.

"Megan. Look at me."

She was a struggling to take her focus off her boss.

"Megan?"

She eventually brought her attention back to him. Her eyes were bright with tears again.

"Take my hand," he said, using as gentle a tone as he could muster.

"What if he sees?"

"That's what I'm hoping for."

"He's glaring at me."

"Ignore him and look at me."

Megan pulled her hand back again and stood up.

"I can't do this."

Without stopping, she picked up her bag and walked from the crowded café. Cam got up to follow. He stopped a waiter as he went past.

"Could you wrap those two meals to go, please? I'll pick them up in a few minutes."

Without waiting for a confirmation, he followed Megan out. Shane had already gone out after her. The man *was* obsessed. And controlling, and, he suspected, dangerous.

By the time he made it outside, Shane had her backed up against the wall of the café. Cam wasn't about to stop and wait to be included in the conversation. He pushed past Shane and took Megan by the hand.

"Sorry, Babe. I'll just pay our bill and then take you home."

"Home?" Shane was not perturbed that they were trying to exclude him. "She's due back at the office."

"She's not well," Cam said, "and I'm taking her home."

He didn't wait to engage in an argument but put his arm around Megan and ushered her back inside the café. "Just stay with me," he spoke in a low tone that might have been considered intimate. "I'll pay the bill and grab our lunch to go."

Megan didn't resist but Cam could tell she was upset. With their meals wrapped and bagged, and the receipt in hand, Cam put his arm around her waist again and guided her outside, past Shane, who seemed to think he could stop them by standing in the way, and towards his car.

"I mean it, Megan," Shane called after them. "If you're not back in the office in ten minutes, you're fired."

Cam felt her whole back tense.

"It's going to be OK," Cam said as he opened the passenger door for her.

By the time he was in the driver's seat, the anger had built again, but he felt removed enough from the situation to be safe from physically attacking the man. Her boss was verging on stalking. Cam faced these sorts of characters regularly, but something about Megan's vulnerability made the emotional impact worse than usual.

"Are you all right?" he asked, as he pulled the car back onto the road.

He saw Megan shake her head in his peripheral vision.

"What did he say to you?"

"He keeps threatening to fire me."

"He can't fire you, Megan. He has no legal grounds and if he tried it, you could sue his butt off for illegal dismissal."

"He knows I have a mortgage, though I didn't tell him about it. And he knew where we were having lunch. How does he know all these things?"

"Are you using your own mobile phone or does it belong to your work?"

"Are you kidding? I can't afford a smart phone like this one. It came with the job."

"Did you set the passwords?"

Megan shook her head.

"He's able to log into your phone. He can track you and he probably reads your emails."

"What!"

"Do you use a private email address on your home computer?"

"I don't have a home computer. I can't afford one, not when I have the work one. I do most of my emails at work and check a few personal ones on my phone."

"Technically, as your boss, he can have access to all the company technology, email accounts, even the tracking on the devices."

"So he's following me through my phone."

Cam put his finger up to his lips, then pulled his car over to the side of the road and took his phone. He opened it to notebook and started typing.

There is a strong possibility he can track your conversations if he's activated the microphone.

"What?"

Cam lifted his eyebrows. All of these technological activities were possible and, as the boss of the company, Shane had the right to go through emails. They were work devices and accounts. That

Megan was allowed to access them for personal use was a privilege, but obviously that came with a risk.

Cam got out of the car. They were near a park and he indicated that Megan should follow him. He took their bagged lunch and left her mobile phone on the front seat of the car.

"So you think he's tracking me through my phone?" Megan asked once they were away from the car.

"That would be my best guess."

"So he knows that we are here now?"

"He knows where my car is parked."

"What am I going to do?" Megan asked. "He's like gone crazy."

"After we've eaten lunch, I'm going to drive you back to your parents' place. I think it's time we called in backup on this one."

The weather was pleasant, and a picnic in the park should have been perfect. Cam couldn't track how he felt. The anger he was familiar with. It had been his nemesis for longer than he cared to remember. But he'd employed the recommended techniques to keep control. So what was this he was feeling? This was a crazy situation. One minute he'd agreed to play a role on the whim of an eccentric mother, but right at the moment, he was being forced to look at his motivations. He wasn't just acting a role. He had real feelings stirred up, and anger was only one of them.

* * *

It would have been nice if this was actually real. Sitting on the grass by a small lake, eating some excellent focaccia with her good-looking boyfriend. Except he wasn't her boyfriend, and the focaccia tasted like cardboard. Shane's threats loomed large over Megan and she couldn't relax and absorb the beauty of the day or the hope of building a friendship with Cam.

Was this what anxiety felt like? It was not an emotion Megan was familiar with. Her charmed childhood had been marked with security and confidence, and yet today she was jumpy, couldn't eat the good food in front of her, and just wanted to run home and hide under the covers of her bed.

"It's going to be OK," Cam said as he scrunched up the sandwich wrapper.

Megan looked at her focaccia which had only three small bites taken from it.

"I can't see how it's going to work," she said.

Cam was sitting quite close and he took her hand in his, drawing her close. She didn't resist but took comfort in the touch. If only it was real.

"Are you going to finish your lunch?"

She held her sandwich out to him.

"I can't eat it. You can have it if you like."

"You sure you don't want it?"

She almost laughed when he took it. "You're like my brother. Always looking for more to eat."

"I don't need it, but I wouldn't want it to go to waste."

That did make her laugh.

"Hurry up and eat. Let's go and see if we can catch my folks before you have to go to work."

Chapter Five

Josiah's muscles strained as he lifted Lady Rosalie down from his horse. She was beginning to come back to her senses but was still unsteady. She would fall over if he set her on her own feet.

"Josiah?"

"Put your arms around my neck," he said, quietly. "You're quite safe now."

"Where are we?"

"Don't you recognize your father's house?"

She seemed to find energy and tensed. "I cannot let my father see me like this. Put me down."

Josiah ignored her plea and mounted the large stone steps leading to the front entrance of the manor house.

"Please, Mr. Landown. I am perfectly strong enough to walk in on my own two feet."

She wasn't well enough.

"Please, Josiah. Put me down. I will be all right."

Josiah allowed her feet to touch the large flagstone step, but he maintained a steadying hand around her waist.

"He will be furious with me," Lady Rosalie said. "I wish you had not brought me here."

Josiah had no scruples about his choice. Who else should care for her other than her own family? He lifted the large brass doorknocker. The sound reverberated inside the main entry hall. He could hear it—thud, thud, thud. The sound of brass against wood, with the edge of metallic tang. Thud, thud, thud.

"Russell, would you get the door. For heaven's sake, I'm trying to write here." Who on earth was pounding on the front door as if the house was on fire? Louise sniffed annoyance as she saved her work and closed her computer. Working from home was supposed to be quiet and safe from disturbance.

Then she heard voices. Megan?

"Mum?" Megan opened the study door and put her head inside.

"Why aren't you at work?" Louise asked.

"Long story. Can you come out and help us sort this thing out?"

"Us?"

Megan did not wait to answer that question, so Louise followed her into the hallway, and then into the kitchen.

"Constable Fletcher!"

"Call me Cam," he replied. "How are you, Mrs. Brooker?"

Speaking of Lord Josiah Landown and wanting to picture him in the flesh, and who should appear?

"Please, call me Louise."

"Tea or coffee?" Russell filled the kettle at the sink.

"I can't drink anything," Megan said. "I'm too agitated."

"I'll have a coffee if it's not too much trouble," Cam said.

"I'm due for a cup of tea," Louise said as she pulled out a kitchen chair to join the others sitting around the table. "What's gone on to get you so uptight? Is it Shane Telford again?"

Megan nodded. "He's gone to another level of creepy now."

"Well, I told you, you should get a boyfriend who will drop in occasionally. That should sort—"

"I followed your advice and even took your lead, mother. Hence, Cameron Fletcher …" she waved her hand at the handsome young man seated next to her as if she was an assistant in a magic show.

Wait! What? "You took my advice and followed my lead? Are you and ..." now Louise waved her hand in Cameron's direction.

"He was sporting enough to play your game," Megan explained. "Came into Telford's posing as my boyfriend ..."

Only posing. Drat.

"And as a result, her boss has stepped up his obsessive possessive controlling routine," Cam said.

"Jealous, do you think?" Trust Russell to say something completely obvious.

"He certainly seems fixated on your daughter," Cam said to Russell. "I thought my uniform might have been enough to deter him."

"But?" Louise asked.

"Instead he's acting like he owns her and has started following her."

"Isn't that against the law?" Louise asked.

"It's a sign he may be stalking her. If we can establish evidence that he's definitely following her, I will give him an official warning. If he persists, we can arrest him and prosecute him. Stalking is a major indictable offense."

"Why can't you warn him now?" Russell asked.

"So far, he's on the thin line between breaking the law and his rights as an employer and the use of his company technical devices. My advice is Megan leave the company and all the technology behind."

"But I can't." Louise could hear the anxiety in her daughter's voice.

"I told you, you can come home here with us," she said.

"I'm a grown-up now, Mother," Megan objected. "I have a real mortgage—a real *huge* mortgage—and I can't just run home to you every time something goes awry. I have to take responsibility."

"Good girl," Russell said.

"However, I'm worried that Shane Telford is verging on dangerous personality disorder," Cam said. "I don't think Megan staying on at that job is safe."

"Really?" Louise said. "Is he that bad?"

"What about you sit down and talk to him face to face and let him know what your boundaries are?" Russell said. "It is a good job. You don't really want to throw it in if it's not necessary."

"Isn't there some Work Safe union or someone who can come and mediate?" Louise asked. "Mind you, I'd be just as happy to see the back of him. I've been worried about you being there for a while now."

"I'm going to have to go back to work tomorrow. There are other people in the company who are dependent on me getting their pay organized each week."

"Will you go with her, Cam?" Louise asked. "Just stay with her while she has a strong word to him about his behavior."

Cam nodded.

* * *

Of course he would go with her. He didn't trust the man from all he'd observed of him, but if Megan felt confident to go and challenge Shane, he would certainly back her up. Besides, he was posing as her boyfriend and that's what a boyfriend would do, wasn't it?

"I don't think you've thought this through," Russell said.

"How so?" Louise looked offended.

"Megan is an adult employee, who needs to address her workplace situation on her own. She can't call in her mother or her 'boyfriend' …"He used air quotes.

Russell obviously didn't buy the 'boyfriend' act either. Joel had said it wasn't convincing.

"But Russell —"

"I can't help it, Louise. Megan has to address this herself unless Shane does something criminal. Then she can call the cops."

"I think Dad's right," Megan said. "This is a workplace issue and I'm a senior employee. I have to deal with it."

"What's the worst he can do?" Russell asked.

"Fire me," Megan said.

Cam could think of worse things but didn't want to alarm her.

"If he fires you, you can take it to the ombudsman for work place issues. He cannot fire you for asking him to respect your personal space." Russell obviously knew his work-place rights.

"You need to document every move that makes you feel uncomfortable, Megan," Cam said. "Time and date it. And don't put it on your work computer."

"I'll talk to him tomorrow."

"What are you going to say?" Louise asked.

"I don't know. That he needs to stop with the innuendo, stop touching me, stop looking through my emails."

"He has a right to look at a work email account, as a boss," Russell said. "Why don't you set up a personal email account?"

"He can hack into anything on her computer or phone," Cam said. "She needs her own personal computer and phone."

"I thought you'd got all your wifi set up at your new house," Russell said.

"I was using hotspot from the work phone."

"What about streaming?"

"I just bought a house. I can't afford things like computers and streaming services at this stage," Megan said.

"Nonsense," Louise objected. "I just upgraded my laptop. You can have my old one for home and you can set up a private free account."

By the time Cam and Megan had left the Brookers' family home, they'd examined just about every angle.

"Are you sure you're going to be OK dealing with this on your own?" Cam asked as he pulled alongside Megan's car parking space.

"I will go back to work tomorrow and schedule an interview just before I leave for the day."

Cam sucked in a breath and held his tongue. Why did he feel so protective about his fake girlfriend? This wasn't real. Suddenly he felt a need to review the way he'd responded to every other woman who'd come through the police station with allegations of sexual harassment or stalking. Was this how he'd felt about all those other cases? Not even close. He knew the procedure and the law and his responsibility in following both, but in this case, he'd already acknowledged he felt something more. Something stronger.

And then he felt alarmed. Was he any better than Shane Telford? He couldn't become obsessive and controlling. She had to call the shots and if she needed him she would let him know.

"I have afternoon shift today and tomorrow," Cam said. "When you're about to have your meeting, send me a text and I'll try to be in the vicinity if you need me, OK?"

"Thanks, Cam. I really appreciate you getting involved like this." Megan gave a warm smile.

"I only hope I haven't made it worse."

"No, I just think you've brought the inevitable to a head. He would have persisted unchecked if you hadn't made an appearance."

"I'm happy for you to text me any time," he said.

"But it would appear I need to use a code if he really has been hacking my phone and email."

"Send me a coffee order and I'll decipher it."

"What, like 'black coffee' and you know he's being difficult, and 'herbal tea' for all is peace and calm."

"That sounds like a great plan."

"OK then." She unbuckled her seat belt and picked up her bag from the floor of his car. Then she paused. What did she want? Was it appropriate to kiss her goodbye?

No! Absolutely not! This was a charade and he would not take advantage, despite the fact he would really like to.

"I'll catch you later," he said instead. "Be careful."

Megan smiled again. Was it sad? Resigned? Reluctant?

Then she got out and straight into her own car. He hoped she would be all right.

* * *

"Sorry I'm late." Cam rushed into the equipment room where he found Joel Baker tooling up ready for their shift.

"Where've you been?" Joel said. "I was about to report you as absent and get them to check on you." He handed Cam his gun belt. Obviously he'd already signed it out from armory.

"Long story."

"Your girlfriend?" Joel zipped his patrol bag up.

"You can quit your smirking. I took Megan out to lunch, yes, and the situation escalated."

"With Megan? She's into you?"

Cam let out a huff and stuffed a torch into his bag, along with the ballistics vest. "Megan's situation escalated. Her boss is on the edge of being served a warning for stalking."

"So nothing happened between you and Megan?"

"Would you get your mind onto the important information? Her boss is probably stalking her and she is vulnerable."

"And you're the knight in shining armor come to the rescue."

"You're impossible, Joel." Cam zipped his patrol bag up and threw it over his shoulder. The pair went from the equipment room towards the briefing room.

"So why have you taken such an interest in her?" Joel asked.

Good question. Why had he taken such an interest?

"Loving the silent response." Joel was grinning like the Cheshire Cat. "It's shouting all sorts of possibilities."

"OK. I like her, all right? Happy?"

"But nothing's going on … yet?"

"As I said, she is vulnerable at present. What sort of lowlife would I be if I swooped in and took advantage of her in this state?"

"You're right." Joel led the way into the briefing room.

Cam kept half an ear on what the sergeant was saying, but his mind was still scrambling to catch up. He should have watched the time and been better prepared for work, but Megan's situation had stolen his focus.

He was assigned with Joel, which wasn't unusual, and they left the briefing to get a car from the fleet. Joel filled in the log book ready for them to commence duty while Cam put the patrol bags in the boot.

"Listen, mate," Joel spoke once Cam was inside the car, fastening his seatbelt, "you need to be careful."

"What? Five minutes ago you were joking about me and Megan being together and now you're all serious and telling me to be careful."

"I don't have a problem with you and Megan being together if that's what comes from this …"

"What's your point, then?"

"This slimy boss character—you know what happened last time, and you weren't involved with the woman on that occasion." Joel started the squad car and drove out of the fleet bay.

Cam pursed his lips. Joel knew him too well. Shane Telford wasn't the first shady character he'd come up against. He didn't have any patience for guys who were nothing more than sexual predators, as Joel had seen first-hand. On that occasion, he'd stepped up to the line and put a foot over it. If Joel hadn't been there, he might have faced some internal investigation and discipline.

"I've done a lot of work since then," Cam said eventually. "My dad got sick and when I spent time with him, he helped me get a lot of things into perspective."

"Like you finding religion."

"It has helped me, Joel. And seeing the counselor when I did. I believe I've got the strategies to cope with … well, you know."

"Rage?"

"Well, yeah. What do you feel about those sorts of blokes?"

"We're in law enforcement, Cam. What we feel has no bearing on how we should act."

"Yeah, I know, and I've never crossed the line."

"You got pretty close."

"So you keep reminding me."

"This is the first time I've brought it up since that incident."

Cam didn't speak. Joel was getting close to emotional stuff he wasn't prepared to discuss.

"I'm sorry, mate. I tease you about Megan because I get that you're interested in her, but then you tell me about her boss, and I get worried that you might want to …."

"What? Hurt him? I do want to hurt him. That thought crosses my mind every time I think about him, but I'm mature enough to use anger management strategies and put my energies into helping Megan find proper solutions. Give me some credit."

"OK. If you say so. But if you feel like you're losing control, you will talk about it, won't you?"

"I daresay you'll interrogate me on a daily basis. I'll let you know."

Chapter Six

A new day, a new attitude. At least that was what Megan hoped she would be able to achieve. Realizing that Shane had been tracking her electronically had really shaken her up. Having taken her mother's old laptop home, she'd done some work towards setting it up for her own personal use and, after several phone calls to her IT geek friend, had managed to get the laptop ready to use online. She was still using her work phone to hotspot the internet and hoped that didn't mean Shane could hack into the personal computer.

Wish me luck! I'm going to face the beast today.

She had sent this private message to Cam and he had pinged back three appropriately themed emojis. The one she liked best was of a small character suited up to engage in a fencing match, saber in hand. Without thinking, she chose a love heart emoji and pressed send. *Wait!* She meant she loved his emoji. The blood rose in her face. Would he read something else into the love heart, like … love? She gave an inner groan that didn't quite make it to the surface. Her emotional energy was needed to face Shane. She couldn't spend time thinking about Cam. More blood charged up into her face. Did she want to think about Cam? He'd agreed to her mother's hare-brained idea of posing as her boyfriend and he was doing a great job. Actually, when she came to think about it he was doing a terrible job. He was turning up at work and going out to lunch, and acting all caring, but if he was really her boyfriend he'd be more … more what? This line of thought was going nowhere. *Stop it!*

Megan closed her new second-hand laptop, picked up her work phone and keys, and left her house. The beast. It was time to face the beast.

* * *

Shane was uncharacteristically circumspect the whole morning. It might have been a blessed relief, except it wasn't. What was he doing? Megan didn't trust him. He was now aloof, almost as if he was sulking.

"Could I have an appointment with you later, if I may?" Megan said to him as he wandered into the kitchen area at lunchtime.

"Is it work-related?"

Was it? Did talking to him about personal boundaries constitute work-related issues?

"Yes." She pulled her shoulders back and tilted her chin up. He would not intimidate her.

"I've got time now," he said.

"I'd prefer the end of the day."

"If you have something to discuss, now is the time, Megan. I won't be available later."

He knew. Cam was not in the area until later in the day and he knew.

"Well?" Shane asked. "What is it you wish to discuss?"

Megan felt her confident stance wilting. She dug deep to find the strength to maintain her best shoulders-back, chin-up intimidation. Was it working?

"Give me fifteen minutes," she said. "I don't want to discuss this over lunch break."

"Fifteen minutes in my office."

And there it was. Not quite a smile, nearly a smirk, definitely a leer. The man was a cockroach.

Short black, and make mine double shot

Megan pressed send on the text to Cam. Would he come? On the one hand, she couldn't wait for him to storm in the front door, brandishing a gun. On the other, she hoped he wouldn't. She had to face Shane herself and make him understand. This was a serious breach of workplace safety. It was sexual harassment. It was stalking. Except it wasn't any of these things. Nearly, but not quite.

"Sit down," Shane barked as Megan came into his office. She didn't want to sit while he was still standing, but she didn't want to appear petulant either. She sat on one of the visitor's chairs in front of his desk. He went to the door, shut and locked it. Locked it!

"Shane, unlock the door."

"I don't want other employees bursting in on this private meeting."

"Un. Lock. The. Door."

There was no one expected in the office, and he knew it. The front door bell would chime if a client came in.

Shane had no intention of complying. He pulled the other visitor's seat around, effectively blocking Megan's exit, and sat with his knees touching hers.

"How can I help you?" Shane said, placing his hand on her knee. She shuddered, picked up his hand and flung it back.

"You know full well what you are doing, Shane Telford."

"I'm not doing anything other than being kind and friendly," he said. "It's you who's reading things into my actions. Sexual harassment indeed."

"I have never said those words to you."

"I know what you've been thinking and about the bogus boyfriend thing. That copper is no more your boyfriend than I am."

"Good! You understand then. You are not my boyfriend and you are not ever likely to be. You need to keep your hands, your comments and your filthy thoughts to yourself. Do I make myself clear?"

"You need to adjust your payroll, Megan. I've just demoted you to office clerk, effective immediately."

"What? That's like a thirty percent pay cut! You can't do that!"

"I don't need to employ an office manager. I can do that myself. You can do reception and payroll. I'll do the rest. I need to make cutbacks and have decided it's a waste of money keeping those positions, especially when the person has no intention of showing any respect for me or the company."

"I can't afford a pay cut of that magnitude."

"Perhaps your boyfriend can shift in and share the expenses." He was definitely smirking now.

"I am a Christian, Shane. You know that. And so is Cam. He won't be moving in until we're married."

"Great. When's the wedding? I hope I get an invite."

Megan stood up. He was insufferable, and he knew that Cam was only posing.

"For your information, Cam has proposed and we'll be getting married early next year."

"Excellent. Then all our problems are solved. He'll help you with your mortgage and I'll make the much-needed economic cuts to my business."

What was he doing now? His hand was on her upper arm and he was leaning forward.

"May I kiss the bride?"

The sound of an open hand meeting his face with a resounding slap rang through the office in concert with the sound of the door-bell chime. Megan looked through the thin-line Venetian blinds and saw Cam walk in, takeaway coffee cup in hand. He was armed and dangerous, and a sight for sore eyes.

* * *

Where was Megan? She was usually at the reception desk. Cam scanned the room and saw Shane's office door was closed. *Please, God, make her be all right.*

Just as he was set to investigate the closed door, it opened and Megan walked out. She was agitated, he could see by her high color, but she also had a smile pasted on her face. Shane followed closely behind. Was that a red hand-mark on his face?

"Hey, Babe," she said, walking straight up to him and kissing him—on the lips! "I just told Shane about our engagement. Hope you don't mind."

Cam was still catching up from the bolt of pleasure that had shot through him at the kiss. What? Engagement?

It felt like an age before he'd pieced it all together and was able to wipe the stunned-mullet look from his face.

"Sure. Good news is meant to be shared, right?" She was standing right next to him holding onto his forearm so he swung it behind her back and pulled her close to his side. The look on Shane's face was priceless. If he was any judge of facial expressions, Shane was telegraphing murderous thoughts. Did he believe Megan's boast of an engagement now? The red hand-mark looked like it was throbbing.

"You don't mind if I steal my fiancée for five minutes, do you, Shane?" Cam asked. "Lovers talk, you know how it is."

"I'm running a business."

"Yes, we know," Megan cut him off. "That's why you've cut my wage, remember? Come on, my darling." She tugged on his arm and directed him outside.

"He cut your wage?" Cam said the moment the door was shut behind them.

"That's all you've got to say?" Megan replied. "I just announced our engagement and you're hung up on a wage cut?"

Right. Engagement should have been the bigger shock. He should have questioned that first. But that didn't seem to be as outrageous as the news about a wage cut.

"How are you going to manage?" he asked.

"Manage a bogus engagement?"

Cam grinned. "No, the wage cut. Was he serious?"

"I don't know." Suddenly her shoulders slumped as if all the wind had gone from her sails. "If I'm reading him correctly, he was calling my bluff."

"Bluff about being engaged?"

"No, that was my raising the stakes. He thinks I was bluffing about asking him to keep his hands and comments to himself. He thinks that by threatening to cut my wage—twenty grand, by the way—I will just capitulate and let him behave however he wants."

"Instead of that, you send an order for double-shot espresso."

"I was feeling cornered even before we started the meeting. He seemed to know you weren't in the area. Aaargh!" She threw her hands up and walked a few steps away. "I don't know what to think. I keep second-guessing myself. And when he touched my knee …"

"He touched you!?" An unbidden burst of fury that had been simmering came to the boil and shot through him. He turned to charge back into the office.

"Stop! Cam. We've got to think straight and sort this out properly." He felt her hand tugging his arm and pulling him back. His muscles were bunched and ready for force, and Megan's hand was around his bicep. Suddenly he was aware of the physical tension. Megan was aware of it too. He felt a slight squeeze against the rock-solid bicep, and then she suddenly dropped her hand, a glow of pink infusing her face.

"Sorry."

"Sorry."

They spoke together. Then an awkward moment when they both caught each other's gaze before first Megan and then Cam broke into a smile. She was gorgeous, especially when she smiled.

Wait. Stop! Supposed to be dealing with obsessive behavior here, not joining the ranks of crazy-stalker Megan fan-boys.

"So you've stepped the charade up a level to engaged?" He had to get this discussion back to the problem at hand.

Megan nodded. "He was baiting me about having you move in to help pay the mortgage, especially since he's just sliced twenty grand from my income."

"So how did it escalate to engagement?"

"I told him you wouldn't move in because we are both Christian and would wait until we are married. The next step was: when's the wedding? And I saw red because he didn't believe me."

"Because it's not true." Cam wanted her to win this but couldn't help pointing out the flaw in her argument.

"I know." She dropped her head and let out a long sigh. Putting his arms around her in a warm comforting embrace just seemed like the natural thing to do. If nothing else, it would add to the charade. Surely Shane was peering out the front window. When she put her arms around his waist and burrowed further into his embrace, he wondered if she would notice his accelerated heart rate.

"Your heart's beating really fast." She'd noticed.

"There's a lot of emotional tension going on," he said, whispering near her ear.

"I know, right?" She pulled away and stood looking at him from an unsatisfactory distance. Of course, it was quite satisfactory, except that Cam was suddenly craving the closeness that the previous embrace had allowed. Crazy fan-boy alert!

"I need to go back in and make sure he's not serious about this pay cut."

"Or else what are you going to do?"

"I'd like to quit and walk out the door, but I can't afford it."

"Why don't you take in a housemate to help with expenses?"

"Who? I can't take you."

"I've been living with my mother since my dad died, but I couldn't anyway …"

"Of course not. Christian morals and all that."

"Well, there's that. Of course, I'm not so sure that telling lies is within the bounds of Christian morals either."

"I know." Megan looked chagrined. "Could you be my boyfriend for a while until we sort this out, and then it won't be a lie?"

"You just told him I proposed and we're engaged."

"Too much?" She was using her big eyes, like a cute three-year-old trying to get her way.

"I don't mind taking on the role for a while, but I'm not sure I could be convincing as a fiancé. I think there'd be less danger to your morals if I actually moved in."

"Oh. Right. Of course."

Shoot. He'd just hurt her feelings. She thought he was saying she was undesirable and not likely to tempt him. Well, that wasn't true. *Oh, the tangled web we weave when first we practice to deceive.*

"What about your sister?"

"Chloe?" Hope began to gleam in her eyes again.

"I thought your dad said she was coming back from an internship interstate. Will she move back in with your folks? Maybe she wouldn't mind sharing with you for a while."

"That's a good idea, Cam." She had a gorgeous smile.

"And hey, after we get married, we won't have to keep paying bills for two places, will we?"

Megan laughed.

Then he had a feeling of panic. "You know I was joking, right?"

She nodded. "Of course."

Bother it. This girl had his thinking in knots. Boyfriend, fiancé, he didn't think he could play either part, not when he wanted to actually be the part. Pretending was no fun but stepping over the line and taking the liberties that belonged to the role was tantamount to becoming Shane Telford. He would not go there.

Chapter seven

Chloe was home. Thank goodness. Megan didn't waste any time dropping by to present her idea. Chloe was ecstatic.

"That's a great idea! I'd love to come and live with you. We can catch up on all those sisterly things we've missed out on the last two years."

"Yes, and you can tell her about your boyfriend and how he's helping you with your work issues," Mum said.

"What boyfriend?" Chloe asked.

"Mum!" Megan objected. "You know that Cam is just pretending."

"Who's Cam?" Chloe's interest was piqued.

"A good-looking young police officer who has been helping Megan out, and I'm not so sure that he's just pretending."

"Of course he's pretending," Megan said. "Don't you go spreading rumors otherwise. The poor man probably can't wait for the day that my Shane Telford problems are over and he can say goodbye to this kooky family."

"Speak for yourself," Chloe said. "And tell me more. How did you meet him?"

"You can ask our mother that question. Mum? Would you care to enlighten the situation for Chloe?"

"He pulled me over for speeding," Mum said. "And I asked him to come to dinner for a research interview." She showed no repentance in either her tone or stance.

Chloe laughed and looked at Megan. "She set you up, didn't she?"

Megan nodded. She wanted to smile. Cam had been such a good sport, and she really liked him—as a friend.

"You like him, don't you?" Chloe teased.

"Of course. He has been nothing but kind, caring and helpful."

"Helpful?" Chloe asked.

"She means that he runs to her aid whenever she summons." Was that a smug smile on her mother's face?

"Megan!" Chloe sounded like a teenager screaming. "The man's in love with you."

"You should take up writing fiction, Chloe. Mum will help you out."

"That man would never have agreed to pose as your boyfriend in the first place if he had not been interested," Mum said. "I give you six months and you'll be engaged."

"Actually, we got engaged yesterday." Megan tried to add an air of confidence to her tone.

"What!" This synchronized response from both Chloe and her mother.

"Not really." Megan smiled at their goggle-eyed expression. "Shane was pushing me, taunting me about how he knew Cam was a fake, and it just came out. I told Shane that Cam and I were engaged."

"How did Cam take the news?" Mum asked.

"He's a good sport. He just doesn't think he should move in. Christian morals, you know."

"Megan, you are so slow," Chloe said, rolling her eyes.

"Why do you say that?"

"He doesn't want to move in because of his Christian morals, right?"

Megan nodded.

"If he was just pretending there would be no danger to his Christian morals. He's in love with you."

Did her heart just stop? No, it was still pumping, perhaps a few beats faster than usual. Did Chloe's round-about logic just make sense? Was that what Cam meant about Christian morals? "I don't think so," she said.

"Mark my words," Mum said. "He's not pretending as much as you think."

* * *

Megan wasn't sure what to think about what her mother and Chloe had said. Cam was attentive and caring, and he came when she called and at other times as well. *The man's in love with you.* Megan smiled as she remembered Chloe's wild exclamation. Was he in love with her? Something warm and fuzzy shifted inside. Should she examine the feeling or keep pretending it was a charade, on her side at least?

Just thinking about Cam was enough for her to send him a message.

When you come by, bring a herbal tea.

That wasn't what she'd wanted to write. *Do you really care about me? Are you really interested in a proper relationship?* Did she really want to know the answer to both of those questions?

"I don't appreciate the amount of socializing you do during work hours," Shane said to her, as she sent the text off.

"That's funny because I don't believe it's any of your business," Megan replied.

"During working hours, it is my business," he said. "I pay you to work, not send off text messages to your fiancé." He pronounced the word as if he still didn't believe it was true. Of course, it wasn't true, but he didn't need to know that.

"Cam never comes unless it's either my tea break or lunch break. Both of these times are my own, and I'm always back at my desk on time. And, you're not paying me that much anymore."

"That pay cut was your own fault, Megan. I can't afford to be paying someone who is not doing the job properly."

"You have no evidence that I was not doing the job properly, in fact, I am still doing all the office management roles I was before. You're supposed to be doing half of it now."

"If you stop being so standoffish and aggressive, I might consider reinstating your former position. Your sister's helping with the mortgage payments is hardly going to make up for the amount of money you lost."

An icy hand gripped her stomach. "How do you know about my sister? I haven't said anything to you about it."

Shane tapped his nose.

He was still tracking her. She had been so sure she'd kept all personal emails on the free account using her mother's old laptop. How did he know so much about her and her life?

Cancel the herbal tea. I think I might need a weak latte.

Megan sent off the text, complete with love heart emojis. She wanted to talk to Cam. Shane might have technically been obeying the rules, but he was slime. She could sense it. He was always watching her and her creep-alert sensor was keenly in tune to an underlying tension she could not shake.

At 12.30pm precisely, Cam walked through the door.

"Shane." He acknowledged her boss with a detached tone of voice. Shane was in his usual position—standing guard like a troll over his lair—and did not respond.

"Hello, my darling." Megan stood up from her workstation, grabbed her handbag and went over to him. It was his rostered day off and he looked less intimidating dressed in jeans and t-shirt than his uniform, but no less wonderful to look at. It was not hard to act like she enjoyed receiving his kiss.

"You forgot her coffee," Shane said.

Megan felt that jolt of alarm again. He must read everything she did on her phone.

"We'll grab one while we're out to lunch," Cam said and gave him a mock salute with two fingers. "Ready, Babe?"

Was she ready? Does a duck like water?

Instead of answering, she grabbed his hand and pulled him out the door.

"Weak latte?" Cam asked the question two steps from the door of the office.

"I had nothing to actually report other than that horrible feeling I have of him watching my every move."

"And his comment about the coffee?"

"Obviously, as he has access to my phone remotely, he must be able to read all my communications."

"But because it's his phone and company time, he has a right to keep in touch with all the business communications."

"You know it's more than that, right?" Megan asked, turning to look him in the eye as they walked side by side.

"I'm guessing it is, but I have to have evidence before I can take any action."

"And I'm guessing he knows that. That's why he's been so circumspect since I spoke to him."

"Spoke?" He laughed as he used air quotes. "I've never seen such a clear handprint on a man's cheek before. Those were some heavy words you used."

"Don't tease me, Cam. He put his hand on my knee."

"And he was lucky it was you there and not me, because a smarting cheek would have been the least of his troubles."

"Don't get yourself into trouble on my behalf," Megan said. "I can handle him."

"Can you?" Cam threw a pointed look in her direction.

It smarted that she wasn't really sure.

"Have you been looking for other jobs?"

She nodded. "There are a couple that seem promising, but applications don't close for another two weeks before I hear back about interviews."

"All I can say is to make sure you're on your guard with him and keep all your personal stuff on your home computer."

Cam held the door of the café open while Megan walked in. Her mother would love how much of a gentleman he was. Chloe wouldn't take too kindly to this protective cosseting. It would go against her independent woman, able-to-open-a-door-herself status. Megan also considered herself to be as capable as any man in any circumstance—except she had to admit that having Cam turn up as that layer of support and show of strength was comforting. Could she deal with Shane on her own? She shuddered. If she were trying to argue with her father about his sexist attitudes, she would say she could easily hold her own. But if she considered releasing Cam from the obligations of the charade, she felt anxious. Was that because she felt she couldn't handle Shane on her own or was it because she was enjoying having Cam's company? Perhaps it was a bit of both.

"Has your sister moved into your place yet?" Cam asked once they were seated and waiting for their lunch order to arrive.

"She has, but Shane said something this morning that upset me."

"About Chloe?"

Megan nodded. "He talked about Chloe being my housemate."

"And?"

"I haven't told him about Chloe and I haven't communicated with her other than with the home computer."

"Do you have your own private wifi?"

Megan shook her head and watched as Cam's frown deepened.

"What?" Megan asked. "I'm using hotspot for internet connection at home."

"Your boss is a wholesaler of electronics, right?"

"Yes, why?"

"And computer hardware and software?"

"Yes."

"It would appear he knows computers and IT very well."

Now Megan frowned.

"He's been able to hack your home computer through the hotspot coming from his internet service provider."

Megan felt a wash of cold from head to toe. "Are you sure?"

"I'm just guessing. But I believe it's possible."

"Cam." Forget independent woman. Megan wanted him to protect her. Was that wrong?

He reached across the table and took her hand in his. His hand was warm and strong and it made those swirls of fuzzy feelings permeate her chest. Chloe would be ashamed of her.

"You need to get out of this job and get rid of all the technology that belongs to him."

"I know. As soon as I get another position, I will be out of that place so fast he won't know what's hit him."

"I'm betting he already knows you're looking."

Megan tried to rein in the anxiety that had been dogging her. This was not who she was—cowered and uncertain. She wanted to explore this friendship with Cam and present herself as the stable and fun-loving person she'd been pre-Shane.

"Can we talk about something else other than Shane Telford for a bit?" she asked.

"Sure. What do you want to talk about?"

What did she want to talk about? Two things occupied her mind most of the time. Shane Telford and Cam Fletcher.

"Let's talk about you," Megan said.

"What do you want to know?"

"I haven't heard you talk much about your family."

"I lost my dad recently."

"I'm sorry." Megan squeezed Cam's hand. It felt natural to show sympathy through touch.

"Yeah, it was tough. He was the stable influence in our family life and I've had to take a long hard look at myself."

"Why?"

"I took him for granted. I didn't realize how much I relied on him always being there to take responsibility."

"Do you have siblings?"

"I have a brother who lives overseas, but I'm the eldest and I feel the weight of looking after Mum now that she's all alone."

"You said you still live at home with her."

"I lived out on my own for several years, but when Dad was ill, I spent those last months with him. I'm glad I did."

Megan squeezed his hand again. She saw the sorrow that was still there in his eyes.

"I haven't felt ready to leave Mum on her own yet."

"You're a good man, Cam."

Cam smiled at her and her heart somersaulted and landed flat on its back. This was dangerous, stirring up feelings she wasn't sure he reciprocated. Was he only playing the part? Should she ask him? What if he said he was only helping and wasn't interested? Best to leave those feelings alone—for the time being at least.

Chapter Eight

Lady Rosalie paced her chamber back and forth. This would wear a rut in the Persian rug if she persisted. Why had he not come? She had been in her father's care for over a month now and had recovered some of her spirits following the incident with Lord Osmond. But she had expected that Josiah would return. He had been so careful of her welfare and treated her with the utmost respect. Rosalie trusted him—and desired him. So where was he?

Rosalie had no wish to repeat an interview with her father. The last time he had railed at her for giving Lord Osmond so much trouble. He had promoted the rakish, jackanapes as an eminently suitable marriage prospect for her. She had shrunk under the fury of his words. Did he have any clue of Osmond's lack of moral fiber? Her father had given Osmond permission to call because he was rich. But he had not listened to her when she had told him what Osmond had done? Why had he sent Josiah Landown away? Lord Landown was a man who could be trusted—who stood head and shoulders above most other eligible men, both physically and in character. Lord Josiah Landown was the man she hoped her father would invite to court her.

"Lady Rosalie?" Her lady's maid, poked her head into her bedchamber.

"Yes, Hannah?"

"Your father says you are to dress to receive a guest."

Rosalie's heart began to pound in her chest. Had Josiah come at last?

"Who has come to call?"

"*That gentleman who was here not so long ago.*"

"*Lord Landown?*" Rosalie could barely contain her enthusiasm.

"*No, my lady.*"

"*Who then?*"

"*It is Lord Osmond.*"

Would the man never leave her alone? Would her father never see through the fake charm? Josiah, please come and take me away from this place.

"*Should I order tea or shall we send out for pizza?*"

"What?"

"Earth to mother?" Chloe said. "Are we just having afternoon tea, or dinner or what? You can't meet your new son-in-law and just send out for pizza. You have to organize something."

Louise laughed. "I've already met him, if you must know. I was the one who introduced him to Megan."

"Yes, I heard the speeding story."

"And we'd probably best not push the whole 'son-in-law' joke. I wouldn't want to scare him off."

Chloe laughed. "If he were that fragile, you would have scared him off just inviting him to dinner the first time."

"You might be right, but I still don't want to take a chance. As far as he knows, we're a normal family."

"You might have a bit of work to do to convince him of that. Anyway, Mother, back to the point, what are you planning to feed him?"

"What time is it?" Louise asked. "I got caught up with my story."

"You're always caught up in a story."

"It's my job, and I have a deadline."

"I know, I know," Chloe said. "That's why I've come around to make sure, since Megan is bringing her man to visit, you're prepared to feed him."

"I thought she was just dropping by."

Chloe shrugged her shoulders. "That may be *her* plan, but you don't want to lose an opportunity to invite them to stay and eat. So what's your plan?"

"I was just going to make spaghetti bolognese. Do you think that's good enough?"

"Depends on what impression you're hoping to make."

"Chloe, you attribute too much power to me—as if you think I really am the matchmaker or something."

"Ha! That's a good one."

"I just introduced them."

"And you have no interest whatever in how it turns out?"

"I shall let love take its own course."

"Come on, Mother. You don't expect me to believe you don't intend to help it along a little."

"I have Lord Landown and Lady Rosalie to sort out. Perhaps I can leave Megan and Cam to you. You seem to be showing a healthy interest."

"Yes, well, I have to admit this mysterious hero from the police department, who is posing as my sister's fiancé, has captured my imagination a bit. I can't wait to meet him."

"Hasn't she invited him over to your house yet?" Louise asked. "I would've thought he'd have been around as often as possible."

"According to Megan, it's just a charade they're putting on for her boss, and there's nothing in it."

"And you're here because …?"

"Because there is *so* something in it, and I want to meet him and see for myself."

"Well, since you're here, I'll put you in charge of getting the dining room set up and you can cut up some fruit to make a dessert platter."

"Excellent. Now that we have a plan, I feel much better."

* * *

"I hope you don't mind coming around to my folks' place again," Megan said, as she fastened the seatbelt in the passenger seat of Cam's car.

"Since your mum was the one who got me involved, I guess your parents would like to know how things are going with operation 'Shane.'"

"You realize Mum has ulterior motives, don't you?"

"She wants to research more about aspects of policing work for her novel?"

Megan laughed. "You keep telling yourself that."

Cam reached across the gear console and took her hand, squeezing it.

"If she is hoping for romance, then you can tell her we're engaged."

"I already told her that."

"Really?" Cam withdrew his hand and Megan's spirits plummeted. There was the confirmation they were only pretending. Why had she let her silly emotions hope for more?

"How did they take that?" he asked.

"They know it's only part of the plan."

"Mmm."

Was that it? Was she reading this situation correctly? Megan wanted to interrogate her fake fiancé. Surely he felt funny feelings—feelings that weren't consistent with an acquaintance who was doing a favor for a famous author. He was happy to joke about telling her parents they were engaged, but he seemed to have withdrawn when he realized they already knew. Did he feel the charade had gone too far? Perhaps it had.

* * *

"Well? Let me see the ring." Chloe didn't waste a moment to jump in on the 'joke'.

"Why are you here?" Megan asked. "You live at my house now."

"I came to meet your fiancé. Hi, I'm Chloe." She brushed past Megan and thrust her hand out to Cam. He grinned as she shook it. "I hope you've bought her a huge diamond ring."

She was incorrigible—almost as bad as Mum. And she wasn't helping.

"You know this is just an image we've adopted to help keep my sleazy boss in line." Megan knew her sister knew but wanted to make sure that Cam knew that she knew that she knew.

"Come in and sit down." Mum finally appeared and pushed past Chloe. "Never mind the teasing. We're all well aware that you're doing our Megan a tremendous favor. Would you like to stay for dinner?"

"No!"

"What're you having?"

Megan's refusal was overridden by Cam's question.

"Good man," Mum said. "It's always wise to make sure it's a good offer before accepting."

"Mum!"

Megan's protest fell on deaf ears as her mother on one side, and her sister on the other, ushered Cam down the hall and into the sitting room. It was her own fault. Chloe was as bad as Mum. How had she expected them to respond to an engagement announcement?

"Hello, Meggsy." Her father appeared in the hallway from his study.

"Hello, Dad." Megan kissed him on the cheek. "How's business?"

"It's going well, especially since Pete's started his own building business and not only gives me design work, but refers me to other builders."

"That's great." Megan kept looking towards the sitting room. What were her mother and sister saying to Cam?

"They won't eat him," Dad said. "I'm sure he's handled more difficult customers than those two in his line of work."

"They've run rampant with this engagement thing," Megan complained.

"Engagement?"

"Mum's told you about it. Don't pretend she hasn't."

Dad shrugged his shoulders. "She might have, but I thought she was talking about characters in her book."

"We *are* characters in her book. We are like her live-action figures."

Dad laughed. "That's a bit harsh, Meggsy. She means well. And besides, I heard you were quite dependent on Senior Constable Fletcher and him standing guard against that villain boss of yours."

"I am." Megan felt her shoulders slump. "If Cam decides we are all too crazy for him and pulls out on me, I don't know what I'd do."

"Has he said something?" Dad asked.

"Not yet, but I really sprang the 'engagement' on him without warning."

"How did he take it?"

"In his stride. He's a good sport."

Her father gave a strange sort of snort, which might have been a muffled laugh.

"What?" she asked.

"Nothing. I'm sure he's a good sport."

"You're not going to join in the band of fiction writers, are you?"

Dad put his arm around her shoulders. "My job is to simply make sure you, your sister and your mother are happy."

"What about Pete?"

"Pete can take care of himself."

"And you don't think that we can take care of ourselves because we're women?"

"No feminist lectures today, Meggsy. I'm sure you're quite capable, but your boss makes me want to forget I'm a peace-loving man."

"You can't come around to the office. How would it look if my father turns up to work to give my boss a good talking to?"

"I wasn't thinking of talking."

"Dad!"

"And so, if Senior Constable Fletcher wants to go undercover and watch over my girl for me, I'm more than happy."

"Are you sure that Senior Constable Fletcher is a trustworthy and decent person?"

"If he wasn't, he would never have made it to fake boyfriend, let alone fake fiancé."

Megan smiled at her father.

"I know you Meggsy. You can spot a rodent from a mile off. Our boy in there," he jerked his head in the direction of the sitting room, "is a good sport, and probably a good man."

"I think he probably is too." Megan accepted the side-hug her father offered and put her head on his shoulder. "I'm going to miss him once we've finished this undercover operation."

Dad didn't reply. Only grumbled something incoherent—man-talk that usually frustrated Megan, but this time she wasn't sure she wanted to know what he'd meant.

* * *

Megan's family was fun. They'd drawn him in as if he really were engaged to their daughter. Cam was enjoying the pasta, the conversation and the good-natured teasing, but wasn't sure Megan was quite so enamored with the game they were all playing. After all, it had been launched as strictly self-protection against Shane and his awful insinuations. It wouldn't do to get too comfortable in this intimate family situation where hopes might rise and lure him into becoming unnecessarily attached—as Shane imagined himself to be.

"Who's at the door?" Louise asked.

"Pete said he was coming over later," Russell replied.

"I wish you'd told me," she complained. "I would have saved him some pasta."

Cam had not met Pete, but knew he was the older brother. He felt like an interloper, having eaten a man's share of spaghetti and was sitting at the table, probably in Pete's position.

"Pete's our brother," Chloe informed him unnecessarily.

"I guessed."

"Where is everybody?" A man's voice called from the kitchen.

"In here," Louise called.

A tall, rugged tradie stepped into the dining room.

"Why are you all eating in here?" Pete asked.

"It's a dining room," Megan said. Was that defensiveness Cam heard in her tone?

"Yes, but you always eat … oh." Pete stopped speaking when his gaze lit on Cam. "Sorry, didn't know you had visitors."

"Pete, this is Cam," Russell said.

"G'day." Pete leaned across his sister and held his hand out. Cam took the offered greeting and felt a strong grip, probably produced by swinging a lot of hammers. Megan had told him her brother was a builder.

"Hi," he said.

"Cam is Megan's fiancé," Chloe piped up.

"Fake fiancé," Megan said. That was a quick response. Cam felt a punch hit his unacknowledged hopes. She didn't want her brother to believe they were a real couple. They weren't, so why did he feel this sense of disappointment?

"Fake?" Pete sat down in the one empty chair at the table and grabbed the last piece of Turkish bread from the middle.

"Don't you ever pay attention?" Chloe complained. "Senior Constable Cameron Fletcher has been posing as Megan's boyfriend to discourage that weasel."

"What weasel?"

"Where have you been?" Russell asked his son. "This has been going on for a few weeks."

"Sorry." Pete ripped a bite of bread from the piece in his hand. "I've been too distracted with Rianne getting ready to leave."

"She got off then, did she?" Louise asked.

Pete nodded. "She flew out yesterday. Touched down in Berlin a couple of hours ago."

"How are you holding up?" Russell asked.

Pete shrugged. "She had this great opportunity to study overseas. I couldn't stop her from going. She would've always resented me for it."

"Rianne is Pete's fiancé," Megan said to Cam.

"Not quite," Pete said. "I proposed, but we postponed the engagement until she gets back."

"When is she due to return?" Cam asked.

"She has a scholarship for two years."

Cam let out a whistle. "That's a long time to wait. Sorry, mate."

Pete acknowledged the comment with a deep breath and a nod, then he turned to Megan.

"Anyway, what's this business about you needing a fake boyfriend to ward off a weasel?"

Megan filled in the basic details for her brother.

"Why don't you just get another job?" Pete asked.

"Why didn't we think of that?" Chloe rolled her eyes, but Pete ignored her.

"I've applied for a couple, but haven't heard anything yet," Megan said.

"You should have said something. I've decided I need an administrator/bookkeeper."

"Really?" his mother asked. "Your business has taken off then?"

"It's crazy," Pete replied. "I can't keep up with everything."

"Is the position still open?" Megan asked.

Pete nodded, as he finished off his piece of bread.

"What would I need to do?"

"Take inquiries, make appointments, organize contractors, send out bills, keep books. Heaps of office duties."

"But you don't have an office," Chloe pointed out.

"Not yet. But if you want the job, Megs, you could work from your home office."

"I don't have internet," Megan said.

"I'll pay for internet."

"Or a computer, or a phone,"

"No problem. I'll write them off as a business expense."

"Make sure you set up your own passwords," Cam said.

She nodded. "I will, but I'm sure my brother isn't going to plague me like Shane has."

"What sort of fella is this Shane bloke?" Pete asked. "He sounds like a proper loser."

Cam wanted to use a few choice expletives to describe Megan's boss, but restrained himself.

"I'm pleased to hear your going out on your own in business is working so well for you," Louise said.

"I didn't think it would take off so quickly, but now that it has … Anyway, if you can get out of your job, I'd be keen for you to start as soon as you can." Pete looked at his sister.

"I better give a couple of weeks' notice," Megan said. "Pete, thank you. This is a huge relief."

"Don't say that until you find out how hard it is to set up and run an office. When I worked for my old company, I took all the admin staff for granted. I have to admit it's a whole lot harder than I'd thought it would be."

"I'll have it sorted out in no time."

Cam could tell Megan was relieved to have found an out from Telford Wholesalers. She sounded as if a great load had been lifted from her shoulders.

"Well that's all worked out nicely," Louise said. "Good timing, son."

"What about Megan's fake fiancé?" Chloe asked.

Suddenly the Brooker family focussed on him and he felt more an outsider than ever.

"I'm glad Megan has found a satisfactory solution to the problem," Cam said, forcing a smile. "She'll be pleased to get her life back."

"Yes. I can't wait," Megan said.

Can't wait? To be out of Shane Telford's office or to be rid of this fake relationship? Cam felt an annoying sense of loss. But he was not Shane Telford and this had been a charade set up by Megan's mother. He would let her go gracefully.

"If you've got time tonight, Megs, I'd like to talk to you about what I have in mind for setting up the office," Pete said.

"Sure," Megan replied. "Can you drop me home after so Cam doesn't have to hang around?"

"No worries."

And just like that, Cam was no longer an intimate part of the Brooker family. He began to understand why Shane had persisted beyond the boundaries. Cam had formed some kind of warm connection with Megan Brooker and it wasn't quite as easy to let go of as he'd thought it would be.

"I'd best get home," he said, once the others had become engrossed in family talk.

"Oh, sorry, Cam," Megan said. "I'll walk you out."

"Thanks for dinner, Louise."

"Any time," she replied. "Drop around whenever you're in the area."

Cam forced a smile. He held out his hand to shake first Pete's and then Russell's hand.

"Nice to meet you," Pete said.

"See you another time," Russell said.

Probably not, but he wouldn't say that out loud.

When they got out onto the front porch Megan looked at him.

"Thank you so much, Cam. I'm sorry this has dragged on so long."

"It's been my pleasure." Well, that wasn't a lie. It had been a pleasure but was proving to be painful at this point of good-bye.

"I don't know what I would have done if you hadn't been keeping an eye on me."

"I hope everything goes well for you working for your brother."

Megan laughed. "We'll probably argue, but at least I can trust him."

"If you ever need me, you know my number," Cam said. He leaned closer and kissed Megan on the cheek. Was that a flush coloring her cheek? Time to leave.

He walked down the garden path, through the gate and to his car. When he'd dropped over with his fake fiancée, he hadn't expected he'd be leaving on his own. A sense of loneliness stole over his heart as he drove away.

Chapter nine

Megan couldn't believe the wave of anxiety that swept over her as she approached Telford's Wholesalers building. She had been happy and positive last night as she and her brother had talked about setting up an office for his business, but that carefree spirit had fled with the promise of facing Shane. It shouldn't be that hard. Just give him written notice, do what she'd always done for two weeks, then she was home free.

Megan had already written the letter of notice the night before at her mother's and had printed it out. She did not want Shane pre-empting her resignation after hacking into her computer.

Two sales reps were in the office when Megan came in. *Thank you, Lord, for the buffer.* Should she give the letter to him while they were still there? It seemed like a sensible idea.

She carefully folded the printed sheet and started to put it in an envelope. Then she thought better of it. The envelope belonged to the company and she didn't want him to start accusing her of using office stationery for personal use.

"Hey, Megan." Domenic smiled at her as he passed her workstation.

"Domenic." She didn't have the emotional focus to engage chatting to the sales rep.

"The boss is on the rampage." He continued despite her lack of encouragement. "Reckons our sales figures are down."

"Are they?"

"A bit, but not enough to warrant his current foul mood."

Megan felt her heart accelerate to the next level. She was going to deliver this letter today no matter what. She wanted to be gone from this office as soon as possible, and she still had two weeks to serve from the point of notice.

"Anyway," Domenic continued, as he packed some files into his brief case, "I'd stay well clear of him today. I reckon this business with his missus has got him all wound up."

"What do you know about that?" Megan asked.

"Sue's filing for divorce."

"Really?" So Sue had finally got the courage to get the legal paperwork done. Megan wanted to cheer Sue on, but her timing was not great for Megan's situation and she could feel her stomach knotting. "That's awful."

"Yeah, poor bloke."

Poor bloke? Domenic had no idea what he was talking about. "What about poor Sue?"

Domenic frowned at her. "She's the one who'll get half the business and the kids and probably the house. She's the one who's taken off on him."

"I don't think Shane is as innocent as you seem to believe."

"He's a good boss, and has always done right by us employees. I hope this doesn't cause him financial trouble."

Domenic was obviously not interested in hearing another side to the story as he put the strap of his bag over his shoulder and left the office.

Megan didn't blame Sue, given what she knew about Shane, but she wished she'd not chosen now to move. Shane would be more volatile and Megan wanted out.

It was nearing lunchtime and the folded letter was still sitting beneath her mouse pad. She'd had plenty of time to deliver it, but no courage. She wanted to text Cam and have him come and talk her through it, but after she'd said goodbye last night, she'd got the feeling their charade was over—not that she wanted it to be over and not that she didn't need him anymore. More that she sensed he felt like he wasn't needed anymore. She should have talked to him about it. But what could she have said? *Don't go. I'm in love with you.* Was she? She felt something about him, but how to put that into words, and did he feel the same way, or was he relieved his role as fiancé was over?

Pete had offered her a job and her first priority was to extricate herself from this position. She would call Cam if necessary, but she had to learn to stand on her own two feet. She had to give notice herself. She would call Cam after she'd achieved this on her own.

She got up from her workstation, letter of notice in hand, and went to Shane's office door. It was closed. This was unusual, but she pushed on, tapping on the door with her knuckles.

"Can I come in?" She cracked open the door enough to put her head in.

"I can't think of anything I would rather have at this moment," Shane said. "Come in and shut the door behind you."

"I just want to drop a letter off for you."

"I'll read it later." He got up from his desk and was fast approaching her. She backed out of the door into the main office area, just waving the letter towards him, a bit like a wand trying to keep a beast at bay. He snatched it from her hand, unfolded it and quickly scanned the page. Megan wanted to run but was rooted to the spot, watching his features as he took in what she'd written.

"Are you serious?" he asked. "What, just because I demoted you? I wasn't for real. I just wanted to make you realize how good you have it here."

"I'll be leaving in two weeks, Shane," Megan said, wishing for a glass of water to lubricate her dry mouth.

"I'll give you your full wage back, plus a raise, and we'll forget you ever said anything about it."

"Two weeks. I'm not staying."

"You'll take the raise or you'll leave this office now—with nothing."

"I will leave this moment if that's what you want, but you'll have to pay me the two weeks, plus the holiday pay I have owing."

"I don't have to pay you anything. You've been socializing during work hours, you've made false accusations and now you're threatening to leave me in the lurch. If you leave, it will be today with nothing."

Megan stared at him. There was not a skerrick of moisture anywhere in her mouth now, and her eyes were stinging with tears, not to mention the lump of anxiety that was now bouncing between her stomach and throat.

"Well, the decision is up to you. Are you going to take the raise?"

Megan struggled to get her thoughts together. He would not let her go in a civil and easy-going manner. But she would not stay. Could not stay. Eventually she managed to shake her head.

"I can't stay."

"You've made your bed." Shane brushed past her and went to her desk. He took her mobile phone and put it in his pocket. He closed her laptop and disconnected it from the monitor at the workstation. "Get out," he said.

"You have to pay me," Megan said. "It's my legal right to the proper pay."

"Not when I've dismissed you for gross negligence and misconduct."

"I have done no—"

"Get out."

Megan was overcome by his powerful personality. He was going to push her if she didn't move.

"I need to get my things."

"No, you don't. Everything here belongs to the business."

"I own my handbag and purse, Shane. You can't pull that one on me."

She had to push past him to get her bag and when she turned around, he was blocking her exit.

"Please move aside," she said.

Shane didn't move but put her laptop on the nearest desk. Then he put his hands on her shoulders.

"Take your hands off!" Megan said.

He ignored her and brought his face close to kiss her. She wrenched to get out of his grasp and turned her face aside so that he ended up kissing her ear. Still he didn't let go.

"If you had stopped being so high and mighty and saw a good thing when it came to you, you could have kept your job and done very nicely," Shane said. "Instead of that, you had to treat me as if I was some kind of sleaze."

"You are a sleaze, Shane. You're a married man, and yet you believe you can treat me as if I am your personal play-thing."

"That is a gross exaggeration. You didn't object to your copper friend touching you whenever he felt inclined."

"That is none of your business. Now please stand aside so I can leave."

Shane held her with an icy stare for a few moments and she feared he was going to make another move. She braced herself ready to defend when suddenly he stood aside. Grasping her handbag firmly against her chest, Megan walked past him, out from the work area and out the front door. When she got to the footpath she burst into tears. She wanted Cam to be there for her, to hold her and tell her it would be all right. But she couldn't even text him. She didn't have a phone and even if she could remember where a payphone was, she had not memorized his number. It was stored in the work phone that Shane had just repossessed.

* * *

Cam had a funny feeling. Was it some kind of prompting from God or was it just he was hungry? Or was it that he missed Megan and wanted to talk to her?

"You shouldn't have let her get to you like that," Joel said, as they ate their sandwich in the squad car. "She was just using you."

"That was what we agreed to in the first place. It's not like she promised me anything more."

"Then stop pining over her. She doesn't need you now, so get your mind back on the job."

Cam heard his partner but wasn't quite prepared to get over her. He wanted to make sure she was all right.

"I'm going to text her to make sure she's OK."

"So, what're you telling me for?" Joel complained. "You never listen to any advice I give you."

Fine. Cam wasn't really concerned about Joel's opinion but he was concerned about Megan.

How has your day gone? Do you need any coffee?

He sent the text off and waited for a reply. Had he gone too far considering Megan had said last night she just wanted to get her normal life back? They had been back on the road traveling towards the next address they'd been given as a lead when his phone pinged. He was driving.

"Do you want me to read it for you?" Joel asked.

Did he? What if Megan said something personal? He didn't want Joel to read that out loud. But he couldn't read a text and drive. That was against the law.

"Pull over," Joel said. "You're killing me."

Cam pulled over and they changed drivers. He buckled in and picked up his mobile straight away, opening the message from Megan.

I'm fine. Don't need your help anymore.

The message was short but packed a terrible punch. He knew her problem was solved by her brother's offer of work, but he'd thought there was some level of friendship that had developed over the weeks they'd gone out together. This short terse message was not at all like the Megan he'd come to know. Or was it? Did he really know the young woman who he'd been building a fake relationship with? Perhaps more than the relationship was fake. Perhaps she was fake.

But that idea hurt. He didn't want to believe that. He didn't quite know what to believe.

"Let it go, mate," Joel counseled from the driver's seat. "We've got interviews to conduct and evidence to follow up. She's moved on. Let it go."

Easy for him to say.

* * *

"You have to follow this up with the Fair Work people," Chloe said over breakfast. "You gave notice and if he wants you to leave straight away, he's still obligated to pay those two weeks plus holiday pay owing."

"I know." Megan felt miserable. As office manager, she was familiar with the Fair Work Act. She knew what was legal and what was not. But Shane was intimidating and she didn't want to face him ever again.

"You have to follow it up, Megan."

"I can't."

"Why?"

"Because he ..." Because he what? He scared her? How could she say that?

"He's bullied you, Megan, and that is another offense under the Fair Work Act."

"I don't know what to do."

"Call Cam. He'll talk some sense into you."

"I cannot call my fake boyfriend whenever I'm facing something difficult to deal with. He's not there to jump at my every beck and call."

Chloe laughed. "I bet he would jump ... if you becked or if you called."

"Beckoned." What was the point in correcting her sister's speech? She was not going to beckon him. Besides, even if Cam did drop everything and rush to her, what was she going to tell him? She was not a kindergarten child in the playground, telling tales on the bully who wouldn't give her ball back. Though that was exactly how she felt. Except telling tales was a fruitless exercise. Cam didn't have any authority to make Shane pay what was owed. She would have to go through the Fair Work department and probably take him to court. It was all too hard.

"I say call him." Chloe got up from the small kitchen table and put her plate and mug in the dishwasher.

"I couldn't call him in any case," Megan said. "I don't have his number."

"You're ridiculous. How hard is it to call the station where he works and ask for his number?"

"No. *You're* ridiculous. What sort of police station is going to give out private phone numbers to random hysterical women?"

"You're his fiancée!"

"I'm not. Chloe! You know this. It was a charade for Shane's benefit."

"Pfft. You keep telling yourself that."

"What's that supposed to mean?"

"You know full well that there was something else going on, other than pretending."

"I don't know that at all."

"Well, take it from me."

Megan blew out a sigh through her nostrils. Like she was going to take Chloe's starry-eyed view on anything to do with romance. She wasn't in touch with the real world. Just like Mum, except Mum got paid for making up stories.

"Well, at the very least, you're going to have to put the hard word on Pete to start paying you sooner rather than later," Chloe said. "I can make my half of the mortgage repayments, and can afford my half of everything else, but I can't support you completely for two weeks."

"I'll call him today and tell him what's happened."

* * *

"Great!"

"Great? I tell you how I'm being robbed blind and all you can say is 'great'?"

"Sorry, Megs." Pete looked uncharacteristically remorseful. "That must have been tough for you."

"It was." Megan watched her brother as he sipped his early-morning takeaway latte.

He'd dropped around ridiculously early on his way to the building site.

"On the bright side, I can get you to work on my office straight away, and for me, that is great." Pete stole a piece of toast from Megan's plate and took a bite. She ignored it. She didn't feel like eating anyway.

"The question is, can you pay me straight away?"

"Hope so. That's your job to figure out."

"Pete! Don't you know how your money looks?"

"I have a vague idea, but that's what I've been telling you. I'm so far behind, it's all got on top of me. I'm hoping you can sort it all out."

"And hoping there will be enough there to pay me a fair wage?"

"I'm guessing there will be. I've been flat out quoting jobs, and I'm running interviews for an apprentice."

"So you're taking on two new employees?"

"Yep. And your experience with HR and payroll is going to be just what I need."

"Well, the first things I need are internet, a phone and a laptop."

"Great. Go out shopping today and get the best deal you can find." He took out his credit card and handed it to her.

"Pete! This is highly unprofessional, running business expenses on a personal credit card."

"I know. That's why I'm employing you. Lots to do, as you can see."

Despite Megan's misgivings, Pete left his credit card with her when he left for work. She shook her head. He was hopeless at administration. She hoped, once she'd spent all his money setting up an office and getting all systems in place, he had the money to pay her.

Chapter Ten

Shopping for a laptop and phone wasn't too hard. She chose the same model of both she had used previously with Telford's. Shopping for an internet connection and a phone plan was not quite so easy. The major internet service providers all boasted great plans, with huge data, calls and texts included. But getting that connection active was another thing altogether. She decided on a company to go with and placed the order. She was even given a sim card to put in the phone. But that didn't mean she was connected.

"You have no idea how frustrating it is trying to communicate with telecommunication provisioning operators," Megan complained to Chloe when she came home later that evening.

"Did they speak English?"

"Apparently, but not any kind of English I could understand."

Chloe laughed.

"It isn't funny. It's frustrating. Do you know how long I sat on hold today, listening to some extremely annoying on-hold music, being tossed backward and forward between different departments, and I swear they were all in offices in some country far, far away?"

"Well, at least you have your phone working."

"Uh-uh. I had to call from Mum's. My phone won't be active for the next forty-eight hours."

"And the good news for the day?" Chloe side-stepped the phone debacle as she pulled out a box of crackers from the pantry.

"The good news is I have a laptop. I don't have any programs loaded, nor do I have any of Pete's business information on it. I will have to find a reputable IT person tomorrow to help me get that up and running."

"You could ask Shane. He's good with computers."

Megan did not stop to think as she threw the kitchen sponge at her sister. "Don't!"

"I was just kidding," Chloe threw the sponge back into the sink.

"That's not funny," Megan said. "Shane is a … I don't want to ever talk about him again. You know what he did."

"I know. I'm sorry." To her credit, Chloe sounded remorseful. "Anyway, I'm going out to a movie tonight with a couple of girls from work. Do you want to come?"

Megan shook her head. "I'm already tired from running around all day and I'll have to do more of it tomorrow, and besides …"

Chloe stopped and looked at her, waiting for her to finish.

"Besides what?"

"Nothing."

"Are you missing Cam?"

Yes. "No," she said instead. "Of course not. I'm not going to go over this again."

"You *so* are missing Cam."

"I need to get an early night, and besides, I don't have the money to spend on a night out."

"Fair call."

Thankfully, Chloe let it drop, and Megan watched as her sister buzzed around the house getting ready. Chloe was right. She missed Cam. How stupid was that? They'd only been pretending and yet the idea of going out to the movies without him held no appeal whatsoever. She wished she still had his number as she was sorely tempted to give him a call.

"Be good," Chloe said, as she picked up her bag to go out. "Don't do anything I wouldn't."

"I'm the one staying in!" Megan yelled after her. That girl was such a whirlwind, it was hard to keep up. Still, Megan was glad she had a housemate—an expenses-sharing housemate.

With Chloe gone for the evening, Megan didn't have the motivation to cook anything for dinner. She opened the fridge twice and toggled between it and the pantry. She finally settled on eating cheese and crackers. Then in a moment of extravagance, she decided to slice a dill pickle to put on top of each one.

She was bored and should have gone with Chloe. It probably wouldn't have cost that much and she could have paid the credit card off once she got Pete's finances working enough to issue her first pay. But Chloe was gone and she was alone. She couldn't scroll through Facebook. She couldn't call her mother for a chat. She couldn't text Cam. Bother this dependence on technology. It ruined a person for normal brain function. The best she could do was watch mindless television or read a book. Eventually, she decided it was time to catch up on some of the devotions she'd allowed to lapse during busy times. The readings were in a nicely presented book her mother had given her for Christmas. She was supposed to read one a day and was only twelve days behind. *Sorry, Lord.* How was it she got so distracted with work and life she often forgot to pray? Thank God her salvation was based on God's grace and not how up to date she was on her devotion schedule.

A knock on the front door drew Megan's attention away from her Scripture reading just as she was beginning to connect.

"Just a minute," she called. She wasn't expecting anyone. Chloe had a key. Pete had told her he was going out with his mate, Andy. Mum and Dad usually called if they took a notion to visit. Cam?

Would he just drop around? Wouldn't it be great if he did? Megan took a moment to look in the mirror. Ugh! Not exactly what she would want to present to the likes of Cam if he was at the door. But she didn't have time to sort her appearance out now. She didn't want him to leave if he was there.

Taking a deep breath, Megan pulled open the front door, then froze. Shane.

"Can I come in?"

"No!"

"Come on, Megan. Just for a while." He began to step forward but Megan quickly closed the door on him. It latched, and Megan turned the lock as Shane tried the handle from the outside.

"You don't need to pretend to be angry. We always got on well together …"

"I'm not pretending, and we did not get on well together," Megan shouted through the closed door. "I don't want you here, Shane. You need to leave now."

"Or what? Are you going to call the police?"

"Yes!"

"With what?"

The telephone. It wasn't connected. What was she going to do? She looked around the house hoping that some sort of inspiration would appear. Her front window blinds were open, so she hurried over to pull them down. Shane was already there looking in.

"Go away!" she called as she shut him out.

"Let me in, Megan. I just want to talk."

Not likely. She rushed to the laundry to make sure the back door was locked. It wasn't, so she made quick work of securing that latch as well. By this time, Shane was back at her front door banging.

God, help me, please. No, she hadn't been in touch with God in recent times, but she had no doubt He was the one to appeal to in this situation. But despite the desperate prayers she was muttering, they didn't negate the panic that had her chest knotted and her pulse racing. Shane continued to knock on the door, calling out to her. She hoped he wouldn't do something macho, like apply his shoulder against the door, as it wasn't the best quality lock she'd ever seen, and she didn't have a lot of confidence it would hold a serious attack.

"Megan?" He called again. "Don't make it so difficult. I just want to talk."

Should she answer or should she pretend she couldn't hear him? What to do? There was no phone or technological communication available to summon help—like in the old days before the light bulb was invented. How on earth had her ancestors of yesteryear managed to fend off random stalkers? But then, of course, the random stalker would not have known where she lived if it hadn't been for his ability to track her phone. *Please go away. Please go away. Please, God, make him go away.*

Megan stared at the front door which had so far been holding the attacker at bay, and even as she stared, it rattled again with what sounded like a screw-loosening thud. The lounge chair. Megan went over and began to wrestle with the large single armchair, shifting it across the living space toward the front door. After she got that firmly in place against the door, she went back and decided to shift the small bookcase. It was too heavily loaded with books, so she took them out, a handful at a time, and then shifted the empty bookcase over and propped it against the chair. Then she took the books and piled them on top of the chair for extra weight. Would that hold him? The table wasn't that big that she couldn't manage to drag that across to add to her barricade. By the time she'd finished, she had as much furniture as she could move from the kitchen living area, stacked in the entryway against the door. Then she sat on the carpet facing the door and stared. She wasn't sure when, but some time ago, Shane had stopped banging and calling. But there was no way she was going to clear the entrance. She might have been tired, but there was no chance she would be able to relax enough to go to bed. In fact, she went around the house and checked all windows and blinds. Were they secure?

Peace. Trust me.

Megan saw her bible, now dumped on the kitchen bench, and remembered she'd been reading about the peace of God that passed all understanding. That's not what she'd been experiencing for the past hour while she rearranged all her furniture. The opposite had been giving her a rush of adrenaline-fuelled strength. Panic—pure unadulterated fear—had gripped her mind, and her body had responded in kind.

Peace.

She heard the word in her spirit again. Suddenly, she realized Shane had gone—from the front door at least. She was all right. He hadn't broken in and she was safe. *Thank you, God.*

But despite her recognition of how panic had driven her into a crazy battening down of hatches, she still felt a bit wobbly on her legs, and not quite prepared to clear the furniture away.

* * *

"Megan! What's going on?"

Megan was jarred from sleep, finding herself curled up on the carpet with one of the chair cushions. Chloe was home, had unlatched the door and was trying to push it open against the blockade.

"Megan? Are you all right?"

"Yes." Megan got up and started pulling the furniture away from the door.

"What on earth happened?" Once Chloe had her head inside, worry was all over her face.

"Shane." That one-word answer was explanation enough.

"What? Did he get inside?"

All of a sudden, Megan couldn't talk. A lump formed in her throat and she struggled against tears stinging her eyes.

"Megan? Are you all right?" Chloe persisted.

Megan lifted the book case away and then helped drag the armchair completely away.

"Megan?"

"He didn't get in," Megan eventually said. "He tried, and he was banging at the door for ages. I couldn't call anyone for help."

Chloe had stepped over the obstacles, come to her sister and taken her in a hug. "It's all right now," she said. "I won't let him get near you."

Megan nodded, then pulled back.

"Come on," Chloe said, taking her by the arm.

"Where are you going?" Megan asked.

"I'm taking you down to the police station to make a report."

"Couldn't we just call the cops and have them come here."

Chloe shook her head. "You've heard Cam tell you how under pressure their constables are, being called to all sorts of domestic disputes and whatnot."

"But Shane came here and tried to get inside."

"Remember what Cam said. Shane has finally stepped over the line. Coming here tonight, uninvited, and refusing to leave, constitutes stalking. We need to make a report so they can serve him an official warning."

"When did you talk to Cam? You only met him once."

"I've heard you and Mum quote Cam ad nauseam. It's all I've heard you talk about."

"I don't think that's true."

Chloe just stared back at her, eyebrows raised.

"Well, in any case, I think Cam said it has to happen on two occasions before they can serve a warning."

"Well, this is the first. We need to report it. And besides, Cam might be at the station, and it wouldn't hurt for you to talk to him."

"I would have called him tonight, but I had no phone connection."

"What did you do?"

"Built a wall and prayed."

"By the looks of the wall, it looks like you might have panicked a bit too."

"You have no idea. I was terrified he would break the door down."

"Was he trying to break in?"

"I'm not sure. But he was definitely trying to get in. It was as if he thought I was going to respond to his pleas. As if. Why doesn't he leave me alone?"

"Get your bag," Chloe said. "We need to strike while the iron's hot."

"So many metaphors, Chloe. Mum would be proud."

Megan walked out, skirting misplaced furniture on her way to the door. The spring evening air was cool and bracing in the circumstances. Megan took a deep breath as she walked to Chloe's car, but then stopped short. Shane's car was parked on the street about twenty meters down.

"Quick, open the car!"

"What's the matter?" Chloe turned to look at her.

"Open the car!" Even as she said it, she saw through her peripheral vision that Shane had started the engine of his car. Was he going to follow them? She heard the car doors click open and without stopping to see what else Shane would do, she got in.

"Hurry up, Chloe," she called. "Lock the doors."

"Was that Shane's car?" Chloe asked. She sounded a good deal calmer than Megan felt. She nodded.

"What a piece of slime."

"You have no idea. What if he follows us?"

"To the police station? I hope he does. That will constitute incident number two and we can get that official warning issued on site."

Megan buckled herself in, rested her head back against the passenger seat and took a deep breath.

"It's going to be all right," Chloe said.

Megan didn't answer but stared straight ahead as they began to drive. Would it be all right? Shane might have been an ordinary sort of boss, a bit clueless and sexist, but his latest actions had elevated him to the level of crazy stalker person, and he'd managed to terrify her.

* * *

As Megan walked into the police station reception area accompanied by her sister, she scanned the whole area. This was the station where Cam was based. Would he be here somewhere?

It was a Wednesday night—Thursday morning, actually as midnight had passed a half-hour ago—and the waiting area didn't seem to be too busy.

"How can I help you?" A young woman of similar age to Megan addressed them as they approached the counter. The police officer looked professional and just a tad intimidating in her dark navy-blue uniform with badges and buttons. Constable Lillian Whitmore, according to the identification badge.

"We want to make a report of stalking." Chloe had spoken before Megan could get the words out.

"Was anyone hurt in the incident?" Constable Whitmore asked.

Megan shook her head.

"Depends on whether you'd call emotional trauma hurt or not," Chloe said.

"I'm all right," Megan said, frowning at her sister.

"You were barricaded in your house and clearly terrorized."

"All right," Constable Whitmore said in a placating tone. "Perhaps it would be best if we found an interview room to take your statement."

Megan followed the police officer and her sister in a bit of a daze. Was she just tired or was her sister right? Had Shane's unwanted attention traumatized her? She hoped not.

Once seated in the interview room Constable Whitmore took out a pad and pen.

"I need to inform you that we will record this interview, as it may be used as evidence in court if the situation persists to a point of prosecution."

Megan nodded. She hoped it wouldn't persist. She hoped Shane would take the hint and leave off.

"Our friend told us if there were two reported incidents of stalking that an official warning can be issued," Chloe said.

"Does your friend work in the department?" Constable Whitmore asked.

"Constable Cameron Fletcher," Chloe said.

"And your name?"

"I'm the one making the report," Megan said. "Chloe wasn't there. I was on my own."

"OK. What's your name?" Constable Whitmore had her pen poised ready to write.

"Megan Brooker."

"Aaah. You're Megan."

Even as the words came out of her mouth, an awkward silence fell.

"What do you mean?" Megan asked.

A shade of red infused the officer's face. Was she flustered?

"I apologize. You're the young woman who was trying to address a case of sexual harassment. Constable Fletcher was helping you … in a non-professional capacity."

"Yes," Chloe responded. "He was posing as her boyfriend."

"Fiancé, last I heard," Constable Whitmore said.

"What? Just wait." Megan held up her hand. "Did Cameron come back to the station and announce our situation to everyone?"

"That's very unprofessional," Chloe said.

"No. Sorry." Constable Whitmore reached across and switched off the recording device. "I think we need to clear something up before we record the statement."

Megan nodded, but she knew her brow was furrowed. She could feel the tension of it.

"Constable Fletcher …"

"Cam," Megan said.

"Cam's good friend and colleague, Joel Baker …"

"Yes, I met Joel a couple of times."

"Joel is my boyfriend."

"So what, you were talking about Cam behind his back?" Megan asked.

"I'm sorry. I've just breached all protocols of confidentiality and privacy. What a mess."

"You can say that again," Chloe said.

"Joel was concerned about Cam, especially when you broke up with him in such a harsh manner."

"What?"

"Sending him that abrupt text, telling him you didn't want to see him anymore."

"Megan!" Chloe turned an angry scowl her way.

"I didn't send Cam any text of the sort," Megan said. "I haven't even had a phone in the last few days."

There was a tense moment of pause as all the pieces began to click into place.

"Shane sent the text," Chloe guessed.

"Well, it wasn't me."

"And Shane is the person who was harassing you at work?" Constable Whitmore asked.

"And who tried to get into her house this evening," Chloe added.

"OK. I've got the picture now. Just before I press record again, I have to apologize for that breach of ethics. I shouldn't have said anything when I recognized your name."

"Your department shouldn't be discussing me and Cam behind our backs, either."

"It wasn't the department. Only me and Joel. Joel was worried about his mate getting a broken heart."

Chloe was smiling. Smiling! "Stop that smirking," Megan complained. "It was a mutually agreed arrangement, organized by our mother, as you well recall."

"She's in denial," Chloe said to the interviewing officer. "She and Cam are so in love, but just won't admit it."

"I can vouch for Cam's side of it," Constable Whitmore said. "Joel thinks he's lost his mind."

"Well, you can reassure your boyfriend that Cam couldn't find a better partner if he's looking for one," Chloe said.

"If you two have finished discussing my private life. I have a real problem of an obsessed former boss who's frightening the life out of me."

"Why didn't you call Cam tonight?" Constable Whitmore asked.

"No phone, remember? I mean, I have the phone and the sim card, but the connection hasn't gone through yet."

"Telecommunication service providers!" Constable Whitmore said.

"You're telling me," Megan replied.

"OK. Now we're all on the same page, we'll need to make the formal statement. Are you ready?"

"Pardon me for throwing a spanner in the works," Chloe said, "I've watched enough crime shows to ask the question."

Constable Whitemore paused and turned a questioning look in Chloe's direction.

"Shouldn't you get a different officer to take the statement? With the personal connection through Joel to Cam to Megan, couldn't someone challenge the report as being influenced?"

Constable Whitmore nodded. "Wait here and I'll send someone else in to take the statement."

"Could you tell Cam I didn't send that text?" Megan asked before she left the room.

"I'll pass the message along." She smiled and left them alone.

Chapter Eleven

He'd found her. She was sequestered with her second cousin in an Italian convent—her father's punishment for refusing to speak to Lord Osmond. Her father's punishment was her haven, but Lord Osmond had found her. Apparently, he had not been offended by her refusal to see him.

"Lord Osmond has sent word that he has come to take you back to England," Sister Maria Bernadette said.

Rosalie took hold of her cousin's hand. "Maria Bernadette, don't make me go. I'm happy to stay here with you."

"You are not even of our faith, Rosalie," the nun replied. Her eyes were sad.

"How we worship is different, but surely it is the same Christ. Surely our hearts are to serve the same Lord."

"Your father has sent word to my mother. They want me to force you to go with Lord Osmond."

"I will not go with him. He is indecent."

"He says he will marry you here in our chapel."

"I will not go. You cannot make me go."

"It is your father's will."

"Not my heavenly Father. He would not require that I make myself vulnerable to such a man. I will stay here and serve the Lord among you."

"But you are not called to the humble life of celibacy and service? You would have to convert to our Catholic faith."

"Your mother converted when she married your father."

"*They were in love, Rosalie. My mother gave up her English faith and homeland because she loved my father. Would you be willing to do the same for Christ?*"

Rosalie thought for a moment. The outward trappings of faith were not a huge concern to her. However, unlike her Catholic cousin, she believed she could be devoted to Christ and love another at the same time. If it had been Josiah who was planning to carry her back to England as his wife, she would be gone in a moment. Lord Osmond was a detestable person. How could she get word to Lord Landown? Who could she trust to deliver such a message, and was it within the realms of propriety for her to send such a letter in the first place? If only she could have one of the bell-tower doves come and take it directly to the man she loved. If only the service provider would make the connection. How hard is it to connect the internet?

"Mum, are you listening?"

"Yes, dear. I imagine it must have been frightening to have had no way of getting in contact with Cam."

"Cam? I would have called you and Dad first," Megan said.

"Would you? I would have thought you'd have called Cam first, given he's a police officer."

"I don't have his number anymore. I didn't memorize it and it was stored on the work phone."

"Maybe I have it." Louise turned back to her computer and started scrolling through her inbox.

"Mum, you really should clear out your inbox. You've got like over fifteen hundred emails."

"I know." She kept scrolling.

"You know you can type his name in the search bar and it will isolate just the emails from him?"

"Really?" Louise put her cursor in the search box that Megan pointed out at the top of the inbox, typed in 'Senior Constable Cameron Fletcher', and just like that, fifteen hundred plus emails turned into three—each one a communication from the man in question.

She opened the first one and scrolled to the bottom of the letter. He had an automatic signature complete with title, the police station address, and the phone number of the police station.

"I already have that number," Megan said, reading over her shoulder.

"Why don't you call him there?"

"It's a bit dodgy. I want to talk to Cam on a personal level and I don't think I should call him on the work number. We already nearly messed up that report because of our personal connection."

"Send him an email."

"I can't, for the same reason. I've just made a report for Shane's stalking behavior. It can be a major offense and he could face jail time, but not if I gum up the evidence with personal calls."

"Fine, I'll email Senior Constable Cameron Fletcher."

"You need to be careful about what you say."

"I'll be careful," Louise promised. "I have a way with words."

"Ha, ha!" Megan put her hand on her mother's shoulder. "See that you are."

"I'll send an inquiry off now while I'm thinking about it. Why don't you go and put the kettle on? See if your father is up for a cup of tea."

Megan left the office and Louise turned her attention to writing the email.

Dear Senior Constable Fletcher,

You may remember me. You were kind enough to submit an interview for research purposes for my novel, and I really appreciate the follow-up you were willing to give when the situation arose. One of my main characters, Megan, recently had a situation where her former boss came and tried to enter her house against her will. I imagine it would have been frightening. I wonder if you would be good enough to help me fill in some of the legal and procedural gaps for my story. You can contact me on this email address or the phone number you see at the bottom.

I look forward to hearing from you shortly concerning this matter.
Yours sincerely
Luella Linley, Author

* * *

"What's the matter with you?" This question from Joel after Cam had uttered a decidedly unchristian expletive.

"Look at this." Cam held his phone with the email open for his partner to read.

"Yeah, Lilly said she was in the other night to make a report."

"Why didn't you tell me?"

"Because Megan told you she didn't need help from you anymore."

"Joel ..."

"But then Lilly told me something that made me wonder if we might not have got our wires crossed."

"What?"

"Megan never sent you that break-up text."

"How did Lilly know about that?"

Joel looked ashamed of himself.

"Who have you been talking to about my love life?"

"There, you see. You admitted it, finally."

"Admitted what?"

"That you were in love with Megan."

"I said 'my love life' or, more accurately, my 'can't find anyone to love' life. I didn't say I was in love with her."

"But you put her in your 'love life' category, which means you were interested and hopeful."

"We already discussed this. I was interested and hopeful until I got her text."

"Which she didn't send."

"It was a reply to a text I sent her. Of course she sent it."

"Sometimes, for a smart and educated man, you can be incredibly stupid."

"Mate, that's harsh."

"She left her mobile phone with Shane because he sacked her on the day she gave notice. He seized all her technology."

"What? How do you know all this stuff?"

"Megan told Lilly the other night when she came in to report the stalking incident."

"Joel, that sounds incredibly unprofessional, and a breach of privacy."

"Well, yeah, and Lilly got someone else to take the statement."

"But she'd already got all of this info first?"

"It's a long story. All you need to know is Megan didn't send you that text and that Shane bloke was at her place trying to get in."

"Why didn't you tell me?"

Joel shrugged. "I didn't think you'd be happy knowing I'd talked to Lilly about it."

"And why didn't Megan call me?"

"No phone."

Cam opened his mouth to throw in another question, but came up short. All the pieces started fitting together. Shane had tried to get into her house and she hadn't been able to call anyone. Another expletive slipped from his lips.

"Mate, I'm not a Christian, but with your recently found religion I don't think those words are appropriate."

Cam let out a loud breath of frustration.

"Are you going to call her?" Joel asked.

"If it isn't the one stored in my phone, I don't know her phone number, do I?"

"Well, you could email the author lady back and get her to give you the new number."

"Or I could go around to Megan's place and see for myself if she's all right."

"Given the pressure she's under with unwanted male visitors on her doorstep, I wouldn't advise it."

Cam's bottom lip rested behind his teeth ready to let fly again, but he thought better of it just in time. "Feather duster!"

Joel laughed. "Very original, and I'm sure your priest would appreciate you made the effort."

Joel was right. It was not wise for him to go rushing around to Megan's without a proper invite. Besides, he was still feeling gun-shy since taking the hit from the text—except she hadn't sent the text. Funny how hard he'd taken it—how hurt he'd been when he thought she'd used him and spat him out when his usefulness was exhausted. And the last few days his emotions had been swinging between the sting of rejection and anger that she'd used him. But none of that was real. Or at least, it appeared that none of it was real based on the most recent intel.

Cam stifled the desire to groan. He needed to hide his frustration. Joel, and now Lilly apparently, were watching him closely and had been discussing the wisdom of his actions concerning Megan. He hated to seem impulsive and emotional. That wasn't his usual form. In the last few days, he'd been reciting a mantra—it was just a charade. There was nothing in it. But she hadn't sent the text. And her mother had sent a veiled plea for help. Or was it a plea for help? His newfound faith was not consistent with his old swearing habit, but he sure would like to express his frustration somehow.

"Go and visit the mother," Joel said.

"What?" Cam feigned surprise and confusion.

"You're squirming around like a perp in the interview room. If you need to find out exactly what's happening, you'd better go find out and, given the mother has sent you the message, I guess that is a legitimate path of inquiry to follow."

"I'll go when our shift finishes."

"You do that. Do you want me to come with you?"

"I think I can manage."

"Good. Can you get your mind on the job, please? We have lines of inquiry relevant to several investigations, and your attention to detail would be highly appreciated."

* * *

Cam was still in uniform when he turned up at Louise and Russell Brooker's home. He should have got changed at the station, but given his impatience to get answers, he let it slide.

"Cam!" Russell opened the door. "Good to see you, I think." He cast his eyes up and down and took in the full uniform. "Anything we should worry about?"

"Yeah, no. I'm off duty. Just thought I'd drop by on the way home. Got an email from your wife."

"About the break-in at Megan's?"

"He broke in?" A band of anger tightened in his abdomen.

"He tried to force his way in, but Megan barricaded the door with every piece of furniture in her living area."

Cam felt cold panic go through his circulatory system, closely followed by hot rage. If he ever got hold of that excuse of a man, he'd …

"Come in and take a load off. Got time for a cup of tea?"

Cam followed his host inside. His mind was ticking over at a ridiculous rate, each thought attaching to rogue emotions that were pinging around, screaming for attention, then stimulating new thoughts.

"Louise!" Russell called as he walked past her office. "Cam's here for a cuppa. Have you got time?"

"Just a minute." Louise's voice filtered back to them.

"She's pushing to finish a manuscript to meet a deadline," he explained as he filled the kettle and switched it on.

"Is Megan all right?" Finally, Cam got his thoughts together enough to formulate a sensible question.

"She was pretty shaken up that night, but Chloe took her down to make a report at the police station, then they came over here for the rest of the night." Russell didn't seem upset as he relayed this information. He opened the pantry cupboard and pulled out a biscuit barrel. How could he be so calm and domestic in such a situation?

"I wish she'd called." Cam pulled out a chair at the kitchen table and sat down, though he couldn't relax. He perched on the front of the chair as if ready to leap up and charge out to the rescue.

"Did you hear about all the fiasco with her being dismissed without pay instead of her serving out her two weeks' notice, and then he took all her technology on the spot."

"I heard a distilled version of it this morning, but I'd like to hear it in full detail."

Russell placed a mug of tea on the kitchen table in front of him and recounted the details of Megan's attempt to give notice, eating a biscuit at the same time. How could he eat? Cam's stomach was in knots.

"She could probably sue for the money owed to her," Cam said.

Russell nodded. "She knows, but you know how difficult it is to follow through on all those details and, at the moment, she just wants to get clear of the man. Pete's willing to pay her straight away, so I think she's just going to let it go."

"Shane shouldn't be allowed to get away with it." Cam's agitation wouldn't let him sit anymore. He walked over to the kitchen window before swinging back around. "He was bordering on sexual harassment as it was, and now unfair dismissal."

Russell nodded again and dunked another biscuit into his tea.

"Constable Fletcher!" Louise came into the kitchen, looking pleased to see him. "Why don't you sit down?" She waved towards his vacant chair.

"Call me Cam." He moved back to the chair and sat down, no less agitated than he'd been a few moments ago.

"I didn't want to presume, given the change in circumstances."

Cam tried to hide his warring emotions with a cough.

"It was a shame she didn't have your number to call the other night," Louise said as she poured hot water onto her teabag in a cup.

"She should have called the police," Cam said.

"She couldn't call anyone," Russell reminded him.

Cam felt awkward, and finally took a sip of his tea to cover for it.

"Can I be frank?" Louise said as she sat down at the table with them. He nodded. He had the distinct impression that Louise Brooker, aka Luella Linley, was used to being frank.

"Do you want to sever communications with Megan now that she's working for her brother?"

What a question to ask! How should he answer it? Honesty equaled vulnerability at this point and he wasn't sure he wanted to go there.

"Because we would perfectly understand if you wanted to put professional distance between you," she continued. "Your playing the part of her boyfriend was a catalyst in the finish."

"What do you mean?" he asked.

"I was hoping it would make Shane back down and behave himself if he believed Megan had a strong man who would be willing to take her part."

"You could have got her father or brother to drop in," Cam said. "Shane might not have become so obsessive."

Russell sniggered. Actually sniggered, almost losing a mouthful of tea in the process.

Cam looked at him. What was he thinking?

"Russell," Louise said crossly. "You said yourself that at least Megan had a clear decision to make now. You're glad she's out of that job, don't pretend you're not."

"I am glad she's out of that job," he reached for another biscuit.

"And that was due in large part to your coming in as you did." Louise looked directly at Cam.

"I'm worried I might have caused Shane to become more obsessive than he was before," he said.

"So, the question is—are you willing to keep the connection? Stay involved?"

"I got a text from her to say she didn't need my help anymore ..."

"What?" Louise sounded alarmed. Russell sniggered again.

"What are you laughing about?" she asked her husband.

"I'm laughing at you."

Louise's facial expressions were telegraphing stern words to her husband. Russell seemed unrepentant and turned his focus on Cam. "You do understand Louise is meddling with hopes of matchmaking?"

Of course he realized this but hadn't acknowledged it openly. Megan had said as much on many occasions. He'd have to be fairly naïve to imagine it was anything else. Did it bother him?

"I am concerned for our daughter's welfare," Louise said. Her defensiveness was obvious in both her tone and the set of her chin.

"Yes, Louise, I realize you're concerned for her welfare, and yes, Russell, I understand this has been an attempt at matchmaking—a reasonably good attempt, I might add."

He watched for Louise's predictable response. Did she look pleased? What was he saying?

"So, you are ...?" She leaned forward her eyebrows raised as if asking for clarification.

"I'm concerned about Megan's welfare. I thought the text saying I should back off was from her. Now that I know it wasn't, and that her phone number has changed, I'm keen to see if there's anything I can do to help."

She looked pleased. There was no missing it. How serious was he?

"Do you know what you're letting yourself in for?" Russell asked.

Cam shook his head. "Do you think Megan is open to continue seeing me?"

"I'm sure she is." Louise's whole demeanor lit up and her shoulders seem to relax, as if she'd got the answer she was looking for.

Cam looked to Russell to see what he thought.

"I'd give her a call and see what she says. Parental meddling might be an introduction, but if you want something to develop, you're going to have to see to that yourself."

Cam nodded. "You don't think she will feel crowded or under pressure if I pursue the relationship, you know, given the pressure she's been under with Shane?"

"Shane Telford is a married man, to start with," Louise said. "And from what Megan has told me, he's been highly inappropriate with his insinuations."

"I think you should give her a call," Russell said. "Let her tell you where you stand. It's no good us trying to tell you what she feels or how she might respond."

"I don't want to make her feel insecure or pressured."

"Ask the question, and I believe she will tell you straight out." Russell got up from the table and put his coffee cup in the sink. Cam took his still-half-full mug over as well. The few steps helped to alleviate the building tension he was feeling.

"Will you do me a favor?" He turned back and looked at Louise. "If Megan tells you she wishes I would disappear or back off, could you tell me straight away? I'd hate for her to put up with me because she was too polite or felt intimidated to tell me the truth."

"I promise," Louise said.

"And I'll make her if she's tempted to conceal evidence," Russell said.

Chapter Twelve

*D*id she have everything she needed to run Pete's business? Megan ran a critical eye around her newly converted spare room. She had installed a new return desk, a four-drawer filing cabinet, a printer that doubled as a photocopier, and a top-of-the-range comfy office chair. And the most exciting installment was the internet modem with flashing lights. She longed for the day the lights would stop flashing and indicate they had connectivity to the World Wide Web, but one could not expect miracles when dealing with telecommunication companies.

"What do ya think, Megs?" Pete put his arm around her shoulder. "Are you ready to turn this into a thriving business?"

"I was under the impression your business was already thriving."

"I'm busy on the tools, with loads of work coming in, but if I don't get a good administration going, the whole thing will fall on its head. You coming on board is going to save my life." Pete squeezed her shoulder in a side hug. "Thanks, Megs."

Not that it was an imposition for her. This job, if it worked out, was her ticket out of Telford's and away from Shane.

Shane.

How was it that he could still shake her confidence? Since he'd tried to gain entry the other night, Megan had been anxious about being home on her own. During the day was not so bad. Admittedly, she had spent a lot of time out with Pete shopping for the office furniture and had made trips home to 'pop in' on Mum and Dad. She was determined. Shane would not win with this intimidation.

Except Chloe was on night shift tonight, and she would be home alone.

"Do you want to stay for tea and perhaps we can go over your books now that we've got them loaded on the computer?"

"Sure."

Pete was at a loose end with his girlfriend on a scholarship studying overseas.

"What do you want to eat?" Megan asked.

"What have you got?"

She went into the kitchen and opened the fridge.

"What if I cook fishfingers?" She could put them in the oven straight from the freezer.

"Wow, this independent living has really helped you develop in the domestic arts."

"Don't be rude," Megan said. "I wasn't expecting anyone to be here for tea. I was going to eat toast."

"Fishfingers will be fine."

Pete flopped down into one of her kitchen chairs. Just like Dad. Men in the Brooker household only prepared food when all the women were sick in hospital or abducted by aliens.

"Do you want a hand?"

Megan raised her eyebrows. That was a surprise.

"Do you want to peel a couple of potatoes? I'll cut them into chips for frying."

Pete got up and took the peeler she held out to him, and waited while she retrieved the potatoes.

"So what happened to that copper fella you were engaged to?"

"You happened."

"What! Why?" Pete stopped peeling and looked at her with a concerned frown.

"He was only posing as my boyfriend/fiancé to help deter Shane Telford from his inappropriate advances."

"What about the other night? The way Mum told it, I'd have thought you would've called him."

"I couldn't call anyone. I might have called you if my phone had been working."

Pete smiled. "I go to bed early and leave my phone at the other end of the house so no one wakes me up."

"My hero."

"So, will you call—what was his name?"

"Cam."

"Cam?"

"I lost his number when Shane took the work phone and I feel a bit awkward going down to the police station and asking for it again."

"I see your point. I'm surprised Mum hasn't found a way to get it for you. Wasn't she the one who introduced you in the first place?"

"You know Mum. I'm sure she won't give up. She hasn't got her happy-ever-after-ending just yet."

"Are you looking for a happy-ever-after?" Pete asked, plonking the second peeled potato on the board next to her.

"I will live happily ever after if I don't have to see Shane Telford ever again."

Pete gave a sniff-laugh. "So not interested in the big fella, then?"

"Cam?" Megan asked, feigning surprise.

"No, Santa Claus. Of course Cam. He was the one you were pseudo-engaged to. You know perfectly well who I'm talking about."

"I liked him. He was nice. But he didn't sign on for a real relationship. He just agreed to Mum's crazy idea of pretending."

Pete sniffed again.

"What?" Megan asked, putting her hands on her hips.

"Guys don't just agree to a pretend relationship if they're not at least half-interested."

"You don't think?"

"Unless we're talking Shane Telford."

"Ugh! Please don't mention that name."

Pete turned and rummaged in the refrigerator. "Shall I make a salad to go with those fishfingers and chips?"

"Speaking of domestic prowess."

"Who's going to cook for me if I don't?" Pete said, pulling a lettuce head, a cucumber and a tomato from the refrigerator.

Megan smiled. Her older brother had been out of home for a few years, making his own way batching with various housemates. The couple of girlfriends he'd had weren't the cook-at-home sort, more than the international-model sort.

Pete was making short work of the garden salad when Megan heard her phone buzz. They both stopped and looked at it as if it had sprouted wings.

"It works!" Megan said. "At last, I'm connected to the world!"

"Except who in the world knows your number?"

"Mum. I gave it to her in anticipation of connection."

She picked up the phone and saw a number she didn't recognize. Wait, maybe she did recognize it. She slid her finger across the screen.

Hi Megan,

Your mum gave me your new number and encouraged me to contact you. I hope that's OK. Would you mind if we caught up sometime soon for a coffee? No pressure if you'd rather not. Let me know. Cam.

"Cam?" Pete asked.

"How'd you know?"

"The dreamy look that came over your face."

"Cut it out. There was no dreamy look."

Pete laughed. "Where's the olive oil and balsamic vinegar?"

"Wow. You really go all out with your food prep. No pre-packaged salad dressing for you."

"Rianne's mother always uses the gourmet condiments." Pete took the bottles from her. "Anyway, Megs, what's the news from Cam?"

"He wants to catch up for coffee."

"Great."

Megan cocked an eyebrow at her brother.

"Well it is great, isn't it?" Pete asked. "That's what you wanted, to get back in contact."

"I think so. Shane has shaken me up a bit, but I felt comfortable with Cam. Of course we were only pretending …"

"You keep telling yourself that."

Megan began to lift the golden-brown chips from the frying pan.

"Are you going to answer his text?" Pete asked.

"Of course."

"So, what are you waiting for?"

"Trying to avoid burning these chips for a start. I'll text him back after dinner."

"You'll have the poor fella worrying that you're ignoring him."

"Sounds like you've got experience," Megan replied.

Pete took the tongs out of her hands. "Do us all a favor, Megs, and text the poor guy back. It's torture waiting to see if you're being rejected or not."

Megan allowed her brother to take over the chips and took up her mobile phone. She'd rather talk to Cam face to face than send a text, but perhaps her brother was right. Best to put his mind at ease.

Hi Cam,

Thanks for your message. I would love to catch up for coffee soon. Let me know when you're free. I'm working for my brother and have set up an office at home, so I'm flexible to fit in with your roster. Hope you're having a great week. Megan.

"Hope you're having a great week?" Pete read over her shoulder.

"Do you mind?" Megan closed the phone so he couldn't see.

"Not 'all my love' or 'I can't wait to see you'?"

"Have you got the salad ready?" Megan asked, ignoring his teasing.

"I think he'd like to know how you feel about him."

"Thank you, Doctor Phil. Now sit down and let's eat."

He might very well want to know how she felt, but she wasn't entirely sure how that was yet. The first thing she had to work out was if he wanted to shift their relationship from pretense to reality.

* * *

She wants to catch up. A charge of electricity shot through Cam's body as he read the text, then a wet blanket of doubt flopped in his gut and squelched every edge of anticipation. What if she just wanted to let him down gently? What if his interest in her amounted to no more than unwanted attention? He needed to make this appointment before he talked himself into an emotional twist. The trouble was, he was on roster this afternoon and then the early shift tomorrow. He wasn't going to be free until later tomorrow evening. By the time he'd got home from work, showered and changed, it would be close to dinner. Should he ask her out to dinner? No, he'd already suggested coffee, so he'd best stay with that plan until he was certain of a way forward. He texted a suggestion for the following evening, and Megan was quick to reply. She had already arranged a family dinner at her parents' place. After several texts back and forth, they settled on a morning coffee in two days' time. Now that he'd made up his mind to see if there was something in the friendship, he was impatient to get an answer.

"Are you still seeing that girl?" Cam's mother asked as he sat down to dinner with her the following day.

"Which girl?" As if he didn't know. Play it cool, man.

"Luella Linley's daughter?"

"Not sure," Cam answered. "Maybe."

"Well, I wish you'd make up your mind. I'd love to meet her mother."

"No ulterior motives there at all."

"It's not every day you find a personal connection to someone so famous."

"Is she really that famous?" Cam asked, "or is it just she is one of your favorite authors and famous to you?"

"Makes no never mind to me. I'd like to meet her."

"Well, you might have to hold your horses for a bit. I'm not sure Megan wants a serious relationship, and you can't go waltzing in as a random person with no connection."

"Do *you* want a serious relationship?" Mum asked.

Cam shrugged. "I'm not sure. Give me a couple of weeks and I'll let you know."

Advising his mother to be patient was one thing but applying that same wisdom to himself was not so easy. He wanted to see

Megan again and gauge her level of interest. Joel had proved to be an unsympathetic friend. Granted they were at work and there was plenty to concentrate on with their investigations, but Cam would have liked his colleague to humor him just a little.

"When you're prepared to introduce her to me properly, and it's settled that she is serious and not just playing you for a fool, then I'll personally organize a double date with you and Lilly and we can chat like old friends. Until then …"

"You're not very supportive," Cam complained.

Joel did not bite but turned the focus back onto the case at hand.

* * *

It was still a day until Megan had agreed to meet and Cam was restless. He'd come home from work, had dinner but could not settle.

"I'm going out for a while," he said to his mother as he picked up his keys from the hall table.

"Will you be back tonight?" she asked.

"I'd say so. Just going out for a drive."

Since he'd shifted back home before to his father's death, he'd not gone out partying all night as he'd done in his early twenties. His father's cancer battle had been enough to help him find a maturity that had been lacking. That and his connection with God. His father's faith in the face of death had made Cam reconsider his eternal destiny. This had led to a decision to open his heart to God and a real faith had emerged. In the past, he might have gone out to the pub or found a mate who'd be up for some beers and computer games. It wasn't that he'd given up drinking altogether, more that he didn't look for it to fill in time.

Besides, if he was honest with his mother, he would have said he was going to drive by Megan's place. Why, was a question he wasn't prepared to answer. Megan was busy tonight and he wouldn't knock on the door. Best not to ask the question and just drive.

Chapter Thirteen

Cam knew where Megan lived. He'd visited there several times during his season as fiancé. It had been fun playing that role, even though Joel had been his Jiminy Cricket, continually reminding him it was a charade.

As Cam pulled into Megan's street he had a moment of self-doubt. What was he trying to achieve? He should wait until the agreed meeting and talk openly. If Megan wanted to investigate a real relationship, then he would have a legitimate reason to swing by her place. Until then, this was a pointless exercise.

He was set to drive straight past when he saw a man standing in Megan's garden, peering in her front windows. Shane. The next few moments, Cam did not register pulling his car over, taking his seatbelt off or getting out of the car. Even when he was standing a few feet from Shane and he began to speak, Cam had not engaged in any sensible thought as rage had consumed his mental energy.

"What are you doing here?" There was aggression in his tone. He had no wish to moderate it.

"What are *you* doing here?" Shane had smug written all over his face.

"Ms. Brooker has made an official report against you for stalking. Stalking is a serious offense."

"I don't see Ms. Brooker here—either of them. And you're not on duty. I don't believe you have any jurisdiction here."

"You need to get off her property before I call the police."

"I don't believe you can make such a call."

Cam glared at him, feeling for his mobile phone. It was still in the car.

"Besides, Constable Fletcher, you are no different from me."

"I am nothing like you," Cam replied, trying to instill menace in his tone.

"Aren't you? Aren't you here for the same reason I am?"

Cam felt a charge of ice water run through his veins.

"Why are you here?" Cam asked.

"The same as you. Trying to get inside that house and into her pants."

Something primeval broke inside. Anger management strategies did not even register. He rushed at Shane and attempted to take him by the front of his shirt, but Shane batted him off. He was obviously more skilled in self-defense than Cam would have given him credit for.

"You don't like it when your own deviant desires are called out, do you?" Shane taunted.

Cam went at him again, this time throwing a punch, then working Shane into a hold that had him on the ground, his arm twisted high up his back. Shane continued to make vile sexually explicit comments about Megan. Worse were the disgusting insinuations that Cam's motivations were the same. The more Shane spoke, the hotter Cam's rage burned, until he found himself over Shane, hitting his face with a closed fist.

"Oi!" Cam heard the voice of another man calling from the road. He suddenly came to himself and stopped his assault. "I've called the cops," the man yelled.

Cam stood up. "I am a cop." The irony hit him. This wasn't part of police protocol. Where was Joel? Where was his good sense? "This man has been stalking the woman who lives in this house."

Shane scrambled to his feet.

"I live four houses down," he said. "This was an unprovoked assault. I hope you're prepared to give evidence when the police arrive."

"What?" Cam looked at Shane like he was a worm. He *was* a worm. There was no way Shane was going to pin an assault charge on him when Shane was the one who was not only stalking and trespassing but had admitted to plans that amounted to no less than rape.

"Are you all right?" the man asked. Cam was about to answer when he realized the man was addressing Shane. He swung his gaze back to his rival and saw that he was bleeding. Cut lip, blood running from his eyelid, and his eye beginning to swell shut. This didn't look right. It *wasn't* right. How had Shane got inside his head and set off that explosion?

"Did the cops say they were coming?" Shane asked. Innocent as a lamb. Cam was appalled. Anything he said and did now had to be carefully measured. Shane had set him up as the villain.

"I will call the station myself and see if they're sending anyone," Cam said. "For a start with, you were trespassing on Ms. Brooker's property after she's filed a stalking report."

"I was minding my own business out the front of my own house when you attacked me for no good reason."

"How come we were on Ms. Brooker's property?"

Why was he being drawn into this argument? The neighbor was swiveling his head back and forth between them. Shane looked like the injured party and had pulled out this story about being out front of his own house. Surely he hadn't …

The sound of a police car siren split the air. This didn't look good. Shane had a witness and several things that would support his story.

Besides, Cam knew well and good that he had no right to have pummelled Shane the way he had. He'd lost perspective. Forget perspective. He'd lost his mind—the moment he'd seen Shane out the front of Megan's house, all sensible thought had fled. When the police car pulled up out the front of Megan's house, he knew he was in trouble.

Gavin Andrews and Julie Reed were the two uniforms who got out of the squad car. Cam hadn't worked too closely with them, but he knew them.

"What's going on here?" Gavin asked the question, and though he hadn't looked specifically at him, Cam decided to take the lead anyway.

"I was just explaining to Mr. Telford that he was on private property and that he needed to move along." Cam indicated Shane with a wave of his hand. He watched as Julie took Shane aside and began to interview him.

"We came in response to a call from a neighbor who said there was a fight. Did you see who it was?" Gavin had his note book ready.

"It was me."

Gavin did a double-take. He looked at Cam—his hands specifically—then looked at Shane, then looked back at Cam.

"Did he attack you?"

Cam shook his head. What could he say?

"You attacked him?"

"It was provoked."

"I can't wait to hear this story. You wait there." He didn't look happy as he joined Julie in listening to Shane's version. Cam didn't bother to step closer. The more distance between him and Shane Telford, the better. Still, he was close enough to hear the conversation.

"What has happened to you?" Gavin directed the question to Shane.

"I just told this lovely young lady."

Cam cringed. The words might have been innocuous, but Shane's tone was enough to make him want to puke.

"I'd like to hear it for myself, if you don't mind." Gavin's jaw had clenched. He obviously knew a slime bag when he came face to face with one. "What happened?"

Cam studied Shane, waiting for his response, and was chagrined to see blood trickling down his face from the cut above his eye, and some blood congealing in the corner of his mouth. He braced ready to hear the accusation.

"Nothing happened. I tripped over."

As if anyone was going to believe that. His facial injuries could not have come from a simple fall.

"Senior Constable Fletcher tells a different story."

"I fell." Was that fear on Shane's face. What was he afraid of?

"Senior Constable Fletcher?" Gavin raised his eyebrows in his direction.

"As I said, I was warning Mr. Telford to get off this property."

"Is this your property?" Gavin asked.

"The owner of this property is a friend of mine. She lodged a police incident report recently when Mr. Telford tried to gain entry to her house."

Gavin's attention swung back to Shane.

"The owner is also a friend of mine," he said. "She and I have worked together for several years. There was a misunderstanding. I recently moved in down the street and thought to see if we could catch up for a meal sometime."

Bull dust. Cam had heard from Louise Brooker how frightened her daughter had been. But right at this moment, given he was teetering on the edge of an assault charge, he decided to keep his peace.

"So the injuries you have sustained are due to a fall?" Gavin directed his gaze back to Shane.

Shane nodded.

Gavin "tched" and sucked in a breath. Even if Cam hadn't admitted to it, it was an obvious fabrication.

"Do we need to call an ambulance, sir?"

"I'll be fine," Shane said. "Can I go? I need to get some painkillers."

"Would you mind if we took your details first, please?" Gavin indicated to Julie that she should take the particulars down, and then turned his attention back to Cam.

"This doesn't look good, Cam," he said.

Tell me something I don't know. "I'd like to make an affidavit saying Telford was on Ms. Brooker's property, gazing in the windows."

"All right. Anything else you want to add—about this incident—while you're at it?"

"There was a fight."

"Obviously."

"But if he's not going to make an accusation, I'm not going to tell you anything else, other than the fact he was trespassing after a stalking complaint."

"All right." Gavin took another deep breath and started a new page. "Tell me what happened from the beginning."

Cam gave as much detail as he could. Megan needed to build the evidence enough so an official warning could be issued to her former boss, then if he continued to stalk her, he could be charged and hopefully jailed. The only thing he left out was how hard he'd hit Shane Telford. The injuries on Shane's face were evidence enough, but would he make a formal accusation?

* * *

When Megan arrived home she saw a police car parked across the street from her house.

"Do you think that's Cam come to visit?" Chloe asked.

"We've got an appointment to catch up tomorrow," Megan said. "I doubt he would just drop by, especially if he's on duty."

"An appointment? Not a date?"

"Chloe! Can you give me a break? I don't know how Cam feels about … you know, about …"

"About you?"

"We had lots of meetups when he was pretending to be my boyfriend, but we never discussed anything like a real relationship. I can't presume. Mum has obviously told him about Shane's attempted entry. He might just be concerned and wanting to know if there's anything else he can do to help."

"Right." Chloe grinned.

"Anyway, that's not Cam coming up my driveway," Megan said. Her tone changed as she felt alarm send a fizzy feeling across her chest.

"Ms. Brooker?" The uniformed police officer addressed her the moment she was out of the car.

"Yes."

"There was an incident on your property earlier. I wonder if you have a few moments to answer a couple of questions."

"An incident?" Chloe asked the question before Megan had a chance to gather her thoughts.

"Could we talk inside?" the policeman asked.

Megan couldn't find any words. She'd reported an incident a few days ago after Shane had tried to gain entry. Without speaking, she led the way inside.

"Can I get you a cup of tea?" Chloe offered the police officer as he sat at the kitchen table.

"No, thank you." He took out a notebook and pen.

"Someone's at the door," Chloe said before the officer had spoken. Megan watched, still speechless, as Chloe went to open the door. It only took a couple of moments before she returned with another police officer in tow.

"This is my colleague Constable Julie Reed. My name is Senior Constable Gavin Andrews."

"What happened?" Finally, Megan found her voice, pushing her anxiety down.

"Do you know Cameron Fletcher?" Constable Andrews asked.

Megan nodded. "What happened? Is he all right?"

"How do you know Mr. Fletcher?" Mr. Fletcher. Not Senior Constable Fletcher? What was going on?

"Cam is a friend of mine," Megan said.

"Do you know a Mr. Shane Telford?"

"We filed a stalking complaint against him a few days ago," Chloe said. "He tried to break in."

Constable Andrews frowned. "Could you tell me more about that incident?"

"He knocked on the front door, I told him to go away but he tried to come in anyway," Megan explained.

"Did he get inside?"

"No, I kept him out, then locked the front door. But he kept banging on the door, begging to be let inside."

Senior Constable Andrews didn't say anything else but wrote a couple of notes.

"What happened to Cam—Mr. Fletcher?" Megan asked again. The worry was killing her.

"According to an eyewitness, Mr. Fletcher attacked Mr. Telford, causing minor injuries."

"What?"

"Here?" Chloe asked. "What was Shane Telford doing at this house again?"

"Mr. Telford claims he is a neighbor. The question is, were you expecting Mr. Fletcher here this evening?"

"A neighbor?"

Chloe asked the question that had frozen in Megan's throat.

"He gave his address as four doors down from you," Constable Andrews said.

"That can't be. He lives on the other side of the city," Megan said.

"So you have a relationship with Mr. Telford, then?"

"What? Ugh! No!" Chloe speaking for her again.

"Ms. Brooker?" The police officer looked at Megan, but technically they were both Ms. Brooker.

"Shane Telford was my boss …"

"Who was harassing her sexually," Chloe said.

"What do you mean by that, exactly?" Constable Andrews asked. Megan didn't know whether to thank Chloe for her help or shove something in her mouth to shut her up. Did she really want to talk about all that awful stress again?

"For months, he was invading my personal space, coming close enough to touch my arm or shoulder."

"Is that all?" The officer sounded concerned that she should tell the worst of it.

"He constantly used sexual innuendo, especially when we were alone in the office, and then he started to stalk me using the work phone. He was becoming obsessively controlling. The day I left he tried to kiss me."

"What?" Chloe stared, open-mouthed. "Why didn't you say something."

Megan didn't answer. She was terrified then and ashamed to talk about it now.

"Did you file a complaint with your HR representative?" Constable Andrews asked.

"We didn't have one. HR was in my portfolio. Cam—Mr. Fletcher—was helping me out, trying to get Shane to back off, but it seemed to be like a red rag to a bull and only made Shane worse."

"Did you report Mr. Telford's behavior?"

"I wanted to, but apparently he got up to the line but didn't quite step over it. Until recently."

"Go on," the policeman prompted.

"I left his employ and left all the technology behind that he'd been using to stalk me. Then he turned up on my doorstep and tried to get in."

"So you reported all this to the police?"

"You bet we did." Chloe. So helpful with her animated interjections.

"What about your relationship with Mr. Fletcher?"

"He's just a friend," Megan said.

"Were you expecting him to visit this evening?"

"No, we were supposed to meet tomorrow morning for coffee."

"Is it usual for him to just stop by—as a friend?"

How was she supposed to answer this? That's what she hoped would eventuate, but the current status was still 'friend'. *What was he doing here tonight?* And had Shane Telford really moved into a house in her street? Given he was going through a dramatic breakup, it was entirely possible he would need to have found another place to live, and that would be just like him, to find a property a stone's throw from her house. She felt sick in the stomach. Surely it wasn't true.

"Ms. Brooker?" Constable Reed sought her attention again.

"If he's moved into my street, how can I report him?"

"We're currently investigating the incident with Mr. Fletcher," Senior Constable Andrews said. "Were you expecting him here tonight?"

Megan shook her head. She couldn't think about Cam at the moment, not when it appeared her nightmare boss was now within spitting distance of her front door.

The police officer asked a couple more questions, mostly answered by Chloe. Megan couldn't concentrate. What was she going to do?

"If you have anything else you'd like to tell us you think would help in resolving this issue, please don't hesitate to call us." Senior Constable Andrews slid a business card across the kitchen table toward her.

"Is Cam in trouble?" Megan asked.

"It really depends on whether you want to press charges for trespass, or …"

"Or?" Chloe asked.

"If Mr. Telford presses assault charges."

"Mr. Telford is a slime bag. You can't believe anything he says." Chloe's vehement spill of information showed loyalty, but Megan knew it held no authority. Chloe hadn't even met Shane.

"Mr. Telford has pushed the lines of appropriate behavior many times," Megan said. "The fact he was on my property gives me the creeps."

"If you wish to file a second report, you can come down to the police station again. We can issue a warning, which, if ignored, means he can be charged with stalking."

"Will that make any difference?" Megan asked.

"That's up to the courts."

"But there are serious penalties for stalking?" Chloe persisted.

"There can be, even a jail sentence if that's what the courts decide."

"Really?" Chloe's eyes nearly bugged out of her head. "Let's do it."

"You need to have evidence. You didn't actually see him on your property, did you? I would advise you wait to see if he tries again. Perhaps Mr. Fletcher managed to scare him enough already this evening."

Megan hoped the officer was right. She hoped that nothing serious would come of whatever had happened on her front lawn.

Chapter Fourteen

Cam was in knots. The vile words Shane had spoken kept whirling around and around in his brain and he couldn't get to sleep. Why had he driven past Megan's house? Was he after sex, the same as Shane had admitted he was?

Cam had slept with a couple of girls in past relationships, like every other young guy he knew. It wasn't until he'd started going to church that he realized Christian culture valued the marriage relationship as the only sacred place to express sexual intimacy. That had been a blow to his usual method of operation. Still, he'd explored the Scripture and the history of marriage as practiced over the centuries and had decided there must be something in the idea of keeping one's sexual expression for one's life partner. That's when his last relationship had broken up. His girlfriend at the time had thought he'd lost the plot when he'd found religion. Since then, he'd kept his eyes forward and on task, and had dismissed passing attractions without giving any thought to flirtation.

Until he'd pulled over Luella Linley for speeding.

When he'd met Megan Brooker, he'd noticed her gorgeous looks, particularly her figure, but he'd pretended it made no difference to him. Now, with Shane's accusations invading in his night-time musings, he wondered if he was just as deviant as Megan's ex-boss had suggested.

No. He totally respected Megan. She was not just an attractive body. She was a funny, kind, interesting person, and he hadn't made any moves on her at all. He hadn't intended to make any moves either, despite what Shane had said.

He took a deep breath. That was settled. Now he would sleep. But self-doubt rose again to accuse him. He wanted her, didn't he?

After another half-hour of tormenting thoughts, he turned the bedside light on and took his mobile phone.

Hi Megan,

I'm sorry for the late notice, but I don't think it's a good idea for us to meet again. I'm sorry for the inconvenience.
Regards,

Cam

His finger hovered over the send button. He so wanted to meet her again and see if there was a relationship worth pursuing. There probably was. But was that honest? Did he want to get to know her and then propose to her, marry her and build a family with her?

Too much, too soon. He wasn't even sure she actually liked him. He deleted the text and wrote a new one.

Hi Megan,

I won't be able to make it tomorrow after all. I'm sorry for the late notice. Perhaps we can catch up sometime later.
Regards,

Cam

This text was better. He needed time to sort out these questions in his mind before he sat in front of her and considered if he was ready to commit his whole life to her. One thing was for sure, he wasn't prepared to get involved in a short-term sexual relationship as he would have done in the past. The tangle with Shane had done more than provoke his anger—it had undermined his usual confidence.

He eventually fell asleep, though it wasn't restful. By the time he'd got out of bed, he was sorry he'd canceled the coffee date. He really wanted to talk to someone about his worries. But then, talking to the girl he was considering a long-term relationship with about whether he was a sexual deviant or not was probably not the wisest choice. He considered his mother as a confidant for about two seconds. Not a good idea. She thought him a sweet, responsible boy. She didn't know about his other girlfriends. He could talk to Joel but he would quickly tell him he was an idiot and if he wanted to sleep with Megan, just make sure it was consensual and use protection. Joel didn't get the Christian moral restrictions—he had said so on more than one occasion. Given Cam's father was no longer alive, that only left one other option.

Cam hadn't seen his counselor for a number of months, but last night's explosion was definitely something that required professional advice. John Glenn was a qualified counselor who also worked as a church pastor and saw clients at his church offices.

"Hello, Cam." The receptionist at the church greeted him with a smile. "Got a day off work?"

"Just this morning. Is Pastor John in?"

"He was on a call before, but I'll check to see if he's free."

"Thanks. If you think he won't mind my turning up without an appointment."

"I'll just check with him. Take a seat for a few minutes."

Cam sat down in one of the tub chairs in the foyer of the reception area. His phone buzzed and he fished it out of his back pocket. He hoped it was from Megan, given they were supposed to have met in half an hour. But then why would she text him since he'd canceled the appointment. Flipping the cover of his phone open he was disappointed. Mum.

Where are you?

I'm down at the church. Catching up with Pastor John.

His mother didn't usually need to know where he was. They'd grown past that years ago when he'd lived out of home.

Everything all right? He typed and pressed send.

"Hi, Cam." He looked up from his phone as John Glenn bore down on him, his hand extended in greeting, and his face swathed in a smile. "Great to see you. How can I help?"

Cam stood up and shook his hand.

"I was wondering if you had half an hour to talk through some things that I'm trying to process."

"Sure." The middle-aged pastor waved Cam through to his office and invited him to sit down.

Cam was confident in talking to John. They'd had several sessions together just after Cam's father had passed away. It didn't take long for the story to start pouring out.

"So, what are you hoping to resolve by coming here to see me today?" John asked at the end of the long story.

"I think I like Megan, but now I'm worried that I'm just obsessed with her, like her old boss. What do you think?"

"Are you obsessed with her?" There was no judgement in his expression.

"That's what I'm hoping you'll tell me. Is my behavior normal, because in some ways, it's not so different from the way Shane is behaving, except Megan has allowed me to call?"

"You believe Shane is only after sex?"

"He's married, to start with, so he's probably not hoping to set up a home and family."

"He already has a family?"

Cam nodded. "But the things he says to Megan are always sexual in nature."

"You've heard him?"

Cam shook his head. "Only what Megan has told me."

"Except the things he said to you when you caught him outside her place yesterday?"

"Megan wasn't there. His language was so explicit …" Cam gritted his teeth, searching for appropriate words to express his thoughts.

"It would make a sailor blush?" John filled in the gap.

"It would make a sailor want to shut him up with his fists."

"Which is what you did?"

"Yeah." It sounded so awful when it was spoken out loud.

"Are you likely to face assault charges?"

"If Telford presses charges, then I'll have to face an investigation."

"Do you believe he will press charges?"

Cam paused. If he knew Shane Telford—or at least the type of man he believed him to be—he would find a way to make something of it. "It's likely."

"So, your major worry at the moment is defending yourself, at least before your colleagues in the force, if not in court."

Funny how that had not worried him as much as wanting to examine his heart towards Megan and make sure it was pure. Punching Telford in the face was nothing, as long as he wasn't a sleaze like Telford.

"Do you want support for this?" John asked.

"What? Facing an investigation?"

The counselor nodded.

Cam shrugged. "I'll see how I go. I was in the wrong, but there were extenuating circumstances, and Telford was—"

"You don't have to defend yourself to me." John cut him off.

"I just want to make sure I'm not presenting Megan Brooker with more trouble. I don't want her to be hurt or compromised in any way."

"I think your behavior towards Megan is the normal behavior of a man who's in love."

John's words hit Cam like he was catching a medicine ball to his chest. "You think I'm in love?"

"The beginnings of love, at least. Of course, love is a much deeper and more committed state than just warm feelings, but at this point, you care more about her than yourself."

Was that true? Was he more concerned about Megan's welfare than whether he ever got to be with her or not?

"If I told you that your behavior towards her was sexually inappropriate, I'm guessing you would step back and leave her alone. Would that be the case, do you think?"

Cam was there to be honest. This was not about him putting on a holier-than-thou pretense for the pastor. He swallowed the saliva that was building in his mouth since he'd forgotten to breathe.

"From where I sit, it looks like you care about what's best for her," John continued.

Cam still didn't answer. Did he love her? It wasn't just about getting sex because the pastor was right. If he thought his actions would hurt her, he would withdraw and leave her alone. Perhaps there was some hope for him after all.

He was about to agree but was cut off by the receptionist knocking on the office door and coming straight in.

"Sorry to bother you, John, but there are two police officers here who would like to speak with Cam."

Rocks fell to the bottom of his stomach. Cam knew how this went down. He'd done this routine a hundred times himself. John looked to him, then back to the receptionist. "Could you ask them to wait, please?"

"No, she can't," Cam jumped in. "They're arresting officers. They're under instructions to bring me in without delay."

"How do you know?" John asked.

"I told you about the tangle with Shane. If he's pressed charges, then they'll send out arresting officers to bring me in."

"How did they know you were here?" the receptionist asked. "Do you have a tracking device attached to you?"

"My mother contacted me earlier to ask where I was. I imagine they were at her place looking for me." He pulled out his mobile phone and, sure enough, there was a reply text from his mother. She had warned him they would be coming after him at the church.

"Why don't they wait until you go in for work?" John asked.

"It'll be a different department and my position in the police force doesn't give me immunity or rights to favorable treatment."

"Send them in," the pastor said to the receptionist.

Once she had left the office, Cam stood up from the couch. "Thanks for your time."

"Perhaps we could pray together?"

Though that would have been nice, and a boost of courage in the current situation, Cam knew there would be no concessions made. The two police officers walked in before he'd even finished the thought. He didn't recognize either of them. Not surprising, since they were probably from the Internal Investigation Section

"Are you Cameron Fletcher?" the first detective addressed him.

Cam nodded.

"We need you to come outside with us to discuss a matter."

"Could you give us a couple of moments to finish our appointment here?" John asked.

"I'm sorry, sir. Mr. Fletcher has been named as party to a serious crime and he needs to come into the station for an interview."

"What is the charge?" John asked. Cam knew they wouldn't tell him.

"Leave it," Cam said to John. "This is the procedure. I'll call you later to let you know how things have gone."

"Do you want me to come with you?" John asked.

Cam shook his head. He was confident he could deal with this alone.

"Lead on, gentlemen." He knew full well if he didn't cooperate, they would put him in handcuffs.

One detective started to walk out and the other indicated with a wave that Cam should follow. He did, without question. It was humiliating, but he knew that Shane had a right to press charges. He didn't bother to call goodbye to the receptionist. He was under arrest, and until the matter had been fully investigated, under a cloud threatening his freedom.

Once in the car park, the leading detective turned to him, with handcuffs ready.

"I'm a police officer," Cam said, realizing they were going to follow procedure to the letter.

"I understand, sir, but we have been advised to follow the process."

"I can drive my own car to the police station and will not resist arrest. I've allowed that a time or two for people of good character without previous."

The detective shook his head. "You're under arrest and we need to follow procedure."

These officers were part of the IIS, a department of cops who were set up to investigate other cops. They were known around the station as the 'toe cutters'—hard, deliberate with no sign of leniency about them. He'd not run into them before, but wasn't about to test the reputation out, so he held out his wrists and allowed them to cuff him. The second detective activated a small hand-held video camera. They weren't taking any chances of being accused of police brutality. The first detective opened the back door of their squad car and pushed Cam's head down as he maneuvred his way into the back seat. The second detective got in the other side with the camera and began to recite his rights. He knew them off by heart, but it was an unsettling feeling being on the other side of the law, trying to attach meaning to those words that usually just slid out of his mouth.

"As an arrested person I must warn you that anything you say may be taken down and given in evidence. Do you understand that?"

As the detective waited for his reply, Cam suddenly understood why some of his arrested persons had been so belligerent. He wasn't feeling very cooperative himself. If he thought a sarcastic comment would not have resulted in a serious reaction, he would have made one.

"Yes, I understand."

"You have been arrested for aggravated assault. Do you understand that?"

Like, duh. Of course he understood.

"Yes, I understand."

"As an arrested person you have the following rights …"

The detective went on about the telephone call, the solicitor, an interpreter. Blah blah blah. He knew his rights. Yes, he wanted to make a call. To Megan. But that was a call he wasn't in a situation to make. He thought about calling his mother, but then he knew she would panic. He decided he would handle the situation on his own.

Once he got to the station, he hoped the detectives would be reasonable when he explained exactly what had happened. Though the detectives didn't talk to him about the particulars of the case and why he was being arrested, he knew. Shane Telford had woven a convincing story of unprovoked assault and had produced the neighbor as a witness. Cam had some talking to do before he was back in control of his keys, his phone and his life.

Chapter Fifteen

"You're taking a long time in the bathroom just for an appointment." Chloe stuck her head around the bathroom door and grinned at Megan.

"Same time as usual," Megan replied. "Why are you here? Shouldn't you be at work?"

"Late shift today."

Late shift. That meant she'd be home just before midnight. Slightly better than nightshift when she was out for the entire dark night. How she wished that, whatever Cam had done to Shane, he'd scared him enough to make him move away. Move far away. Move so far away she never saw him ever again.

"So, coffee with Cam?"

"Yes, Chloe. I'm going to meet up with Cam for coffee and I'm going to ask him about last night. I'm also going to see what else I can do to get Shane out of my life."

"Not going to ask him if he loves you and wants to marry you?" The grin on her face looked even more ridiculous reflected in the bathroom mirror. She determined to ignore the teasing.

"Where are you meeting him?" Chloe asked.

"Not sure. He said he'd send me a text to let me know."

Chloe reached over to the bathroom bench and picked up Megan's phone, then opened it.

"What's your password?"

"As if. The idea of a password is so only I have access to my phone. Besides, if there was a text, it would show up on the screen when you switched it on."

"There's no text here."

"I'll call him shortly, once I'm ready."

"So, what do you think about last night?" Chloe asked, closing the phone and putting it back on the bench.

"Something happened, but those two police officers weren't very forthcoming with information."

"Do you think Shane has really moved in a few doors down?"

Megan dragged in a deep breath and exhaled dramatically.

"You better keep your eyes open for him," Chloe said. "If he so much as sets a toenail on your property, you call Cam."

"If I understand correctly, I should be able to make another report if I even see him lingering outside my property."

"Though, if he *has* moved into the street, he may contend he's just going to and from his own house."

"I'm going to talk to Cam about it. Surely, the fact he's even taken a lease in the street has to be somehow a breach of the law where stalking is concerned."

"What time are you meeting Cam?" Chloe asked.

"He was going to confirm, but I thought he'd mentioned around eleven o'clock."

"Tick Tock! It's after ten now. You never take this long in the bathroom."

Megan took a final look in the mirror. Did she look all right? Did it really matter? Of course it mattered. She might not admit it aloud to her sister, but she was hoping something real might develop between her and her former pretend fiancé. Would it make any difference? They had enjoyed several date-not-dates and she hadn't taken any extra care on those occasions. He'd seemed to like her and had been happy to see her but had that just been part of the act or was there something real?

She unplugged the hairdryer and put her make-up away in the top drawer.

"Right," she said as she slid the drawer closed. "Has he sent a text yet?" She picked up her phone. Chloe came across and peered over her shoulder. Nothing new.

"Call him," Chloe said.

"Why didn't I think of that?" Megan performed a reasonably good gasp of surprise and gratitude.

"No need to be sarcastic."

"No need to state the obvious."

"Well hurry up, already. I'm keen to see how this turns out."

Megan shook her head and gave a half-lidded eye roll.

She exited the bathroom and headed to her bedroom, hoping to shake her sister. She had Cam's newly-programmed number on screen and pressed call. Turning around, she almost knocked Chloe over. Megan frowned at her tailgating sister.

"Go away." She mouthed the words and shooed with a wave of her hand.

"What?" Chloe asked. "I want to hear what he says."

The phone was still ringing in her ear and Megan began to wonder why Cam didn't answer. Another ring and it switched through to voice mail.

"Hi Cam. Just calling to confirm the time and place to meet this morning. I'll hear from you shortly."

She ended the call. Her sister was still looking at her.

"Send him a text," Chloe suggested.

Why hadn't he answered? A wave of self-doubt swept over her. Was she kidding herself? Was their meeting only about what to do with the Shane problem and nothing to do with a possible relationship?

"Text him," Chloe persisted.

Megan opened the green text speech bubble and was about to open a new message when she saw there was an unopened message waiting in the inbox. It was from Cam. She put relief on hold until she'd read what he had to say.

"He's canceled the date," Chloe read over her shoulder.

"I can see that," Megan answered. "You should really let me read my own texts in private, in case he'd said something sensitive."

"That's what I was hoping for. I love you, will you marry me? Stuff like that. Instead of that—I'm sorry for the late notice. That's not what I want to hear."

"Me either." Did she say that out loud? She hoped not.

"Well, that's a downer. You're all dressed up and nowhere to go," Chloe said.

"I have work to do for Pete in any case."

"Yes, but no one is going to see how carefully you did your hair and applied your make-up."

"You saw it. Now go and do whatever you do when you're waiting for afternoon shift to start and leave me to get on with sorting out Pete's business."

Megan went into the newly set-up office and opened her computer. The internet connection was still not working properly. How many times did she have to call her service provider? It was so frustrating. Or was it that she found small things like dodgy internet connection frustrating because she was trying to pretend that Cam's canceling their date was not a disappointment? All right, she would admit it—to herself at least—she'd been looking forward to the meeting and had raised hopes that something would emerge by way of a personal relationship. Now all she had was a load of self-doubt and a pile of communications that she was going to have to get done with the slowest internet known to mankind. Carrier pigeons would be more effective.

* * *

Though the routine was familiar, the rest was an exercise in perspective. It was different being the one who had to ride in the back of the police car, who was escorted into the police station in handcuffs by two officers, and who had to surrender his phone and keys without so much as a 'please' or 'thankyou'. He remembered being new on the force and having done this job plenty of times. Some of the people he'd brought in had come literally kicking, swearing and screaming. Others had been sedate and cooperative and, he suspected, were being brought in for questioning over an incident they had nothing to do with. Being on the receiving end was not nice—even roused a certain level of anxiety. But then, he wasn't completely innocent of the charge he knew he would hear.

Once the arresting officers had delivered him to the duty sergeant, he was processed for fingerprints, having each of his fingers held and rolled over the ink as if he was a child in kindergarten. And the mug shot. The same as those dreaded drivers' license shots, except in this case, he had no wish to smile.

But he didn't complain, question or resist. It was easier to submit to what would be done whether he protested or not. Hopefully, the process would go quicker.

"Cameron Fletcher?" Detective Jimmy Morang slapped a case folder onto the table in front of him and pulled the chair out. "Got yourself in some bother over a woman, have you?"

Cam didn't answer. Jimmy Morang. Why did it have to be Jimmy Morang? They'd been through the academy together years ago, and their mutual dislike had not improved during the training years when they'd been forced to compete on various levels. Jimmy had gone farther than Cam by way of promotion and had achieved detective with Internal Investigation. This wasn't a particularly endearing piece of information.

Jimmy had another detective with him, who set up the video camera.

"This interview will be recorded and anything you say may be taken down and used as evidence. Do you understand?" the second detective started the spiel of all the rights, each one punctuated with the standard question: "Do you understand?"

"It is your right to have a solicitor, relative or friend present during any interrogation whilst in custody. Do you understand?"

"Yes, I understand," he replied. He was getting impatient with the pages of procedure. *Just get on with it.*

"Do you wish to have someone present?" He wished Megan was here, but then he didn't. He wished he'd gone and had coffee with her earlier and told her how he felt. Now that he was sitting under the restrictions of custody, he wished he could just get up and leave. Remembering other interrogations he had sat in on, he began to understand the level of frustration and anxiety the accused often revealed in tone, body language and, on occasions, foul language.

"Do you wish to have someone present?" the detective asked again.

"No."

The rest of the rights were read as per usual practice, and Cam managed to answer at the appropriate times.

"So, tell me about last night," Jimmy leaned back in his seat, arms folded across his chest. Even though Cam knew he had the right to refrain from answering any questions, he wanted the matter cleared up.

"I was passing by a friend's house, knowing she'd recently reported her former boss for stalking and, as I came past, I saw him peering in her front window."

"Who was peering in the front window?"

"My friend's former boss."

"Were you on duty? Did you call for back-up?"

"I wasn't on duty. I guess I've been keeping an eye out for my friend, especially when I heard how he'd tried to gain entry into her house a couple of nights earlier."

"An attempted break and enter is a serious offense. Why didn't you arrest him?"

"He was not trying to break and enter. Just peering in the window."

"You just said there was a police incident report on him for stalking."

"I have not read the report, nor was I at the scene in the first case. I only heard about it from my friend's parents. I needed to ascertain what the circumstances were."

"Go on."

"I stopped, got out of my car and confronted the man."

"What was the man's name?"

"Shane Telford, owner and manager of Telford Wholesalers."

"And how did he respond?"

160

"He was full of bravado and filthy language, particularly about my friend, Megan Brooker."

"How did you respond?"

"I told him to get off her property."

"Is that all?"

"No. He continued to make sexually explicit threats against Megan, and I tried to grab him by the shirt front."

"Why?"

The truth—he'd lost the plot—but that was not a good answer in this situation.

"I hoped to shake some sense into the man."

"And did you—shake sense into the man?"

Cam shook his head.

"For the record, please," the second detective prompted.

"No. He evaded me quite successfully."

"How did that make you feel?"

"This isn't a psychological counseling session," Cam said.

"No, but I need to ascertain whether you were in control of your temper at the time of the incident."

"Alleged incident," Cam said, "And it wasn't his ability to defend himself that made me angry."

"So you were angry?"

"I've been supporting my friend for a number of weeks while she's been trying to figure out a way to stop him from making sexual innuendo and basically sexually harassing her."

"Basically. Either he was or he wasn't."

"His behavior had escalated from innuendo, but not to the point where there was evidence to take to the police."

"Did you witness any of these alleged incidents of harassment?"

Had he? He'd seen Shane pull the overbearing boss routine, and he suspected he was stalking her through her technology but had he seen actual evidence of sexual harassment?

"I only have the statement from my friend."

"Which you believed?"

"Yes, I believed her."

"But there are the work-safe procedures she should have followed."

Cam shook his head. "She was the HR rep and he was the boss. She needed to get out, but he had her over a barrel financially."

"How close are you to Ms. Brooker?" Jimmy asked.

"Fairly close."

"Are you in a relationship with her?"

"No. Just friends."

Detective Morang opened his folder and pulled out a couple of photographs and put them on the table in front of Cam. Wow! He had packed a harder punch than he'd thought. Telford's eye was swollen shut and his lip was sporting a cut that was also swollen. And there was bruising. Cam rewound the incident in his mind trying to recall if his actions could possibly have done this much damage. He had to admit he'd been wound quite tight from the verbal provocation—just recalling what this man fantasized doing to Megan sent a charge of flammable fuel through his system again. He had to keep a lid on it.

"How do you explain the injuries to Mr. Telford's face?" Jimmy asked.

"At the risk of being crass, may I outline for you what threats Mr. Telford made with regards to Ms. Brooker?"

"Go on," Jimmy said.

Cam hated even thinking about what had been said, let alone being forced to verbalize it and having it on record.

"I assume you have given an affidavit testifying to Mr. Telford's behavior?"

Cam nodded.

"Do you think Mr. Telford's inappropriate words were sufficient justification for the attack?" Jimmy asked.

"They were more than inappropriate words. I caught him peering in her front window, and he had no scruples telling me he basically planned to rape her … and this after Ms. Brooker had filed a stalking report."

"Let me rephrase. Do you think Mr. Telford's alleged words and alleged behavior gives you license to assault him when it is within your rights and jurisdiction to call yourself back to duty to effect an arrest?"

"Alleged physical assault," Cam said.

"We have interviewed a witness who says he saw you attack first, and you were the one who wrestled Mr. Telford to the ground, and you were the one who was attacking him with your fists until he called out that he had phoned the police."

Though the details of the incident were foggy in his mind, Cam knew what the detective said was more than an alleged attack. He remembered the rage. Could still feel it even now. He didn't say anything else.

"I'm afraid the evidence against you is overwhelming, Cameron, and I have no choice but to charge you with aggravated assault. This matter will have to go to court."

Cam knew the drill.

"I assume you wish to exercise your right to apply for bail?" Jimmy said.

Cam nodded.

"Is there anything more you'd like to say, Cameron?"

There was plenty more he wanted to say—none of it useful. He shook his head instead.

"We'll go and see the charge sergeant then." Jimmy got up from the interview table and the second detective turned off the video recorder.

Cam's hands were re-cuffed and he was led from the interview room, past a waiting area where there were too many curious eyes looking at him. Thankfully, he was dressed in jeans and pullover and didn't look like a cop who was being dragged to the cells. The cells—down to the basement, through a long, windowless corridor that was all dismal grey concrete. He hadn't thought too much about this place when he'd dragged charged persons down to be processed, but it was a cold place where the smell of body odour mixed with the smell of hand sanitizer. A place where the lights were never turned out and every room had a camera watching every move you made. Walking in with hands restrained made this place suddenly scary. He was not free to leave for a while yet.

At the end of the corridor came the 'drive-through' window, only here they didn't take your order for burger and fries, but they were good at taking your dignity. He fronted up to the Perspex window.

"Cam?"

Of course he knew the charge sergeant. They'd shared a beer more than once at the odd police function. Of course there was surprise in his tone. Cam didn't make any comment.

"Who have we here?" the charge sergeant asked the two detectives standing behind him. "And what are the circumstances of his arrest?"

Cam waited while Jimmy outlined the situation, then waited while the charge sergeant brought out the standard questionnaire given to anyone being taken into custody. Twenty or thirty questions, one after the other. Did he have any mental health issues? Did he have any health issues, was he a risk to top himself while in custody?

"What property do you have?" the charge sergeant asked.

The second detective put Cam's phone, keys and wallet on the counter.

"Just that," Cam answered as he indicated the small pile with his head.

Nevertheless, he was asked to hold his legs akimbo while the second detective patted him down. It wouldn't do for him to smuggle a small knife into the cells.

"I assume you're applying for bail?" the charge sergeant asked.

"Yes." Even to his own ears, his tone sounded resigned.

A few moments later the charge sergeant turned the bail application around on the small shelf jutting out from the Perspex window. Cam took the proffered pen to sign his name.

"OK then. Now that's done, you'll need to wait in one of the cells for a short time while I work out the application."

The detectives took him to the steel-reinforced door that let into the cells, which was opened by one of the cell guards. Still cuffed, Cam was ushered into his new digs. Even though he knew it would be probably only thirty minutes to an hour, he felt a band of anxiety tighten his chest. This was a place where all rights were forfeit. He couldn't bring himself to look at the other waiting prisoners in adjoining cells. Did they know him from past tangles with the law? It was entirely possible. There were a host of repeat offenders who made regular visits through this facility.

The small cell was inhospitable. A hard bunk, a toilet and a basin. This was not the Hilton and Cam wondered why anyone would re-offend. He sat down on the bunk and dropped his head into his now uncuffed hands. It was hard to pray in a situation like this. Almost impossible, but he managed to utter one word.

"Jesus." And not as an offhand curse, but a genuine calling out to his Savior for strength.

It was only thirty-five minutes but eventually he was called from the cell by the cell guard and back before the charge sergeant.

"I have processed your application for bail and it is granted on the following conditions."

Cam had guessed he would get bail, but having it said out loud was a relief.

"You must reside at your home address," the charge sergeant read. "You cannot leave the state. You will have no contact with the victim of your attack. You will forfeit your bail money to the crown if any of these conditions are breached."

Cam read these conditions as he heard the bail sergeant read them aloud.

"And pending an internal investigation, you will be pulled from active duty and will be on administrative leave."

Not that he should have been surprised, but his life for the next two or three months until a court appearance meant he could sit at home and cool his heels. He wondered if he had any chance of forming a defense.

Chapter sixteen

Chloe left for work as promised, in time for the late shift. Megan was like a caged lion. She tried to concentrate on Pete's bookwork and even took a couple of calls for him. She even thanked God for the incompetent internet service provider, because she spent an hour with ineffective communication to at least three different departments in different countries, and while she was focused on this frustration, she was not thinking about the fact that Shane Telford apparently lived right down the street.

But by the time the sun went down, she had run out of things to do for Pete, had grilled her cheese on toast for tea, and was left to contemplate the silence. Or at least contemplate every tiny sound that punctuated the silence.

She jumped when a text message pinged on her phone. Chloe.

Don't forget to put the bins out. It's recycle night.

Brilliant. She felt a small measure of security barricaded in her house, but the bins had to be put out on the road as collection was usually before they roused from bed. The recycle bin was full of cardboard from all the packing boxes that had protected the office furniture when it had been delivered. Now she would have to go around the back of her house and roll the two bins down the dark driveway and put them on the side of the curb.

Would Pete come over and help her? *Don't be ridiculous.* She knew he went to bed early in time for his five am rising, and she knew he kept his phone at the other end of the house so it didn't wake him. No Pete. What about Dad? How would he respond if she asked him to come and help her put the bins out? She looked at her watch. It was already ten pm and way past the time she could have called to ask him around for a cup of tea and a chat.

Perhaps Cam was on duty. Perhaps he would respond if she sent one of their old coded messages. This was not really a short black situation, probably more in the line of weak latte. Actually, if she were honest with herself, it was probably a herbal tea situation, but her imagination had engaged with her fight-or-flight deck and everyone there was on tenterhooks, ready to man battle stations.

"This is ridiculous!" She walked to the pantry to change the bin liner and gather the rubbish. "How old am I? Do I have any faith at all in God? Why am I letting him get to me?"

Having pulled out the full bin liner and knotted it, she then pulled a clean liner from the roll in the bottom of the kitchen drawer.

"Shane Telford, you will not rule me with your intimidation. This is my home and I am safe here."

Having recited this loudly for no one to hear, Megan picked up the rubbish bags and took them outside the back door to the wheelie bin. She flicked on the outside light as she passed by. It would be no good tripping over things in the dark. Taking a deep breath, she pulled the rubbish bin behind her, opened the side gate, and rolled it down to the curb.

"There. That wasn't so hard." She took a quick look up the street first to the left, and then to the right.

And then it hit her. That was Shane's car parked on the side of the road about four doors down. Without stopping to see anything else, she turned tail and ran back down the side of the house, past the recycle bin that still needed to go out and into the back door. She slammed it shut and turned the key in the deadlock.

Megan's pulse was hammering in her chest and her breaths came fast. He was there. Out in the street. She reached for her phone and didn't even think twice before calling Cam.

The ring tone buzzed in her ear once, twice, three times. *Pick up, Cam. Please, please, pick up.* Four times and then it switched through to voice mail.

"Hi, this is Cam. I can't take your call right now, but please leave your number and I'll get back to you as soon as I can."

Megan waited and heard the tone indicating she should begin recording, but then couldn't think what to say. She breathed deeply then realised she probably sounded like a prank caller.

"Hi, Cam. Can you call me back? Thanks."

She hung up. Why hadn't he answered her call? He hadn't responded earlier in the day either, when she'd called about their date. Had his text been a gentle let down? He didn't want to see her anymore. Like two different weather systems, her fear and disappointment clashed and a storm of emotion broke over her. She burst into tears and fell into a nearby armchair, crushing a cushion to her chest.

Two hours later, Chloe opened the front door and Megan was still in her fetal position on the chair.

"What's going on?" Chloe demanded. "And why didn't you put the recycle bin out?"

Megan got up and stretched the cramps out of her joints. "Shane was in the street."

"Did you call Cam?" Chloe asked.

Megan nodded, then tears welled in her eyes again, followed by a wobbly jaw that would not hold the emotion back.

"Did he come?"

Megan shook her head.

"Did he send another cop car?"

"I didn't speak to him," Megan replied. "It just went through to voice mail again."

"Did you call another cop?"

Megan shook her head again.

Chloe gave a sniff of disgust, threw her keys on the kitchen counter and plonked her work bag on the couch before sitting down next to it.

"Did Shane approach you again? What did he say?"

What did he say? Megan couldn't remember. That was because she hadn't seen him.

"He didn't say anything."

"That doesn't make any difference. If he was on your property."

"I didn't see him, only his car parked down the street."

Chloe got up and went to the back door. "Come on," she said. Boy, did she have authority in her tone when she got fired up. "And bring the recycle bin with you."

Megan's courage gradually regrouped having her sister, the general, shouting commands in the house. Why had she let Shane get to her again? Why had she let Cam's refusal to answer get to her?

Without waiting to investigate those questions deeply, she went out to the back porch and retrieved the recycle bin. Chloe had already switched on the lights and led the way down the side of the house. Megan had no doubt that anyone standing in her way would come off second-best.

Dragging the yellow-lidded recycle bin behind her, Megan followed in her sister's wake. Chloe had already stepped onto the road and was marching down the street in the direction of where Shane's car had been parked by the time Megan got the bin to the curb. Megan wanted to call after her and ask what her plan was, but she still had waves of anxiety threatening to overwhelm her when she saw the car still parked where it had been earlier in the evening. Instead of following Chloe, she came partway and then stood to watch what her sister would do.

Chloe made her way straight to the driver's side and peered inside the car. Was he sitting in there, staking out their house? Chloe moved to the back passenger door and rubbed the window of any collected moisture, then peered in. She didn't yell or thump on the window. Either he wasn't in the car or he had held up a white surrender flag.

"It's just his car," Chloe said, wiping her hands on her work pants as she walked back towards their house.

"Are you sure he's not sitting inside?" Megan asked.

"Go look for yourself." Chloe stopped and waved her hand back toward the car like a TV game show host.

"I'll take your word for it."

"Look, Megs, if he has moved to the street, it's probably one of those units in that block of flats and I'm guessing he'll have to park his car on the road."

"But I don't want him anywhere near me. Anywhere!"

"And Cam didn't answer your calls today?"

Megan shook her head, swallowing back a lump in her throat that seemed to be attached to a sliding weight, straight down to the pit of her stomach.

"He was probably busy," Chloe said. "He did say he would have to cancel the date. There must have been a reason."

"I don't think he wants anything to do with me and my dramas anymore."

"You don't know that."

Megan shrugged. She didn't know, but she didn't have the courage to pursue it any more. If he wanted to call her back, he would. In the meantime …

"In the meantime," Chloe said in chorus with her thoughts, "you need to call the police station and report the car."

"But he's not in it."

"Still, they need to know the situation, and they will advise you."

Megan nodded. She would do as her sister suggested but couldn't help the sadness that was taking root in her heart. She'd hoped Cam would stand with her, not just in dealing with Shane, but in friendship, in relationship, in love.

"And another thing," Chloe said as they came back inside, "I'm concerned about your mental health."

"What? My mental health? I'm fine."

"You're not, Megan. You're showing signs of anxiety and stress—"

"Well, it was stressful working for Shane."

"But your situation is different now. The thing is, you're … fragile, and I'm concerned about it."

"But … Shane … Cam didn't answer … I was scared."

"You're not the anxious sort, Megan. You've always been confident and secure. I think you should go to your doctor and talk about the situation."

"Why? Do you think I'm losing the plot or something?"

"No, I think you might have a form of PTSD."

Megan shook her head. She hadn't been on the front line of a war zone or faced an armed bandit or anything like that.

"When Shane tried to break in, along with the way he treated you before you left his work, I'd say there is enough trauma there to have affected you. I'll come with you to the doctor's if you're not sure."

Megan watched her sister. Chloe was serious. Was she anxious and stressed? A quick review of the evening before her sister got home only confirmed the diagnosis.

"OK. I'll make an appointment tomorrow if you think it'll help."

Chloe gave her a firm hug. "You're stronger than this, Megs. I think a little help will get you back to normal."

Chapter Seventeen

Josiah could hear rats scurrying about in the dim, dank depths of the hull of the ship. How had he come to this? He was a gentleman of some means, titled and with a wealthy estate. Yet by some twist of fate, he was sitting chained to the splintery wall of a ship, deep in the hold, other convicts chained to his right and his left. The only thing he had to be thankful for was that this ship was one of the abandoned hulks left to rot in the moors outside London and not one of the able sailing ships already on the waters between England and the convict colony of New South Wales.

This was Osmond's doing. He'd gone to retrieve Lady Rosalie from the convent in Italy but had not returned. When Josiah had eventually inquired, he'd found his lady love still ensconced within the walls of the sacred home, apparently having refused to wed the brutish Lord Osmond. His heart had soared that he might yet have the opportunity to woo and court her, but those moments of joy were soon dashed. The local constable and magistrate had visited his home, bringing with them the news that Lord Osmond had disappeared, feared dead, and the suspicion of murder had fallen on Josiah's shoulders.

There had been no body, but there had been small pieces of evidence that all pointed to Josiah as having done away with the man who was his rival. But all the evidence was manufactured. None of it was true, yet the magistrate had believed the rantings of Osmond's mother. The woman claimed she had heard Josiah threaten to kill her son.

Not that the thought had not crossed his mind, but he was a man of integrity and honor. If he were to have killed Osmond, it would have been in the duel to which the blackguard had challenged him. But that had come to naught. Several thrusts and parries, and their coachman had rushed in to tell them to desist on threat of arrest by the authorities.

Blast it all. He'd had a chance to settle it face to face, but the change in public opinion about the practice of settling disagreements with the sword made it a risky pursuit. At least Osmond had gone away with blood coming from an injury to his arm. That had made Josiah feel better for the moment, but apparently, that blow had been enough to enrage the injured lord, and now he had found a way to exact extreme revenge on him.

Here he was, sitting in a rotting prison, and if he did not die from a fever in this putrid environment, he would find himself sailing to foreign climes. And Lady Rosalie did not even know where he was—or that he loved her with all his heart.

"Sometimes these young people need someone to spell things out for them," Louise said as she leaned back on her office chair, stretching her stiff shoulders by holding her arms high above her head.

"What was that?" Russell called from the neighboring office.

"These young people," Louise shouted back. "They need someone to give them a good talking to."

"Sounds a bit harsh."

Louise shook her head as she let out a sniff of frustration and pressed save on the document.

"Have you heard from our Constable Fletcher?" she asked before she'd left her own office and entered her husband's. "He's MIA and Megan is eating her heart out."

"How do you know?" Russell swung his office chair away from his drawing desk as his wife walked in.

"What, that he's MIA?"

"No, that she's eating her heart out."

"A mother knows these things."

"Are you sure it's not just your fervent imagination?"

"Thank you very much, Russell. I can see I'll have to help our daughter in her hour of need without your assistance."

Russell laughed.

"I'm sure she's sitting by her phone waiting for you to call."

"That may well be, but I think I shall call our Constable Fletcher first."

"Can we have it on record that I advised against it?" Russell said, replacing his computer glasses on his nose and turning back to his architectural drawing.

Louise went back to her office and flicked through past emails. Now that she knew how to filter a search through her cluttered inbox, she went straight to Cameron Fletcher's last email and got his mobile number. She wrote it down on a fluorescent post-it-note and took it out to the kitchen to ponder her plan of attack.

With the kettle boiled and her cup of peppermint tea steeping on the cupboard, she decided the best form of solution was to openly address the situation. Putting the number into her phone she pressed the green dial button and waited. It began to ring—once, twice, three times, and after the fourth went through to voice mail.

"Constable Fletcher," she said, after the tone, "Would you kindly return my call? I have something important to discuss regarding my daughter, Megan."

"Well, that was subtle," Russell said as he came into the kitchen. "You know, if he has decided that our Megs is not for him, your stalking him is not going to make one whit of difference."

Louise shook her head. "He hasn't decided anything of the kind. You heard him last time he was here. He was interested and wanted to see how things turned out. Something went wrong after that night with the incident with that weasel, Shane."

"Well, I guess we shall see. I'm putting money on the fact that he won't return the call."

"If you were a betting man, Russell Brooker," Louise said.

* * *

"Your phone just rang."

Cam hardly acknowledged his mother as she placed his phone on the table in front of him.

"Aren't you going to see who it was?"

"Not at the moment." He had no wish to know what his mates at work had say about his arrest and subsequent release.

The message alert ding appeared intent on reminding him there were people outside his home who were determined to communicate with him.

"Cameron." Mum was back using her scolding tone and it was about to drive him crazy. But there was no escape. He was basically under house arrest. Couldn't go to work. Couldn't go on a holiday. Couldn't go and visit Megan.

"Do you mind if I look at your messages just to make sure there's nothing important you should attend to?"

"Will you leave me alone if you do?"

"I know you're feeling sorry for yourself, but you have no one to blame but yourself. You shouldn't have gone around there."

"Mum! Don't go on about it."

The reminder ding punctuated the tension in the air.

"Fine!" He pushed his phone across the table to her. "Check my messages. I don't really want to know."

"Password?"

He snatched the phone back and used his fingerprint identification to unlock the phone, then handed it back to her. Then he got up from the table and left the room.

To say he was agitated was an understatement. He'd contacted a solicitor to represent him but hadn't heard any new information that suggested things would go his way. He went over the incident again. Was he sorry he'd driven past Megan's place? On the one hand, he knew he should have waited for their meeting the following day, and nothing would have happened. On the other hand, he could not bear the thought of that slimy Shane Telford being on Megan's property and trying to find a way to get to her. Especially after Shane had made it clear what he hoped to do to her. His blood boiled again. Every time he thought of it, he couldn't think of any other way he could have responded.

"Cam?" Mum put her head around the doorway. "You've had three calls and two texts from the Brookers."

Cam lifted his head and looked at his mother. Was he interested?

"Megan called a couple of times, sounding a bit panicked."

"When?"

"The day after the incident."

"Too late now."

"She also sent a text. Don't you think you should call her back?"

Should he? He wanted to, but his current state of disgrace suggested he sit down and stop pretending he was anyone's hero.

"And her mother has asked that you call her back."

"When did she call?"

"Just a few minutes ago."

Cam sucked in a deep breath and let it out riding on the discouragement he felt.

"Can I call her back for you?" Mum asked.

"Will that set your mind at ease?"

"You're being awfully snappy, Cameron Fletcher, and for a man who is sitting in his mother's house under the cloud of an assault charge, I would think you should have a bit more grace."

"Go ahead and call Mrs. Brooker, and please apologize that I'm not up to speaking to anyone at the moment."

Mum had the phone and was pressing buttons, obviously intent on calling Louise. She would enjoy that, talking to her writing hero.

"Oh, and your friend Joel left a message to say they've served a warning to that Shane person. Hope that's good news."

Cam nodded, but his mother wasn't watching. She was already concentrating on connecting a call to the enigmatic Luella Linley.

So the department had put his affidavit together with Megan's first report and decided it was enough to issue a warning. From now on, if Shane so much as stood outside her house or tried to contact her on the phone, he could be arrested and charged, and if the courts were in good working order, be put behind bars. He hoped Megan understood all the intricacies of the law and how she could call the police for the smallest contact now that the warning had been issued. But they would have told her that in the follow-up. Surely.

He wished he could call her. He wasn't the one on a warning to sever all contact with her—but he was the one who could not go within fifty meters of Shane Telford, and since Shane apparently resided fifty-five meters down the road from Megan's house, that was definitely off limits for him, according to his bail conditions. How were Megan and her family faring?

Given his mother was now on the phone to the Brooker household, he figured the best way to find out was to listen in.

"That would be lovely," he heard his mother say, with a good deal of enthusiasm. "What can I bring?"

"Bring where?" Cam asked, even though his mother was still listening intently to whoever was on the other end of the call.

"Oh, I'm sure he would love to come."

"Come where? Are you making arrangements for me?" He stood nearby, trying to pin his mother's attention with a glare, but she cleverly avoided him.

"Yes, I'll tell him. Thank you so much. Yes, we'll see you tomorrow then."

She disconnected the call, turned and smiled at him.

"I'm not going," he said in as firm a tone as he could muster.

"Not going where?" she asked.

"Wherever it is you've just promised we would go."

"Don't be such a spoilsport. Mrs. Brooker, Luella Linley, has invited me over for dinner tomorrow night and I'm not going to turn an invitation like that down, no matter how much you're sulking and feeling sorry for yourself."

"Sulking! Mother, do you have any idea the humiliation it is to have been arrested and charged and sat in a holding cell?"

"You do that to people every day as part of your job. Now you know, next time you can have more empathy for their condition."

She was impossible. And she was smiling. It was not a laughing matter.

"Well, I'm not allowed to visit Megan Brooker, anyway."

"Who said anything about Megan? Luella … Louise, I mean … has asked me to dinner, and she asked if you would like to come as well."

"So this is just a social occasion to discuss books?"

"For me, but she indicated she and her husband would like to talk to you about Megan's situation and what they're allowed to do."

"The attending officers would have given her all the information."

"They just want to talk to someone they trust, to put their mind at ease."

Why was he arguing? He wanted to go.

"All right, I'll come. What do we need to bring?"

"Nothing."

Sure. Nothing. How would that look?

"I'll go out and buy some chocolates."

* * *

The moment she walked through the front door, Megan had that funny feeling she was being set up again.

"Are you expecting guests?" she asked her mother as she opened the oven door and saw a roast browning inside.

"Yes."

No information. She was up to something again.

"Who?"

"A lady who is interested in my work and wants to talk about my novels."

"Mum, you never allow fans into your personal life. Is it Mrs. Fletcher?"

"Janine Fletcher, yes."

"And is she bringing Cam?"

"I believe so."

"Why didn't you just tell me? Are you afraid I'll run away or something?"

"Frankly, yes. I cannot understand what went wrong between the two of you."

"Nothing went wrong. You suggested I get a fake boyfriend to intimidate Shane, you brought Cam around as a suitable candidate, he agreed to play the game and we even raised the stakes by pretending to be engaged."

"So what went wrong?"

"He was pretending, and when I got another job, there was no need to continue."

"What about you? Were you pretending?"

Megan narrowed her eyes. Her mother was too perceptive by half.

"What should I assume by your silence?" Mum persisted.

"You should assume that I was enjoying the charade and hoped it might become something real, but it didn't, and since then, I haven't spoken to Cam. So I assume he was happy to end the arrangement and get back to his normal life."

"Mmm."

She was plotting. Megan knew that look and that non-committal hum of hers.

"Mum, please don't force Cam into something he doesn't want to do."

"Who said anything about forcing? I invited and he accepted."

"Does he know you also invited me?"

"He will when he arrives."

Megan shook her head. To tell the truth, she wanted to see Cam again. She wanted the opportunity to talk and see how he was feeling, not just about his recent brush with Shane, but also how he felt about her—about them. Since her visit to the doctor, she was feeling a heap better, knowing that the anxieties she'd been experiencing were a symptom and she would get back to normal. And she hoped her normal would include a relationship with Cam.

She didn't bother to continue fussing about her mother's underhanded tactics. Secretly, she was pleased with the opportunity, though there was no need to admit that. Instead she helped set the table and prepare the vegetables.

"You here for dinner too?" Dad asked as he came into the kitchen.

Megan kissed him on the cheek. "Where have you been today?" she asked.

"I had a meeting with some clients, needing to approve some new plans." He pulled a seat out and opened a bottle of soft drink.

"Do you know what mother has planned for this evening?" Megan asked.

"No idea, but I'm guessing by the amount of effort being put into dinner that she has people coming and I'm also guessing that being as you're here, she's managed to convince your police constable to be one of them."

"Not much gets past you, does it?"

"And how will you respond—to your police constable?"

"I think I will decline to answer."

"Very wise."

Chapter Eighteen

Cam's heart skipped a beat. Megan's car was in the drive. He wanted to see her but had lost confidence from the moment he realized what he'd done to Shane. Recalling Shane's words didn't help. They were not a justification for what he'd done, and they called his own motivations into question. Those awful words always rose up to sully any pure thoughts he might have had for Megan. He could not seem to banish them from his mind. The best he could do was utter a prayer and try to focus his thoughts on something other than Megan.

But she was here and he wanted the opportunity to speak with her, to at least explain, if he could find the right words.

"Smile," Mum said, as she got out of the car. "You look as if you're about to face a firing squad."

Ironic. He was scheduled to face a court, but before that, he needed to face himself and how he felt about Megan.

"I'm quite excited about this dinner, Cam," she continued. "Please try to be pleasant."

He gave a tight smile and waved her forward along the path leading to the Brookers' front door.

As he'd been there a couple of times before, he took the lead and knocked on the door. What if Megan answered? What should he say? How would she respond to seeing him again?

"Cam." It was Russell.

"Russell." He shook the hand extended in greeting. "May I introduce my mother, Janine."

Cam was amused to see his mother tongue-tied and flustered. She really was star-struck. What did Louise—Luella Linley—write that was so engaging, even addictive? Perhaps he should read one of her books.

Once they had moved through the hall to the family room, Cam tried not to look too eager, but the moment he set eyes upon Megan, he couldn't help smiling.

"Hello," he said.

"Hello, Cam. It's good to see you." There was a shade of pink in her face. And when he became aware that both mothers were looking at him, he realized his own face was probably flushed. How ridiculous. He was not a wet-behind-the-ears schoolboy.

"Are we ready to eat?" Russell asked. Either he was oblivious to the emotional undercurrents or he was hungry. Or he realized that Cam needed a rescue.

That *Matrix* moment where everything seemed suspended and all focus was on one subject—Megan—broke and the room erupted back into activity.

"Come in and sit down." Louise exuded charm and hospitality. "I'm Louise." She held her hand out to Mum. "You must be Janine."

Mum barely spoke but had a stunned sort of smile on her face. The power of celebrity.

"Cam has told me all about you," Louise continued.

"I'm a huge fan." Mum eventually broke her silence. "I just love your books."

"Thank you so much," Louise said. "It's always an encouragement to know the work I do in the quiet of my office is appreciated out in the wide world."

"I should say so," Mum replied. "I always have to pre-order your books to make sure I can get a copy when they're first released."

Talk about fan-girling.

"Mum," Cam said, using a tone he hoped would drag her attention back to the real world. "Can I introduce you to Megan? Megan, this is my mother, Janine, who is a huge fan of your mother's books, and Mum, this is Megan."

He'd intended to get his mother to stop fawning over Louise, and it worked. She now switched targets.

"So you're Megan. I've heard so much about you." Mum went up to her and reached out her hands, which Megan graciously took. Mum then leaned in and kissed her on the cheek—kissed her! Mum was never demonstrative with affection, and certainly no public displays of affection. She just kissed Megan on the cheek and still had her hands in her grip. How awkward.

"I can see why my boy has been so distracted lately."

Good gravy. What was she saying? Cam felt heat rise in his face. He couldn't recall having talked about Megan at all … well maybe a few times, when he'd told her he was trying to sort Shane Telford out.

"It's very nice to meet you," Megan said.

For goodness sake, Mum, let her hands go. Who knew his mother could become so socially awkward. She'd never shown signs of it before. But then, Cam hadn't gone out with her much since he was a kid, even since his father had passed away. She obviously needed to get out more.

"Can I get you a drink?"

Thank goodness, Louise had come to the rescue.

"Thanks," he said. "Mum?"

"Just a cold water, if that's all right?" Mum replied. But it was enough to distract her from smothering Megan.

"Do you want a drink?" Russell asked Cam. Decisions. He didn't want to offend Russell, who was obviously an ordinary bloke who enjoyed sharing a cold one with another bloke, but then he didn't want to offend Megan or her mother by entering into the usual men at one end, women at the other—à la the outdoor barbeque. He might need to keep his mother in check for one thing and he wanted the opportunity to talk to Megan as well. But before he could answer, Russell had opened a long-neck bottle and placed it in his hand.

"So, tell me about this business with Megan's old boss," Russell said, beckoning him aside from the women. Outdoor barbeque style. There was no fighting it.

"Did you hear about the incident outside her place?" Cam asked.

"I heard there was an incident, but not what it was or how the police responded to it."

They didn't know about his arrest. Did he want to tell them?

"How are they going to deal with this pest?" Russell asked. "Can't they warn him off or something?"

Had Megan not told them about the official warning? Did Joel misunderstand the situation when he sent the message? Cam cast a look across the room to Megan, who was being smothered by his mother again.

"There's a lot to this situation and I don't want to double up. Could we include the others in the discussion?" Cam asked.

"Right. Yeah. Of course." Russell took a swig from his bottle, then sat down on one of the lounge chairs. "So while we wait for them, how's your work going?"

They hadn't heard. Cam felt anxiety do a turn through his intestines, like a kid sailing through a tubal water-slide.

"I'm currently on leave," he said. Forced leave, but he couldn't bring himself to say that out loud.

"Excellent. You got much planned? Do you surf? What do you do when you're on holidays?"

As a matter of fact, he did surf, but he wasn't in a position to be going anywhere to find good swell. Should he tell Russell? Of course, but he wanted to tell Megan first. This was so awkward.

"My son, Pete, surfs when he can find the time. He reckons the surf coast in Victoria is the best spot but likes the one down at Port Elliot best of the local beaches."

"I'm not that good," Cam said. "I only go for the mid-sized waves down at Port Willunga." Cam guessed if he talked about surfing, he would not need to answer the question as to whether he was going on a trip.

Russell continued on the small talk that included surfing and the end of the football season. Thankfully, Cam was able to contribute to each subject. Apparently, he was a normal bloke.

* * *

Mrs. Fletcher seemed nice. There was no mistaking her passion for reading—particularly for reading Mum's Regency romances. Megan smiled at what she hoped were the appropriate places but kept casting furtive glances towards where her father and Cam were sitting. What were they talking about? She wanted to be part of that conversation.

Finally, her mother decided to get everyone seated at the dining room table and asked her to help serve. Dad was given the opportunity to carve the roast, which was amusing, given he hardly ever carved the roast or had anything to do with food preparation. But Mum had the table set up in Regency format, with lit candles and embroidered tablecloth. Mrs. Fletcher was loving it. What was Cam thinking?

"That was a lovely meal, thank you," Cam said after they'd finished the chocolate soufflé. "Can I help with the dishes?" He stood up from the table and began to collect the plates.

"Thank you," Megan replied, and stood up as well.

"Don't worry about it," Russell said. "Sit down and have a cup of tea."

"I insist." Cam continued to pick up plates.

Megan waited for her mother to object but saw that calculating look. She knew how to play the game.

"Janine and I are going to my bookshelf to talk about all things Regency."

Megan watched her father's face. He was about to do the martyr thing and agree to help with the dishes.

"Why don't you go into the lounge and watch the sports news?" Megan said quickly.

"I don't mind helping," he said. As if. He hated helping in the kitchen, and of all the times, now he decides he needs to pull his weight.

"Can I talk to you for a moment?" Mum took his arm and drew him aside. Mrs. Bennett to the rescue. Megan couldn't hear what her mother was saying, but she could guess. She would have come up with some hare-brained thing that her father suddenly needed to attend to. At this moment, it didn't really matter. She needed time alone with Cam and finally, she had it.

Cam continued to clear the table and she helped. She didn't want to be in the kitchen alone when she wanted to be near him, to begin catching up on all that had gone on in the past couple of weeks.

"Thanks for coming," she said, by way of opening. "It looks like your mother is as conniving as mine."

"To be honest, she genuinely wanted to meet her writing hero, but she didn't have to bring me."

"Did you want to come?" Megan asked. May as well get straight to the point.

"Yes and no."

What did he mean by that? She had to wait while they pushed through the swinging door between the dining room and kitchen. She put her pile of glasses on the cupboard, ready to load in the dishwasher.

"There's been a lot going on since the night of the incident," Cam said. Was there discouragement in his tone? He looked like he had the weight of the world on his shoulders.

"What's wrong?" she asked. "What happened?"

"You were interviewed by the police. You know I was there?"

Megan nodded. "I heard. I was surprised you came by."

"But you know why they were interviewing you?"

"They said there'd been a fight or something. Were you OK? Did you get hurt?"

Cam smiled. But it wasn't a cheery smile.

"They would have told you that I attacked Shane?"

"They said something of the sort. I was not really listening, to be honest. I was so shocked and terrified to know that Shane had moved in a few doors down."

"I found him on your front lawn, peering in your windows."

Megan felt the blood drain from her face. She knew Cam had made a statement and that had been enough for a warning to be issued, but she didn't know everything that had happened. The doctor had said that she may experience triggers every now and then and this was a trigger. At least now she knew how to recognize signs and that helped her bring her emotions back into order.

"I'm sorry."

Megan looked up and saw him looking at her. His facial expression was a mix of genuine concern, but something else. It looked like sorrow.

"What's the matter, Cam? What happened?"

"I was arrested and charged with aggravated assault."

"What? That's ridiculous!"

"It's not. I lost it. I hit him."

"Well, he should toughen up and not be such a princess. He needed a hit to get him off my lawn."

"I hit him hard. Too hard."

Megan watched his demeanor. His eyes were searching hers. He was really troubled by this thing.

"All I can say is I'm glad. And glad that nothing has come from it."

She tried a smile, but it fell dead between them. His jaw muscles were working hard and she could see his Adam's apple working as he eventually forced a swallow.

"I'm on administrative leave waiting to face court."

"What do you mean?"

"I mean I've applied for bail, so I don't have to spend the intervening months in prison, and will have to face court, probably in a couple of months."

"But court for what? What did you do?"

"I applied unnecessary force—lost control in my anger—and caused physical damage."

Megan just stared at him. She couldn't understand what he was saying.

"That's why I canceled our date."

He'd called it a date. She'd wanted it to be a date, but he'd canceled it. And what was he saying? Canceled because of this ridiculous fight with Shane? He deserved everything he got.

"I had wanted to see if there was something between us that was worth pursuing …"

"Me too." Megan jumped in. She felt as if this conversation was going downhill and she wanted to prevent that if she could.

"But I don't think I can go any further," he said.

Megan wanted to shout, *why not?* But the look on his face was hard and pathetic and sad and, all at once, she felt she should go gently.

"I hope you understand," he said.

"I'm not sure I do," she answered.

She sought his gaze, but for some reason he was determined not to meet hers, busying himself putting dishes in the dishwasher instead.

"Cam?"

"Not now," he said, still without looking. "Things are not good and I don't want to drag you into it."

Megan opened her mouth to object but was cut off by the kitchen door swinging open.

"I've come to put the kettle on," Russell said as he came into the room. "Not interrupting anything, I hope."

Yes, you're interrupting! Get out! But Megan didn't say anything. Cam had already closed down and having a fit of hysterical proportions was not going to help him open up again. She tried one last time to gain his attention by looking at him, but he avoided it. Well, now she knew. There was no use hanging onto false hope, dreaming that something might happen. Her heart sank.

"If you're both ready, let's talk about this 'Shane' situation with everyone over coffee," Russell said. "That all right with you, Cam?"

Cam nodded and left the kitchen without looking back.

Chapter Nineteen

"For heaven's sake, Megan! You can't just tell me it's over, and then give me no good reason," Chloe said.

"I didn't say it was over."

"You did."

"We hadn't even started anything yet."

"Pfft." Chloe walked out of the living room, her workbag over her shoulder. "You keep telling yourself that," she shouted. Megan heard the door of her room slam.

"There was nothing official!" Megan yelled back at her. What was the point? Chloe had already built up a romantic finish in her mind and it didn't seem to matter what Megan said, her sister thought it rubbish.

"But what did he actually say to you?" Chloe asked, coming back into the living room, having changed from her work uniform. Her tone was calmed a few degrees.

"I can't remember."

"Try."

"I don't know. Something about it not being a good time and him not wanting to drag me into trouble."

"Well, there you see." Chloe smiled and rummaged in the refrigerator.

"There you see, what?" Megan got up from her lounge chair and took the kettle to the tap to fill it up. "That sounds like a classic brush-off line to me."

"He said it wasn't a good time *at the moment*. That doesn't mean forever. Just for now."

Megan sighed. "I'd like to enter your fairyland, Chloe, but honestly, what if he just means he's not interested?"

Chloe rolled her eyes. What was the point saying anything? She wasn't listening.

"You said he was facing a court charge."

"That's what he said."

"What, like a criminal?"

"Assault. No, aggravated assault, he said. Not sure what the difference is."

"So he got aggravated and hit Shane. Is that all?"

Megan shrugged, facing her sister, who was pulling dip and carrots from the fridge and placing them on the counter.

"It can't be all that bad, can it?" Chloe asked.

"It was like he was under a black cloud of discouragement."

"Well, if you ask me, I think he's probably stressed and discouraged from being made out to be the bad guy when really he jumped in to defend you."

"Do you think so?" Megan asked.

"Did you sit down and talk it through with him?"

"There wasn't an opportunity, with all the parentals there coming in and out, and then they had a family conflab to ask all the questions about my legal rights where Shane is concerned."

"But you didn't get a chance to have a private talk with Cam about you and him?"

"Just what I told you. And he didn't seem to want any more time to talk about it."

"Can't you give him a call and ask him to explain it to you properly?"

Could she? She had his number and knew he wasn't at work. Should she? He seemed to think it best they didn't pursue anything. The days of the fake relationship were over and the days of a real relationship had been cut off before they'd had a chance to begin. Despite her sister's optimistic enthusiasm, Megan struggled to find the courage to call. He'd said it wasn't the right time. She wasn't prepared to force it with so little assurance that he was interested beyond the game they'd been playing for Shane's benefit.

Chloe brought a plate of snack food to the coffee table before flopping into the couch.

"How are you coping with the other thing?"

The other thing. "'Mental health problem' isn't too hard to say, Chloe."

"I know. There's still a stigma attached to it though, isn't there?"

"You're the one working in the health sector."

"How are you going with it?"

Megan brought her cup of camomile tea over, put it on the coffee table and sat down next to her sister.

"Thanks for making me go to the doctor. Now that I've talked about it and they've given me information and a support line to call if I need, I feel as if I'm getting back to normal."

"I'm glad. Your reaction last week was so uncharacteristic I began to worry."

"Thanks, Chloe. I'm not quite back to normal, but I have strategies when triggers set off anxiety. Now that I know what it is, it's getting easier to get the anxiety under control."

"Now, if only we could sort out your love life, I'd be a happy girl."

Megan picked up a couch pillow and hit her sister, crushing the cracker and dip she had in her hand ready to eat.

"Megan!"

"Let that be a lesson to you."

* * *

"She seemed like a lovely girl." This was the fourth time Mum had made mention of Megan.

"Mum," Cam complained. "We're not together."

"At the moment. From what I saw there is a young woman who would be willing to support you through thick and thin. You did tell her about the arrest when you were in the kitchen?"

"I told her."

"And how did she react?"

"We didn't have time to discuss it before Russell called us into the dining room."

"She seemed attentive when we were talking. Not like she wanted distance or anything."

Cam shook his head. There was no explaining it to her. She hadn't been with him when they'd put handcuffs on and pushed him in the back of a police car, when they'd taken his fingerprints and mug shot, when they'd locked him in one of the holding cells. If she didn't understand the gravity of the charge, he did. It was a criminal offense. If he was found guilty, he might face jail time—up to four years. Would the court take the provocation into consideration? The fact that he was a police officer—a disgraced police officer—would probably not go in his favor. The department and the courts tended to hold law enforcement officers to a higher level of accountability. He couldn't find any reasonable defense for his loss of control. Shane had not attacked him—physically at least. He'd been clever in his provocation, using words, particularly focused on Megan. It was as if Shane had known how he felt about her, that he cared for her, that he loved her.

Did he? Did he love Megan? Was love an excuse for trying to beat the stuffing out of a man who threatened harm against his woman? But she wasn't his woman. There had been the possibility she might have agreed to start a real relationship. It might have turned into something deep and lasting, but what was the use of even investigating the idea now? He didn't want to start a relationship that would have to be continued during spasmodic visits through Perspex glass. He wasn't prepared to put her in that position.

"Well, I enjoyed spending time with Luella."

"Louise." Cam corrected. "Luella is her pen name."

"I was talking to the author most of the night."

"I'm glad you had a good time," Cam said. He meant it too. His mother hadn't had a lot of good in her life since his father had become ill and since he passed.

"Louise said she thought you were interested in Megan."

"I thought you said you were with the author all night."

"I did talk to the mother for a little while. She likes you."

Cam smiled. He'd known that from the moment he'd met her, writing out a speeding ticket.

"So are you interested in her?"

She was not going to let this drop. Since he couldn't go storming out the house to work or somewhere else, he decided he'd better get the discussion over and done with.

"I was—am—interested, Mum, but what happened the other night effectively disqualifies me from even considering going forward. And before you start to argue, you need to know I'm in serious trouble and it's going to be hard enough on you, let alone dragging someone else into it."

He watched for her reaction and was surprised when she didn't wind up to promote her argument.

"Do you understand, Mum?"

She took a deep breath and pursed her lips.

"You're a good man, Cam. This business is not a true reflection of who you are."

Cam felt a small surge of courage, but then remembered that of course his mother would say that. However, her opinion would hold zero influence with the magistrate or a jury if he had to face one.

"I appreciate you taking an interest," Cam continued, "but in all honesty, I'm not going to be calling Megan or making any effort to see her, not until this court case is over, and even then …"

"You really think they'll find you guilty?"

"How can they not? I physically assaulted the man."

"You're going to plead guilty?"

Cam shook his head. "I'm going to defend myself on the grounds of provocation, but I have doubts that will hold as much of a defense."

Mum shook her head and let out a breath through her nose.

"It's wrong," she said as she left the room. "It's just wrong."

If only a mother's opinion were worth anything in a court of law.

If only he could stop thinking about Megan Brooker.

No. He would not start a relationship with her until he knew how his next few years were going to look. If he was going to serve time, it was better she moved on from the likes of him.

Chapter Twenty

"Pardon me, my lady."

Rosalie looked up as Roberts, their butler, came into the drawing-room where she was reading.

"What is it, Roberts?"

"A letter has just been delivered for you. The boy said to tell you it was urgent."

She waited as Roberts brought the silver salve across, the sealed letter perched neatly on top.

"Thank you, Roberts. That will be all."

Rosalie took the letter and broke the wax seal. It was a communication from the man her aunt had engaged to investigate the disappearance of Lord Osmond. Not that she ever wished to see him again. On the one hand, she hoped he *had* perished, but on the other, the man she loved was awaiting transportation. Convicted of having supposedly murdered Lord Osmond, Josiah was bound for New South Wales—a dreadful, ferocious place, where convicts faced a fate worse than death. She knew that Josiah had clashed with Osmond, and that he'd breathed angry threats of revenge at the way Osmond had treated her. But she did not, for a single moment, believe he had killed the man. There had been no body, only an accusation from one of Osmond's men, and some conveniently placed pieces of evidence that seemed to suggest Josiah had arranged for the man's demise.

If Josiah was sent to that place, Rosalie wondered if she might find a way to go as well. It was no picnic, she knew, but she had heard that some free settlers had left the shores of England in search of a new life.

She read through the letter carefully. There was news. The investigator had found evidence that Lord Osmond was alive.

"Roberts!" She called, hoping he was standing just outside the door, and rang the bell cord as well, just in case he was not. "Roberts! Order a carriage, and have my maid bring my cloak."

The office door flung open.

"Mum! Get off your computer." Chloe burst into the room and hovered over her mother.

"Where's the fire, Chloe? For goodness sake. You're interrupting my train of—"

"Never mind that. You do know that everything between Cam and Megan is about to disintegrate?"

"Chloe, bless you."

"Mum!"

"You shouldn't meddle with your sister's love life. If it's meant to be—"

"Would you listen to yourself? You were the one who set them up. You were the one who invited him over to dinner the other night. If that isn't meddling ..."

"What have you heard that has you all het up?"

"They're not going to pursue the relationship."

"How do you know? They talked for quite a while in the kitchen after dinner last night."

"Megan told me that it's all off."

Louise frowned. "Are you sure?"

"That's what she said."

"I find that hard to believe. Cam told us he was serious. He took her number to follow her up."

"That was before."

"Before?"

"The incident at our place. The fight on the lawn."

"How should that change his mind? Wait. Was it Megan who called it off—because of the fight?"

"No! Mother! I can't believe you haven't been paying attention. Didn't Cam's mother tell you what happened?"

Louise shook her head. "What happened, other than the fight?"

"Cam was arrested and charged with assault and is now facing a court case and possible jail sentence."

"What?" Shades of Josiah all over again. "Do they have evidence or is it just Telford's word against his?"

"I cannot believe you don't know all this. Where have you been?"

"Megan didn't say anything to me."

"She only just found out at dinner last night."

"Janine didn't say anything either."

"His mother?"

Louise nodded.

"Well, if she's trying to promote her son as a good catch to possible in-laws, she's hardly going to come into the house and say: 'Guess what? My son is a criminal.'"

"No, I suppose not. But I'm surprised no one said anything when we were discussing Megan's situation."

"You knew about the fight?"

"Yes, we discussed that, but Cam didn't say he'd been arrested, only that Megan should report any little thing to do with Shane."

Chloe paced around the office, obviously agitated.

"Well, what are you going to do about it?" She finally stopped and looked at her mother.

"Chloe, I get the feeling you believe I have some influence in the matter."

"Well, don't you. You're a famous author. You're always plotting and scheming for your characters. Can't you think of something to help sort this out?"

"And by sorting out, do you mean getting Cam and Megan together, or do you mean helping Cam out of his dilemma?"

"Both! I can't believe you're just sitting there."

Louise laughed. Yes, she was a famous author, with magical powers, apparently. But then, when she thought about it, perhaps there was something she could do if she had all the facts before her.

* * *

Megan finished the call from yet another possible client who was looking for a building quote. The phone had been ringing non-stop all morning. How on earth had Pete managed his business before and done actual building work at the same time? She went back to his accounts and the answer was there before her. He hadn't managed. His accounts were a mess. He had money owing to him left, right and center, and it was never going to be paid if he didn't send the invoices. At least she knew he was going to be able to afford her, and she was going to earn her money.

She was distracted from the invoices by a knocking on the door. There was a flash of anxiety—one of those triggers. *Stop it.* She picked up her phone and had the number for the police on speed dial, just in case, but she had to get back to her normal way of life. She did not want to become a basket case, living and breathing fear. *Thank you, Lord, for your strength.*

Drawing her shoulders back and taking a deep breath, she approached the door with confidence. She was going to get back to normal.

"Hello, Meggsy."

"Dad." Relief and joy flowed in to fill in the gaps on her pretense of bravado. She opened the door wide and threw her arms around him in a warm hug.

"Glad to see me, then?" he said with his usual dry humour.

"Come inside. You haven't been around to visit for ages."

Russell stepped into the entry and waited while Megan shut the door.

"Do you want a cup of tea?" she asked.

"Coffee, if you have it."

Megan led the way to the kitchen area and pulled out a pack of coffee pods, putting one in her espresso machine.

"How's Pete's business?" Dad asked.

"It's thriving, though he would have lost the lot if he hadn't taken me on. His accounting and invoicing are a mess."

"I'm glad that's worked out for both of you."

"Me too." Megan put an open packet of Tim-Tams on the counter in front of her father. "So, what brings you around to visit on a Wednesday morning? Dropping something to a client in the area?"

"I've come specially to see you," he said, taking a Tim-Tam and biting into it.

"Usually you and Mum come together."

"Your mother and Chloe are at home freaking out over how you and Cam have broken up."

Megan took a deep breath ready to speak, but her father cut her off.

"I understand, Megan. You don't have to justify it to me."

"What do you understand, Dad?"

"Cam is facing a serious criminal charge and may end up in jail. He would have gone past stressed to depressed by now, if he's a normal bloke."

"You think so?"

"I do. Listen, Meggsy, Cam told me he was interested in pursuing a relationship with you. That's why we gave him your number."

"But the fight occurred before anything could happen." A wave of regret flowed over her—or was it longing?

Dad nodded. Megan placed his coffee on the counter in front of him.

"You need to give him time, Megan. Let him sort out this charge. He hasn't got the emotional energy to be starting a serious relationship, and I don't believe he's the sort to drag you into something so precarious and distressing in any case. He's taking his own responsibility for a mistake he's made, and you need to give him the time and space to do it."

"No matter what Mum and Chloe say."

"Particularly despite what your mother and sister say."

That made good sense. She filled her own coffee cup and sat on a bar stool next to her father.

"Are you upset with me?" Dad asked.

"No. That makes sense."

"Good, because I haven't finished yet."

Megan sat up straighter and watched his expression closely. She could tell he was going to speak sternly on a matter. She hadn't seen that look in years.

"You should be taking your former boss to court over the way he has treated you. You should not allow him to get away with it."

"Dad—"

He held up his hand. "Let me finish."

Yep. He was back in his stern father mode.

"Shane Telford has broken the law on several fronts. Firstly, with the Fair Work Act, dismissing you without properly paying your owed holiday pay and the weeks in lieu, despite you having given notice, according to law."

Megan nodded. It rankled, but it was too hard to follow up.

"And I believe you should sue him for emotional distress due to his sexual harassment and stalking."

Megan took a deep breath. Her father sounded like a general rallying his troops.

"I know it's a difficult process, Megan, and that's why I've come around here to help you do it."

"Really?" She felt her courage and confidence surge.

"I'm your father, and who should help his daughter beat this injustice if not me?"

"I don't know what to say."

"Say you'll work with me to fight this thing. You need justice and I mean to see that you get it."

Megan stood up and put her arms around her father again. He was not usually a hugger, but he responded and held firm. Tears sprang to her eyes as she felt the weight of Shane's offenses begin to lift from her.

"Thanks, Dad," she said. "I love you."

"I love you too."

Megan smiled. This lovey-touchy-feely thing might not be his usual style, but it felt good.

Chapter Twenty-one

Cam couldn't believe how bored he was sitting at home, unable to go anywhere. He could have gone to the shops or the gym or for a run in the park, but truth be told, he was feeling sorry for himself. He wanted to visit Megan, but even if he hadn't called it off, she lived and worked in the forbidden zone, as outlined in his bail conditions. Too close to Shane's residence.

"I'm going out for a while," Mum said. "I've got ladies' fellowship morning at church."

"OK." One thing was for certain, he had no intention of going to ladies' fellowship.

"Will you be all right?"

"I'm fine, Mum. I'm a grown-up."

She picked up her handbag and keys and went to leave the house. Cam felt a surge of guilt. It wasn't her fault he'd been put on administrative leave.

"I'm sorry for being snappy," he said, just before she went out the door.

"I'm sorry too," she said. "I'm only trying to be encouraging."

"All right. I'll see you later. Will you be home for lunch?"

"No. I'll go out for lunch and do some grocery shopping while I'm out."

Cam settled back into the living room couch once the front door closed. It had been less than a year since Dad had passed away and he'd come back home to live. Cam had wanted to make sure his mum coped all right. It wasn't a perfect living situation. He was nearly thirty years old and too old to still be at home. He knew what it was like to live independently. Was it time for him to move out again?

He had thought about his living arrangements while he and Megan were playing their game. It would be nice to marry and set up a new home together. Joel had teased him about it several times, and he'd reacted in the usual way of pretending it was the most unlikely thing in the world. But it wasn't. Something had sprung to life between him and Megan, and he had intended to follow it through. But now, sitting under the cloud of a criminal conviction, he wasn't going anywhere. Sitting in his mother's lounge, watching stupid daytime television and shopping channels seemed to be defining his status and his frame of mind. Until the court case came up, this would be how his life would look—unless he stopped feeling sorry for himself, got off his butt and found something positive to do.

Mum had gone to ladies' fellowship at the church. Cam hadn't been to the church since the arrest but wondered if he should go and catch up with Pastor John, just to let him know how things had turned out.

Pulling himself up from the couch, he retrieved his mobile phone and looked up the number.

John was keen to catch up and, given the church building was overrun with ladies at the fellowship morning, they arranged to meet at a local café.

"I'm glad you called," John said. "I've been worried since the day you were marched off in cuffs."

"Sorry. I should have let you know." Cam ducked his eyes and scanned the café menu.

"So, I take it they sorted it out and you're free to go."

Cam let out a sigh. "Not quite as easy as that, I'm afraid."

The pastor looked at him, eyebrows raised.

"I've been charged with aggravated assault and am facing a trial in a couple of months."

"Oh, mate! I'm sorry to hear that. So are you still working?"

"I'm on administrative leave—forced leave."

John sucked in a large breath through his nose, held it a couple of seconds and then blew it out through loose lips. "That must suck."

"And then some," Cam replied.

"Can you get off? Is there evidence that will help you?"

Cam shook his head. "Unfortunately, in this instance, I'm guilty as sin, pardon the expression."

"I heard the story about what the other fellow said, mate. Surely they have to take that into consideration."

"I gave an affidavit outlining that particular conversation—"

"Hardly a conversation."

Cam nodded. "The best result is that he's been officially warned. Any further breach of the Unlawful Stalking act and he's in worse trouble than I am."

"That's a relief for Megan."

Cam nodded again.

"How are you getting along with her, following the incident? Does she understand?"

"I've only seen her once, but I've called it off."

"Because?"

"Because I don't want her mixed up in all the legal nastiness that's coming up, and if I go to jail ..."

"Do you think that's possible? Surely a man of your standing in the community, and first offense—you haven't had anything like this in the past, have you?"

"Not anything I've been charged with. I got involved in another incident years ago that could have turned bad. I was saved by my partner who defused the situation."

"Yeah, I remember now that you mention it. That was when you first started seeing me?"

"Yes."

"You've grown heaps since that time. That incident won't influence this case, will it?"

"I hope not."

"Surely, they'll only give you a suspended sentence or something."

"Maybe. But our Internal Investigation Section is known to be harder on members of the police department than perhaps another individual."

"Why?"

"They don't ever want to be accused of police corruption by being soft on their own."

"Mate." John took another deep breath, held it, then let it out.

Cam stopped and gave a lunch order to the waitress who had come to their table, and waited while John did the same.

"Anyway," Cam went on, once the girl had left with their orders, "I guess it wouldn't hurt for me to catch up with you a bit, if you're free. I could use some prayer, and I'm so bored, it's driving me around the bend."

"Anytime. And if you have some time on your hands, I have loads of community service work that needs doing."

"Small problem."

John frowned a question.

"Churches need to have all volunteers cleared to make sure they don't have any criminal history," Cam said. "You know how much focus has been on institutions like the church regarding child abuse."

Cam watched John form his lips as if he wanted to swear, but he didn't. Cam had been practicing keeping his language in check as well and knew the signs of a man who was frustrated.

"Sorry to be a fly in the ointment, but neither the community nor the church wants to find themselves under that sort of intense scrutiny again," Cam said.

"That sort of thing should never have happened in the first place, and God only knows how the folks who suffered abuse will ever be able to find healing."

Cam nodded. God only knew. In the meantime, the law was now in place to protect everyone from a similar event happening again.

"OK. So, no community service," John said, "but there's no stopping you coming in for prayer and counseling. If you happen to help me move some boxes or file some paper, that can hardly be considered community service, can it?"

Cam smiled. This charge was going to affect him in all areas of his life, even if he didn't go to jail. A good reason why he should learn to deal with the things that Shane had said.

"You might have to help me learn to forgive."

"Forgive? Shane Telford?"

"I'm struggling with it at the moment. The things he said spring to my mind in full-color detail every time I think about him, and sometimes when I think about Megan."

"Yep. We're gonna have to help you sort that out. We'll definitely need some counseling to help you process those thoughts. I can give you some tips and pointers on how to win the battle of the mind."

"I think I'm going to need it."

Cam was encouraged from the time he spent with John. The pastor seemed sure there were ways he could deal with his thoughts, and he wanted to do that more than anything else. He wanted to think about Megan sometimes and perhaps hope for something in the long-term future, but he didn't want Shane's perverted and disgusting suggestions encroaching.

On the way home, he decided to stop in at the gym and pump some iron. He needed the physical activity as well. His body was beginning to creak and groan from lying about too much.

By the time he pulled in the driveway, he saw his mum was home, and there was another car. He didn't really want to face any visitors, but there was no other place to go. He opened the front door with his key and hoped to make a polite excuse so he could go to his room and read.

"Hello, Cameron." He was greeted by Louise Brooker, who stood up from the kitchen table, where she'd been drinking tea with his mother.

"Louise." He found a smile came easily enough. "How are you?"

"I'm well enough."

There was a huge 'but' implied in the pause that followed. Should he bite?

"OK." He put his keys on the key ring by the refrigerator.

"Do you want tea or coffee?" Mum asked.

"I'm right, thanks. Thought I'd go and read for a bit." Actually, he was panting for a coffee, but this was an extension of ladies' fellowship, and not really for him.

"Would you mind if I chatted with you for a while?" Louise asked. "I brought chocolate cake."

The way to a man's heart.

"How can I say no?"

"To the cake or the chat?" Louise asked.

"The cake, of course, but I think I can spare some time for a chat as well." He knew there was something. Louise did not hide her ulterior motives well. Cam pulled out a chair at the kitchen table and sat down.

"I'll get you a drink," Mum said.

"I think I will have a coffee, thanks, Mum."

It was excellent chocolate cake, oozing with chocolate icing on the top and fresh cream and strawberry jam in the middle layer.

"So tell me about this fight with Shane," Louise said.

Cam pressed his lips together and breathed deeply. Talk about putting a man off his cake.

"I know you were arrested, and I know you're facing court," she continued. "I just want to know the details of how it happened."

"Why?" he asked. "I hit the man with excessive force and he suffered some facial injuries as a result."

"But why would you do that? You don't strike me as the sort of man who's reckless—quite the opposite. I would have had you pegged as a man who took his responsibilities extremely seriously and a person who had excellent control of his temper."

"That's right!" *Bless you Mum for your support.*

"To hear there is evidence of an alleged assault surprises me to no end. I want to know what he said to you that caused you to flip out."

"No, you don't," Cam said. "You most certainly do *not* want to know what he said."

"It was about Megan, then?"

Cam was silenced momentarily. There was no hiding things from this woman.

"Louise, you should go into the police force. Your interrogation skills are excellent."

"What did that worm of a man say?"

"I would not like to repeat it in the company of ladies."

"Pfft! Cut that out, young man. We are strong-minded and capable women and are not likely to go into a faint at the first sign of strong language."

Mum giggled. She actually giggled.

"Why are you laughing?" Cam cast accusing eyes in his mother's direction.

"I've read Luella's novels. Her heroines always faint."

"That is fiction," Louise said. "And sadly, what society expected of females during the Regency period."

Cam kept his lips hidden. At least talking about Regency romance distracted them from the subject he didn't want to talk about.

"And, you may as well know, women of that period probably fainted because their corsets were laced up too tight. *We* ..." she waved her hand to indicate Mum and herself, "do not wear corsets."

Cam felt the heat rise in his face. Talk about mental images.

"And by the flush on your face, young man, I would say you have finer sensibilities than we do."

Mum's giggle escalated to a snort. This was not amusing.

His cake was beginning to wilt, Mum had forgotten about the coffee, and a pair of middle-aged women had him in the cross-hairs of a first-class glare. The first one to speak loses.

He shrugged his shoulders helplessly. "I can *not* repeat what Shane Telford said."

"Will you tell the court as some form of defense?" Louise asked.

"I'll have to. It's my only defense."

"Given that both your mother and I will be sitting in the gallery during the trial and we'll hear every word then, you may just as well tell us now."

Cam picked up his fork and attacked the cake. He shoved a very poorly shaped piece into his mouth.

"Where's the coffee?" he asked around the mouthful.

"Don't go all male chauvinist on us now, Cameron. I know you're a decent and fair-minded human being."

Louise Brooker was relentless. The words 'grand inquisitor' came to mind. He kept hacking at his cake, failing to enjoy the taste and texture he had been anticipating earlier.

The sound of one finger tapping on the tabletop began to annoy him. They were still giving him the 'I'm waiting' stare.

"All right, but you'll be upset and horrified. And you'll know why I flipped out."

"Why don't you give us the edited version," Louise said. "Just so I know what we're dealing with here."

"We're dealing with a sexual pervert," Cam said. "And the words he said I want to erase from my mind as soon as this court case is over. I want rid of them completely. I love and respect your daughter, Louise, and when I think of what he said, I sometimes get so angry, I want to hit him again."

"Cam!" Mum looked shocked.

"That's why I don't want to talk about it," Cam looked at his mother. "And that's why I've arranged to go back to counseling, so I can deal with the whole emotional situation and get some closure on it."

He felt as if he had some sense of control of the discussion now—that both mothers understood what pressure he was under. He carefully chose his words to indicate the kind of things Shane had said, without actually repeating the words.

"Thank you, Cameron," Louise said. "Now I know how to act."

"I don't think there's anything you can do," he said.

She raised her eyebrows at him and gave him a look that said: *really?*

"Thank you for caring, Louise," Mum said. "I really appreciate your taking the time."

"You heard the man," Louise said, waving her hand in Cam's direction. "He loves my daughter. You don't think I'm going to let that opportunity slide past without some effort on my part."

Had he said that out loud—and to her mother? Good grief. There was no going back from here.

Chapter Twenty-two

Chloe was on night shift again and Megan made a deliberate decision to analyze the situation—how she felt, what things presented as triggers, and sensible steps she could take to combat any sense of encroaching anxiety. With this plan and God's help, she would beat this thing. The brochure the police constable had given her, outlining the Unlawful Stalking act, sat on the kitchen bench. She had the relevant telephone numbers highlighted and knew she could call at any moment if she so much as saw Shane, and they would respond with an arrest. She almost hoped he would happen by so she could make the call and be done with it. Dad was looking into the legality of his having moved into her street and whether that might end up being extra evidence in a suit against him. Good old Dad. He was being so encouraging. It was doing wonders in rebuilding her self-confidence.

Her phone rang and Megan jumped. She rolled her eyes at her ridiculous reaction, took a deep breath and answered.

"Pete. Do you want to come over?" She didn't wait for a response before blurting out the invitation.

"Yeah."

"What's the matter?" She could hear the heaviness in his tone.

"I'm parked outside your house, so I'll tell you when I come in."

Well, that was the answer to one problem. She now had company and wouldn't have to be constantly fighting shadows. If only she could talk her brother into staying overnight.

"What on earth's the matter?" she asked as she let him in the house. He looked worse than he sounded, shoulders drooping and dragging his feet.

"Not sure I want to talk about it. Have you got food?"

OK. Megan turned on her heels and headed back to the kitchen. He wanted comfort food. She would provide comfort food.

"You're in luck. Chloe was in a cooking frenzy this afternoon and has a whole heap of food in the fridge."

"Good." Pete walked straight past her and opened the fridge. He pulled out a bowl of cold pasta, grabbed a fork from the cutlery drawer and started forking it into his mouth.

"Why don't you microwave it?" Megan asked.

Pete just shrugged his shoulders.

"Being as I'm in charge of your financial records and your current job schedules, I know this slump of spirits is not about work … is it? Your apprentice didn't fall off the roof or anything, did he?"

Pete shook his head, having just filled his mouth with another forkful of pasta.

"Well, anyway, I think my life is in worse shape than yours."

No answer, only the sounds of more food being shoveled in.

"I have a stalker living down the street and now the relationship I hoped would turn into something serious is over, and I'm sitting here on a week night fighting the jitters because I'm scared to stay home alone."

Pete stopped chewing for about three seconds and looked at her. Then started chewing again.

"So, is your situation worse than mine?" Megan asked.

"Probably not. But it feels like it."

"Are you going to tell me or are you just going to consume everything in the fridge and leave Chloe without lunch tomorrow?"

"You didn't tell me it was her lunch," Pete said, putting his fork down.

"She will make more, don't panic."

He picked the fork up again.

"Is it Rianne?" Megan asked. "Are you missing her?"

Pete put the fork down again. "She's broken off our engagement."

"I didn't know you were engaged!"

"We'd agreed that we'd make it official once she got back from the study exchange."

"So what happened?"

"She met some European guy and has just told me they're getting married."

"Seriously! That *is* worse than my situation."

"Glad you think so."

"Here, let me get you some trifle."

Megan got up and pulled out the fruit and jelly trifle her sister had made during her afternoon domestic blitz. She spooned large serves into two bowls and brought one across to her brother.

"Let's eat our misery away," she said.

Pete actually gave a half-smile. He was easily placated with trifle.

"So the big guy decided against you?" Pete said once he'd scraped all but the floral pattern from the plate.

"The big guy got involved in a fight with the stalker and he's been charged with assault."

"Who's been charged? The stalker or Cam?"

"Cam."

"You're kidding?" Pete sat up straight and looked wide-eyed at his sister.

"Don't tell me Mum hasn't called you and given you all the details?"

"I haven't spoken to Mum in nearly a week."

"Well if you neglect her, you're going to miss out on all the family happenings."

"So you dropped him because he got into a fight and was arrested?"

"There was no dropping. We didn't have an actual official relationship."

"Well, who backed off from whom? And why?"

"He called it off."

"I thought you said there wasn't an official relationship."

"All right he backed off."

"Because?"

"Because of the legal battle and possible jail time."

"Seriously?"

"Seriously, Pete."

"Well, at least it wasn't because he fell in love with another woman."

"I'm sorry, Pete. I feel miserable enough, but I know you and Rianne had been fairly serious."

He shrugged.

"Will you stay over for the night?" she asked.

He nodded. "Yeah. I don't fancy being on my own at the moment."

"Me either."

* * *

"Josiah Landown?"

Josiah opened his eyes and tried to see in the dim light of the dark, dank prison. This was it. Time to be transferred to a moving ship, one that would set sail to the antipodes, separating him forever from his home, his love, his freedom. He was in no hurry to answer.

"Josiah Landown?"

"He's over here." One of the other prisoners, chained a couple of men down, called out.

"Is he still alive?" the new voice asked.

"Oi. Landown. You all right, mate?"

"As right as you can be, chained to a rotting ship and bound for New South Wales." It was hard to keep the sarcasm out of his tone.

"Lord Landown?" In the dim light, Josiah could see a well-dressed gentleman peering around the space. He had woven his way between the other chained, miserable convicts to be standing a few feet in front of him. Wait, he'd addressed him by his title. He hadn't heard any formality or deference for his position in the months since he'd been arrested and tried.

"Who are you?"

"My name is Gullington. I work for Lady Wordall."

Lady Wordall? Rosalie's aunt.

"What is your business here?" He had nothing to lose by being cautious and wasn't prepared to engage in pleasantries until he understood what he wanted.

"My business has been to find evidence that Lord Osmond is alive."

Osmond. That detestable man. If it wasn't for the fact that he'd been charged with his murder, Josiah would have been just as happy to know he was dead.

"Have you found evidence?"

"Come along, sir. This is no place to be discussing personal business."

"I'm not sure if you have noticed, but I am not at liberty to be moving to the library."

"There is no need to be rude, young man. I am here on a mission that is for your benefit. I would appreciate your cooperation."

"*Even if I believed you, I can hardly move to scratch myself.*" He lifted his manacled wrists and the chains clanked and rattled in objection. "*I am in no position to move to another place.*"

"*Now that I know you are here, I will see to the necessary paperwork, and have you removed from this appalling place.*"

"*Can you fill in a paper for me too, mate?*" one of the other convicts said. "*This 'ere place ain't no Windsor Castle.*"

Paper work. Well that was the blight of the Twenty-first Century. But if this idea worked, writing a couple media releases would be paperwork well worth the effort. And she was a writer, so writing some emotionally moving pieces shouldn't prove too difficult. Being a famous author had its perks, and the glossy women's magazine had offered her payment for this candid interview. All she had to do was craft the story in a way that would move the readers—one reader in particular.

With the two manila folders tucked in her briefcase, Luella Linley, dressed in her best media-ready outfit, got in her car and drove to the address she'd found on the internet.

So, this is where her daughter had worked for nearly two years. Telford Wholesalers. The office had gold lettering set on a salmon-colored render. With the large, black-tinted, plate-glass windows the building exuded a classy image. Shane Telford might not have valued his marriage or his employees, but he valued his business. The whole presentation told her that.

Louise Brooker was not a native to high-heeled shoes, but Luella Linley determined she would walk into this office with a commanding presence. Flat shoes would not do the job, so she had to expend extra energy to make sure she didn't twist an ankle. One thing she was sure of, high-heeled shoes were invented by a man and were probably a conspiracy to keep women from taking over the world. What a ridiculous invention. But when image counted …

"Can I help you?"

A fresh-faced young woman sat behind the reception desk, looking up at her. Was it too much to hope that she was dazzled by the media image she was trying to impose?

"I would like to speak to Mr. Telford, please," Luella said.

"May I ask who is calling?"

"You may tell him that Luella Linley from Division Publishing is here to talk to him about a promotion possibility."

"Please take a seat and I'll see if he's in."

Of course he was in. She could see him sitting at his desk behind the thin-line Venetian blinds. The point was, would Shane Telford take the bait she had thrown out?

Luella pulled out her compact mirror, opened it and checked her make-up. She should be on the stage. She only ever wore make-up to church, then never as much as Chloe had pasted on her face this morning. And the compact mirror had sat rusting in the bottom of her author briefcase for years. She'd been given it as a token gift at one of those women's conferences, where every woman got a gift. Shades of Oprah. Shame it hadn't been a car.

"He will be with you in a few minutes, Ms. Linley," the reception-ist said, once she came back.

"Thank you."

"Could I get you a coffee or tea?"

"A glass of water would be wonderful, thank you."

The receptionist—Megan's replacement—went through another door, obviously a staff room or kitchen, and was back within a few moments, a glass of water in hand.

"Thank you. And I have some reading material for you." Luella held out two pamphlets from the Safe Work SA Office, one addressing sexual harassment in the workplace and another on protecting the worker's privacy. "Make sure you're familiar with that information, Marie," she said, reading the girl's name badge. "Don't be afraid to exercise your rights if you need to."

Marie looked at the titles on the brochures and a shade of pink climbed into her cheeks. Had she already encountered Shane Telford's inappropriate behavior?

"Thank you," she said and returned to her desk.

Luella sipped the water in a lady-like manner. She then crossed her leg over her knee like a professional woman, glad she was wearing some classy trousers and not the short skirt Chloe had suggested.

"Ms. Linley." The man himself. The person who had dared intimidate and objectify her daughter, and who now stood in the way of all her romantic plotting.

"Mr. Telford. Please call me Luella." She placed her glass on the coffee table and stood up, holding out her hand in greeting.

"My receptionist tells me you're from a publishing company."

"Could we talk in your office?"

"Please." Shane stepped aside and directed her towards his office with a wave of his hand. Luella swallowed. She was all front, and suddenly felt a wave of second thoughts—sensible, logical, questioning thoughts. What was she doing? Too late now. The charade was in motion.

"Please have a seat," Shane said.

Luella sat in the brown leather tub chair on one side of the room and Shane took the other tub chair opposite, with a small coffee table in between.

"I believe my receptionist said you wished to speak to me about a promotion opportunity."

"Yes, actually. You may not have heard of me, but I'm a well-known author …"

"Oh?" Shane's eyes widened, and his eyebrows rose. "What do you write?"

"Regency romance fiction, as it happens."

His eyebrows went down and his eyes narrowed. Had Megan ever told him that her mother wrote Regency romance? Too bad. She was in for a penny, in for a pound now.

"I have a wide reading audience—quite popular, you know."

"I see." His tone had cooled. He knew she was Megan's mother.

"I've recently been approached by two leading women's magazines asking for a candid story about the person behind the stories."

"Ms. Linley, how does this have anything to do with me or a promotional opportunity for my business?"

"Oh, but it does." She reached into her briefcase and pulled out the two manila folders. She placed them on the coffee table and opened them up, placing the two single typed sheets of paper on top of each folder.

"Would you care to read these media releases?"

The look on his face told her he wanted to get rid of her, but the papers were there begging to be read. Eventually, he shifted his eyes down and began to read.

Luella Linley comforts daughter following sexual harassment

Favorite Regency Romance author, Luella Linley, has had a difficult year in her personal life, having to spend time with her daughter who was severely traumatized by several incidents of sexual harassment. When the perpetrator, Shane Telford, of Telford Wholesalers, was confronted, the harassment escalated to stalking and intimidation.

Mr. Telford has been warned by the police that if he breaches any conditions of the unlawful stalking act, he will be arrested and possibly jailed.

Luella had written more in this report about how this had affected her and her writing, but she hadn't needed to. This passage had been enough to have Shane stand up, his face red with anger.

"You can't print that!"

"I won't be printing it. The publisher of the magazine can, though, after they've done some investigation to verify the facts of the case."

"I'll sue you for defamation."

"A case you will lose. We all know there is sufficient evidence to dismiss any liable case. And besides, you will be busy answering your own suit that my husband intends to bring against you on our daughter's behalf."

"Get out!"

Luella wondered why she wasn't intimidated by his aggression.

"Aren't you interested in how you can prevent me from releasing this to the magazines?"

Shane calmed at this, though his color was high, his jaw clenched and his breath coming in deep heaving motions.

"Read the other media release." She pointed to the second sheet.

Luella Linley's year of joy, preparing a romantic wedding for her daughter

Favorite Regency author, Luella Linley, has taken time from her busy writing schedule to help prepare for the wedding of the year. When pulled over for speeding, she met a young police officer who was the very image of her current romantic hero, Lord Josiah Landown. Through some careful arrangements, Luella orchestrated a meeting between him and her daughter, and today is overjoyed to be preparing for their wedding.

"This is nonsense," Shane said. "You set him up to try to intimidate me."

"Does it matter?" Luella said.

"You can't release this either, as Cameron Fletcher is due to face court and he'll probably be jailed."

"Well, that is very much up to you, isn't it?" Luella said.

"How do you mean?"

"I mean, you have two days to make that charge go away or I will be sending the first media release to the magazines."

"Are you trying to blackmail me?"

"Nothing of the sort. My husband and I will see justice for my daughter, suing you for the emotional distress you've caused. How that case goes might well depend on how you deal with Constable Fletcher. Then what am I going to tell my loyal readers about my personal life? My pain at seeing a daughter's joy destroyed by a sleazy, sexual pervert or my joy at seeing her united with the man she loves. The end of the story is in your hands, Mr. Telford. How do you want it to end?"

Luella watched the man who had the power to destroy Megan's state of mind and prevent her happy-ever-after ending. Would he capitulate? It was like a Mexican standoff, watching him watch her. His eyes were narrow, his teeth clenched and his jaw ticking like it was in a spasm.

Finally, she couldn't take the tension anymore.

"Well, it's up to you," she said, as she scooped up the papers and put them back into the folders. "If I don't have word within two days that Cameron Fletcher has been released from this charge and is back at work, I'll send the first media release. It shouldn't be that hard to make a phone call to your lawyer and let him know you're dropping the charges."

Shane still didn't speak.

"Oh, and I'd also like to hear that my daughter's rightful pay due to her when she left your employ is deposited into her bank account. That at least can be dropped from the law suit if you see to it straight away."

She walked out the office door. "Good afternoon, Mr. Telford."

She nodded to the receptionist, walked out the front door and collapsed against the wall outside. Did she just do that? She had more front than Harrods.

Chapter Twenty-three

Cam was working out at the gym when his smart-watch buzzed. Without breaking stride on the treadmill, he glanced at his watch. Joel.

Call me ASAP.

He didn't feel he needed to talk to him immediately. He was on leave, and anything Joel wanted had to be work-related. He kept running, watching his heart rate on the treadmill monitor. It was hammering away at an acceptable rate for a cardio workout, and he was glad to have something to focus on other than his looming date with justice.

The watch vibrated again and Cam glanced at it. His lawyer was calling his mobile number. He never had any good news, so Cam decided to ignore him and push on to his limit rather than lose momentum.

The watch vibrated a third time. He recognized the police station's office number. What was going on? He decided to wind the pace back to a point where he could manage a phone conversation.

"Where's the fire?" he asked Joel.

"Where are you?" Joel returned. "You sound like you're out of breath."

"I'm at the gym, on the treadmill. I wouldn't have answered, but there was a raft of calls all at once. Is something wrong?"

"Mate! Have you not spoken to the boss?"

"There was a call from the station, but I haven't returned it yet."

"Well, get off the phone and call him back."

Joel disconnected the call abruptly.

"Idiot," Cam said under his breath. Why couldn't he just have said what the commotion was about and saved him having to make another call?

He slowed the treadmill right down and allowed his heart rate and breathing to return to a resting pace. Wiping sweat from his face and neck, he threw the towel onto his gym bag. He took out his mobile phone and pressed the missed call number, the police station first.

"I missed a call from the office," he said to the on-duty sergeant who answered the phone. "Do you know who called?"

"Hold on, I'll check."

Cam was annoyed at being placed on hold and wondered if it was worth breaking his training to answer this call.

"Cam?"

It was the chief inspector. What more trouble could he get into, beyond the administrative leave?

"I missed a call from the office."

"Have you heard from your lawyer?"

"Not recently," Cam said, "though I think he tried to call me a few minutes ago."

"Well, get off the phone and call him back."

What was with his work colleagues? Why couldn't they just tell him what was going on? Like Joel, his boss didn't wait for Cam to ask clarifying questions but hung up.

"Fine, I'll call the lawyer."

It was annoying that he'd chosen the wrong order to return the calls.

"Cameron?" George Reed spoke the moment the call connected.

"Sorry I missed your call," Cam said.

"Did you listen to the voice mail?" George asked.

"No, sorry. Just called you back."

"It's over," George said.

"What's over?"

"The court case. The aggravated assault charge. It's over. Gone. No more."

Cam felt the bottom fall out of his stomach.

"Cameron? Did you hear what I said?"

"I don't understand."

"Mr. Telford has dropped the charges, so the case cannot be taken to court."

What was going on? Cam couldn't understand it. He began to feel dizzy.

"You all right, mate?" One of the gym trainers came across and put his hand on Cam's shoulder. He must look bad for a bloke to be so concerned.

"I'm all right," he replied, though he reached a hand out to steady himself against the wall.

"You don't look great. Better sit down for a minute," the trainer said.

"You still there, Cameron?" George's voice continued to come from the mobile phone that was now away from his head. The trainer took the phone out of his hand and put it to his ear.

"Your man isn't looking so good at the minute," the trainer said into the phone. "I'd like to check him out and make sure he's not having a heart attack or something. He'll call you back later."

Suddenly, Cam found himself sitting down, a bottle of sports drink thrust into his hand. The trainer took his pulse and checked his pupils and announced he didn't think it was a heart attack, but he still wasn't happy.

"I'm calling an ambulance," he said.

"No. That's fine." Cam felt embarrassed by the attention.

By this time, he'd attracted a small group of onlookers.

"Call the ambulance." A female trainer had joined in. "You can't take chances with these macho guys who never take care of themselves."

It was too late to stop it. The ambulance arrived before Cam had a chance to gather his thoughts and, before he knew it, they'd hooked him up to heart monitoring equipment and blood-pressure cuff.

"I've just had a shock, that's all," he tried to explain.

"Better to be safe than sorry," the young female paramedic said to him, as she analyzed the results.

"Do you think you need to take him to hospital?" the trainer asked.

"That's our procedure. Any hint of heart attack has to be checked out." The paramedic waved her partner, wheeling a stretcher, over to where Cam was seated.

What were they talking about? He'd just finished a heavy workout session, then taken a call that had shocked him. He still wasn't sure he understood what George had said.

"Who can I call?" the trainer asked.

"Constable Joel Baker, he works out of the southern areas police station," Cam replied. He doubted he was having a heart attack, or a stroke, or an epileptic fit, but the paramedics had him in hand and he didn't have the confidence to fight them. He had ambulance cover. He'd take a trip to the hospital and Joel could bail him out.

As the ambos loaded him into the back of the ambulance, he debated which was more humiliating—being stuffed into the back of a police car in handcuffs or being strapped to an ambulance gurney, bare-chested with electrode pads stuck all over him, and a female paramedic constantly monitoring his vital signs.

"I think I'm fine," he said as she sat in the seat next to him in the back of the ambulance.

"We'll let the doctors decide."

Brilliant.

"Do you mind if I make a couple of calls?"

"It'd be better if you didn't. Just wait until the doctors have run some tests."

Cam took a deep breath. He concentrated on his chest. Did it hurt? It was a bit tight, but then he'd just been doing some heavy weights, prior to the running, and he was usually a bit stiff after a workout. His breathing didn't hurt. He was now in a half-recline and didn't feel dizzy anymore. What on earth had George said? He wanted to believe the charges had been dropped, but he was too scared to buy into that just in case he was getting hopeful for nothing. But what if it was true?

"Are you all right?" the paramedic asked.

"Why?"

"Your heart rate just increased."

"I've been under some stress lately. I was just thinking about something."

She pursed her lips and nodded. This was ridiculous.

By the time they had rolled into the emergency ambulance bay, Joel was at the back of the ambulance waiting when the door was opened.

"Mate! Are you all right?" Joel asked as he walked with the gurney into A and E. He was apparently still on shift as he was in full uniform. His presence wasn't questioned as he followed the team inside.

"It's nothing," Cam said. "I just had a bit of a dizzy spell straight off the treadmill."

"What are all the heart monitors about?"

"You know if someone says the word 'heart-attack' they won't let you go until they're sure it's not."

"Sir, if you could let us attend to the patient." A young doctor spoke to Joel.

They wheeled Cam into one of the cubicles and left Joel standing in the corridor.

"Shall I call your mother or Megan?" Joel asked before they pulled the curtain to shut him out.

"No. There's nothing to tell them. Just wait a bit until they let me go."

Waiting for a bit turned into four hours. After an electro-cardiograph, a chest x-ray and a blood test the doctor returned to speak to him.

"Have you been under a lot of stress lately?" he asked.

"And then some," Cam replied.

"The good news is there is nothing wrong with your heart."

Surprise. Cam wanted to make a sarcastic comment but decided it wouldn't be helpful.

"I'd suggest you need to do what you can to lessen the amount of stress you're under."

"Good idea." He couldn't help it. Sarcasm was the only response he felt capable of since he'd been kidnapped by paramedics.

"I'll send someone in to sign the release paperwork and then you can go. Do you have someone who can give you a lift home?"

Cam nodded. Joel had gone to the hospital café to eat dinner. While he'd been waiting for results, Cam had managed to talk to him about the phone call. Joel seemed to think it was true and that the boss wanted him back at work, but Cam was reluctant to believe it until he saw the paperwork in front of him. Still, he was hopeful.

"Look what I bought you from the hospital gift shop," Joel said as he walked into the cubicle. He held up a bright red t-shirt with a corny medical joke on it.

"Excellent."

"You could go home naked. You should thank me."

"Thanks, mate. I need to drop by the gym and pick up my gear and my car."

"And then you need to call your lawyer back and hear it from him. This business with Megan's ex-boss is over. Trust me."

"I hear you. I'm hoping it's true, but I'm finding it hard to believe."

"Yeah, well, you never were very quick on the uptake."

Cam didn't reply. He was surprisingly tired from the day's ordeal.

"Are you gonna call Megan?"

Was he? He just wasn't sure about her anymore. Too much had happened since they'd actually gone out together, and none of it had been good. That hadn't been her fault, but he didn't know how she felt or what she wanted. And he still wasn't sure he had fully dealt with all the mental stuff Shane had thrown at him.

"I'll take that as a 'no'," Joel said. "I'm sorry. I thought you really had something there."

"I'm not sure, so let's just leave it for the moment."

He couldn't think about Megan. Not yet. Even if George's news was true, he still had to sort his head and heart out.

Once Joel had dropped Cam off at the gym, he gathered his gear from the locker, but couldn't find his t-shirt. He should be thankful he had the gaudy red shirt to wear, but it didn't fit with the image of a confident, well-adjusted officer of the law.

He retrieved his phone from the gym bag and looked at the unread messages lined up in the inbox. His boss wanted him in at the station pronto. He'd better go and face the music sooner rather than later.

"Glad you could make it," the chief inspector said, once he got into his office. "Love your shirt."

"I've just been released from hospital."

Cam tried not to grin at seeing the shock on the boss's face.

"What for?"

"Suspected heart attack." He was being cruel, and he knew it. He was as fit as a mallee bull, but it was true he'd been delayed by the hospital trip.

"Are you all right?" Was that care and concern in his tone?

"My heart's fine. They think I just had a few symptoms because of stress."

"Well that should be sorted out now, shouldn't it?"

"I didn't finish the phone call with my lawyer when the dizziness came on, so I'm not really sure what the verdict is."

"Your trash-talking stalker has withdrawn the assault charge, so you won't be going to court."

By the tone of his voice, Cam sensed a major 'but' coming. Not quite time to rejoice yet.

"Just because this won't go to the magistrates court doesn't mean it should not be dealt with. There was evidence that you actually assaulted the man."

Cam nodded. "I did."

"Yes, and having read the report you filed, I understand you were extremely provoked by what he said to you."

"It wasn't an excuse. I understand that."

"You're correct. But do you understand, particularly as this was a personal situation for you, that you should have called in back-up?"

"He was on her property, looking through her windows."

"It would have been legitimate for you to call in and put yourself back on duty to take action, but given the personal nature of it, you needed one of the team there with you."

"I know that in hindsight. At the time, he knew my weak spot and went straight for it."

"Your weak spot being the woman?"

"Megan is her name." Cam felt a charge of emotion. Megan wasn't just 'the woman'. She was a special and beautiful person.

"That's all very well, but you know we can't just turn a blind eye to the incident, no matter how justified you felt."

"I don't feel justified. I'm sorry I lost my head. I know you need to take action."

"Quite so. As you haven't acted in accordance with police values and what we represent, I need to impose some penalties. Do you understand?"

"Yes."

"You will need to pay a fine and you will be demoted from senior constable first class, to senior constable."

The chief inspector looked at him with his eyebrows raised as if he expected him to object. He wasn't going to. A fine and a decrease in pay was a whole lot better than a couple of years in jail.

Chapter Twenty-Four

Josiah's clothes hung on him, but he didn't want to waste time going to a tailor to get a new suit two sizes smaller. Mr. Gullington had negotiated with the governors of the prison hulk and he'd been released. The first stop had been to an inn where Gullington supplied him with clean clothes and soap.

"Could we not get straight on the road?" Josiah had asked.

"My apologies, Lord Landown, but you look and smell like a convict."

That was because he had been a convict until several hours ago. He had gotten used to the appalling smell.

After the bath, he went to a barber where the months of shaggy facial hair were shaved and his hair trimmed in the style of a fashionable gentleman. But nothing could be done about his gaunt condition. He was weak from months of poor food, no light or fresh air, and little to no exercise. He looked awful in the baggy clothes, but he was not about to wait around to fatten up.

"Could we get underway to Rosedown Park?" He was chafing to get out of London and back to the country home where the woman he loved was waiting—he hoped.

"We will go first to Lady Wordall's home in Grosvenor Square."

Josiah didn't have the energy to object. If it were Lady Wordall's wish that she see him first, as she had paid the investigator, then he would go.

But what on earth was causing the delay in getting them together? It had been two days and Louise had not heard that Cam had been let off the hook. If that Telford fellow hadn't dropped the charges, she would do as she had threatened and send that media release. The whole situation was affecting her work and she needed to clear her mind so she could finish Josiah's and Rosalie's story.

"Why are you so restless?" Russell asked as she left her office and walked past his office door.

"Why do you say I'm restless?" She paused and put her head in the door.

"That's the fourth time in the last half hour you've got up from your desk."

"Is it?"

"Something's bugging you, I can tell."

That was her man. He could tell after thirty-three years of marriage. Funny how he couldn't tell when she wanted him to take the rubbish out.

"Are you going to tell me or just continue to haunt the hallway?" he asked.

"I should have heard from Cam by now."

"Why?"

"I told you how I visited that Telford fellow."

"Yes, you told me, but even if he fell for your little intimidation tactic, why would Cam call you? How would he know what caused Telford to change his mind?"

"I guess you're right." Louise deflated like a soggy balloon.

Russell raised his eyebrows at her.

"There's no need to look at me in that tone of voice. I tell you when you're right."

He gave a stifled laugh and turned back to his drawing board. "Call his mother," he said without looking back.

"Good idea! Russell, you're on fire this afternoon."

She turned back to her office to get her phone.

"You could reward me with a kiss or something!" Russell called after her.

"I don't want to disturb you while you're working."

She heard him mumble something else, but her focus was on solving the mystery about Constable Cameron Fletcher. She was trying out ideas of what she might say to Janine Fletcher as she found her phone number and entered it into her phone.

"Hello, Janine," she said when the call connected. "This is Louise Brooker."

"Hello, Louise." She sounded surprised. Well, it wasn't like they'd pretended to be best friends or anything. "How are you?"

Moment of truth. Should she dither about with pointless small talk or come straight to the point?

"How is Cameron?" she asked. "I've been worried about him."

So, straight to the point. She didn't have an alternate story to go with in any case.

"It's funny you should call," Janine answered.

"Oh?" Did her surprise sound fake? It was fake, but that wasn't the point.

"Yes, he came home last night and told me he was going back to work because the charges have been dropped."

"Really?" That elation wasn't fake. Her tactic had worked. "Did he say what happened?"

"Apparently his boss took the matter in hand and has taken disciplinary action as a result of internal investigation."

"Oh?" Was that better or worse than going to jail?

"He is so relieved at only having a demotion in rank. It's been a stressful time for him."

"I can imagine."

"And I'm relieved. He's a good boy—man, I should say—I doubt I would have managed after my husband died if he hadn't come to help me get used to the loss. Wondering if he would be found guilty of that assault was a real worry."

"I'm glad to hear the good news. We've all felt bad about how it happened while he was trying to defend Megan's honor."

"She seems like a nice girl," Janine said. "It's a shame it hasn't worked out between them."

"Oh? I thought he had pulled back because of the court case."

"Well, I'm sure I don't know. You know how these young people like to work their own lives out. I don't like to interfere."

Louise held her tongue. If she hadn't interfered, they would never have met. And if she hadn't interfered, Cam would still be under the cloud of a criminal court case. In theory, she agreed with Janine, but she wasn't sorry she'd used her position to influence the outcomes.

"Anyway, I'll tell Cam you called."

"Yes, please do. Tell him we're all pleased he has been reprieved. And I personally am thankful that he involved himself to help Megan get a resolution to the problem with her boss."

"Thank you, Louise. And thanks for calling."

"What did she say?" Russell called out.

Louise closed her phone and walked back to her husband's office. She stood inside the door but didn't say anything.

"I don't like that frown on your face. Didn't your plan work?" Russell said.

"No."

"What? So that man wasn't scared off by your threat to expose him as a sexual pervert in a national magazine?"

"Yes, he dropped the charges."

"Well, what's the frown about?"

"I haven't heard from Megan, which means she hasn't heard from Cam, which means my plan didn't work."

"Good heavens, woman. What was your plan?"

"To get Cam and Megan back together."

"They weren't together in the first place, remember?"

"They were well on the way until that stupid incident tipped everything off track."

"Leave it alone. If it is meant to be it will be."

Louise let out a frustrated breath and left his office.

"That shows how much you know."

"Leave it alone, Louise." Russell's voice followed her down the hall.

* * *

Megan was making progress with Pete's accounts and filing, and she had her professional voice when speaking with potential clients and arranging quotes down to a tee. And finally, she was making headway with the invoicing.

Thanks to Dad's regular meetings with her and help sorting out legal representation, her confidence was growing almost back to her pre-Shane state. She still had the police on speed dial but thankfully she hadn't seen hide nor hair of the revolting man.

The one fly in her ointment was she hadn't heard from Cam. She understood what her Dad had said about the court case but couldn't help hoping he might still call her as a friend. Pfft. Friend. She wouldn't be happy with friendship status. Best to be honest about it. It was such a pain that their opportunity to explore a relationship had been swallowed up by drama. She wished she could call him up and meet for lunch, and just encourage him.

Her mobile phone rang and she had a moment of anticipation—perhaps he was calling just as she was thinking about him. She looked at the screen.

Mum.

Was it wrong to feel so disappointed?

"Hey, Mum. What's up?"

"Why do you always ask me if something's up? Couldn't I just be calling to say hello?"

"It's just a saying," Megan said, feeling annoyed that her mother always asked that same question. She should remember to get another phone greeting in line for when her mother called.

"Anyway," Mum continued, "I just heard from Janine Fletcher that Cam has some good news. Has he called?"

Megan felt the rock of disappointment get heavier and sink to the bottom of her stomach.

"I haven't heard from Cam since we were over at your place for dinner a couple of weeks ago."

"Oh." Megan heard her mother's disappointment, but it hardly matched her own. Why hadn't he called if there was good news? It just supported the theory that he'd decided there was nothing worth pursuing between them.

"Do you want to hear it?" Mum's voice rode over the top of her melancholy thoughts.

"Sure."

"The charges have been dropped, and he's going back to work."

"What?" A jolt of elation bounced off that rock and shot up through her chest. "What does that mean? Does he still have to go to court?"

"No. Without a charge, there's no case to answer in court."

"Who dropped the charges?"

"Only the person who brought the charges can drop them."

"You mean Shane dropped the assault charge against Cam?"

"Didn't I just say that?"

"But *Shane*?"

"Apparently, he had a change of heart."

Megan went silent. The Shane she knew never let up. If he felt he could get his way, he would pursue it to the end—he'd move in several doors down, stand on her lawn and gawk in her windows.

"That seems very unlike him. I don't trust him. He could be playing a game."

"He's not."

"You sound very certain."

"I am."

"Mum! What did you do?"

"It doesn't matter. The point is, Shane is unlikely to renew the charges as he values his business reputation too much, and exposure in national media is not something he was looking for—not in the format I presented it, anyway."

"You're impossible," Megan said.

"Megan, that man had no intention of letting Cam off the hook. He would have pursued it to the point of seeing him behind bars for the maximum sentence. He needed to see sense."

"The sense being …?"

"That he's lucky he's only being sued for damages and that people should know about his perverse ways, and if they surface again, I won't be so quiet about it."

Megan had a million different emotions warring inside. Why hadn't *Cam* called her to let her know? Was he really free of the charges? Would Shane really back off and leave them—her—alone? How embarrassing that her mother had to meddle in everything.

"Are you there?"

"Yes, Mum. I'm here."

"You don't sound pleased."

"I am pleased that Cam is free."

"But you're disappointed that he hasn't called."

"Of course."

"Perhaps if I call …"

"Wait. Stop." Megan suddenly found her voice. "Look Mum, I know you thought Cam was a great catch and set us up. And he was—is—a great catch, but I don't want you to interfere anymore. If there's ever going to be anything happen between us, I want it to happen between *us*. You need to leave it alone now."

Now her mother went silent. Had she hurt her feelings? Probably.

"I'm sorry if that hurts you. We had fun at first, and it really did put the wind up Shane, probably too much, as it turns out. But now that everything has happened I think it's best if we just leave it— leave him—alone. If he ever wants to call me, he has my number."

"I wouldn't say anything …"

"Mum! No! That's enough now. Leave it alone."

"You sound like your father."

"Well, he's not entirely stupid. You could pay attention to him for a change."

"Ouch. That's a bit harsh."

"You're right. Sorry. Look, I love that you are keen to see me happily settled in a stable and loving relationship. I want that too. But you've had your go with Cam. Just leave him for now and let things take their own course."

"What if I prayed about it?"

"Pray as much as you want, but remember, prayer is not about manipulating God to do your bidding."

"You really are being harsh today, Megan."

"I know. I'm sorry. But I just want Cam to make his own decisions where I'm concerned if he's ever going to call or visit."

"All right."

"Promise?"

There was a significantly long pause.

"Mum?"

"OK. I promise."

"I'm calling Dad and telling him to make you hold to it."

"Spoilsport."

"Go back to Josiah and Rosalie and sort their life out. You have complete control over them."

Chapter Twenty-Five

It was great to be back at work, and he was glad he'd been given the demotion and raking over the coals by the chief inspector. It meant there was no whispering behind hands, at the station, that they thought he'd got off lightly. Most of his mates knew the circumstances, and they were all keen to hear a report that Shane Telford had stepped over the line so they could arrest him and bring him in. But thankfully for Megan, there had been no sign of an infringement.

Megan.

She was never far from his thoughts, but he didn't dwell on her often. He wanted to but inevitably, once he thought of her and developing a relationship with her, Shane's words intruded from left field and damaged the purity of what he wanted. Cam called Pastor John and they had a meeting scheduled after work. He couldn't wait to talk about it.

"So you're saying that your thoughts keep straying to territory you consider immoral? Impure? What exactly?" John asked, once Cam had talked about his frustration.

"I keep thinking about what Shane said. He basically saddled me with his disgusting and perverted ideas, telling me I was no different from him."

"But you are different?"

"I hope so, but I have to admit in my younger years, I didn't protect my mind from certain images."

"Like, you mean, porn?"

Cam nodded. "I didn't know the dangers of it, and even though I knew my parents would have hit the roof, I didn't value their moral ideals back then. I just thought it was harmless entertainment."

"You think differently now, I assume."

"Mate, if I could destroy every porn website and magazine out there, I would. You wouldn't believe how young the boys are who are becoming addicted to it. Thankfully, I gave it up in my early twenties. These kids are shaping their whole view of intimate relationships based on the distorted and manipulated images that are put up. And the makers of these websites are often using and abusing young women who don't know what's happening to them."

"You've done some research on this?"

"I've seen too much in the force by way of sexual abuse to pretend this industry isn't an influence."

John took a deep breath. "You don't have to preach to me the evils of that particular industry. However, today, we have to look at how you're dealing with images and suggestions in your own mind."

"Yup. I don't want to live life like this. I don't want to be a Shane Telford. I want to love and respect my wife."

"So, you're serious about Megan Brooker?"

"Not until I get my head together."

"So you need to learn how to win the war in your mind."

"I guess that's one way to put it."

"Sitting and talking to me is a good step. When you bring something out from the hidden places into the light, it no longer has the same power over you."

"I guess that's true."

"Also, you need to not be quite so hard on yourself. You do realize that most people struggle with wrong thoughts?"

"Not like these."

"Maybe, maybe not. Bad thoughts take all different shapes and sizes."

"Do you have to battle with your thoughts?"

"I think we all do. I realize you having viewed some images and material means you have fed something there, but if we pray and repent of those things, and ask God to help us, I believe we can come to a place of even-keeled living."

"Do you think so?"

"Think of it like this—a bird can come and land on your head, but you don't have to let it build a nest there. Shoo it away. The same with wrong thoughts."

"That makes sense."

"Let me give you a couple of scriptures to keep handy to help you with this."

Cam waited while John wrote down a couple of verses on a piece of paper.

"I recommend you keep accountable with this for a while, just to help you work through that last situation. I think it affected you more than you know."

"I think you're right. Are you happy to keep seeing me?"

"It would be my privilege."

John prayed with Cam and, with the two Scriptures in hand, he left the office. Strangely enough, he felt more confident about the way he could manage his thoughts. He looked at the paper again before starting his car. 2 Corinthians 10:5. He could take every thought captive and make it obedient to Christ. He could do that. He would do that. The other scripture, Romans 7, was a huge encouragement. Apparently, the Apostle Paul battled with doing what he knew God wanted him to do and had to admit he needed the spirit of God to help him. If the Apostle Paul had felt overwhelmed by it all and had still managed to find a way through, surely he could as well.

The visit with Pastor John lifted Cam's spirits. He felt hopeful he'd be able to get on top of the things that had been threatening to poison his thoughts. He could and he would.

* * *

The last time Megan had broken up with a boyfriend, her high-school relationship of three years, she'd felt like her heart had been ripped out and it had taken months to get over the loss. That was one of the reasons she'd been reluctant to get involved in another relationship. Now twenty-eight, she should be mature enough to manage her emotions in a relationship. Mature or not, the phone silence from Cam was about to make her explode.

She'd told her mother to cease and desist but was tempted to call her back and ask her to reactivate Operation Cameron Fletcher. Why hadn't he called? She didn't call her mother, of course. Common sense told her that if Cam wanted to reignite the spark they'd felt, he would. But it was so depressing.

"You haven't cooked a proper meal in over a week," Chloe said as she opened the fridge and saw nothing.

"I don't feel like eating much at the moment."

"What's the matter?" Her sister came and sat down next to her on the couch, bless her.

"It's nothing. I just feel a bit blue."

"You've been doing so much better with your anxiety. Do you need to go back to see the doctor?"

Megan shook her head and gave a wan smile. "I'm all right."

"Is it because of Cam?"

"Did Mum call you?" Megan sat up and fired the question at her sister. It would be just like Mum to go behind her back.

"Calm down. I've spoken to Mum, yes, but not about Cam. Why? What has she done?"

"Then you don't know?"

"That he's going to court for an assault charge?"

Megan shook her head. "That was last week's news. Shane dropped the charges."

"Oh, that's wonderful. Why didn't you tell me before now?"

Megan slumped again and breathed out a deep sigh. "I thought he would have called to tell me."

"Well, how did you find out?"

"Mum called his mother."

Chloe shook her head and sniffed. "She is such a meddler."

"You would have done the same thing. Admit it."

"Not the point. Anyway, at least you know."

"Yes. I know. He's back at work."

"Are you sure?"

"Well, that's what his mother told Mum. So I assume he's back at work."

"But Mrs. Fletcher didn't tell you about the heart attack?"

"What?" Megan stood up this time. "What heart attack? What are you talking about?"

Chloe clapped her hand over her mouth and rolled her eyes from side to side in a suspicious manner.

"What do you know?" Megan pushed.

"I'm not supposed to say anything. Patient confidentiality."

"Well, you just did say something. Who had a heart attack? Was it Cam?"

"I shouldn't say."

"It was Cam, wasn't it? A heart attack. Are you sure?"

"Megs. I saw them wheel him in on a gurney. He had all the heart monitors on and they rushed him into a cardio unit straight away. They only ever do that with serious cases like heart attack."

"Did you go in and check?"

"He wasn't my patient and he had another cop with him."

Megan began to pace the lounge area. "Oh, God. Please let him be all right."

"Maybe that's why he hasn't called. Perhaps he was admitted to the ward."

Megan stopped pacing and faced her sister. "But his mother would have told Mum."

"Maybe this happened after Mum's phone call."

"Honestly Chloe, didn't you go in and check on him?"

"It was a ridiculously busy afternoon in A and E. I couldn't leave my patients, and when I went by his cubicle, the curtain was drawn."

"Is that a good or bad sign?"

"It really depends. He looked healthy and alert when they wheeled him through."

"What do you mean healthy?"

Chloe blushed, and Megan noticed. "What do you mean healthy?" she persisted.

"He's a nicely built unit, which was on display, since he arrived sans t-shirt."

"Chloe! Did you check him out?"

"It was difficult to miss."

"But he was alert?"

"He was talking to the cop as they wheeled him through the foyer. He didn't look too distressed."

"Then maybe he's OK?"

"Why don't you call him and see?"

Megan flopped down on the couch again and blew out a breath through her nose.

"I can't."

"Yes, you can. You have his number."

"I can't, Chloe. If he wanted to tell me, he would have called, but I haven't heard a peep. No text, nothing."

"Well, if I were you, I'd bake a cake and take it around to his house, and tell him you'd heard he's been sick. There's nothing wrong with caring about someone who's been ill, especially if it was a heart attack."

* * *

It seemed to be working. Cam had put the advice into practice and was brushing troubling thoughts aside like flies. He realized that the Apostle Paul had talked about walking in the spirit and not in the flesh, so when he tackled his thoughts, he prayed at the same time. He shouldn't have been surprised, but was, when he realised the thoughts had less and less power over his mind. *Thank you, Lord*.

His mother had just left the house for ladies fellowship morning, and he got ready for bed. He'd had a hectic night shift and hadn't been able to sleep when he got home until he'd done some paper-work and a couple of other chores that needed doing. Now he felt he could sleep uninterrupted for at least four or five hours. He put his phone on silent, pulled on his boxer shorts—bought specially to preserve his mother from shock should they encounter one another in the middle of the night—and got into bed. A quick prayer, and he felt his mind drifting.

Two seconds later, he jolted awake, his heart hammering in his chest. He glanced at the bedside clock and realized the two seconds had in fact been two hours, and someone was knocking at the front door. He wanted to roll over and forget it, but it persisted.

Who would bother to keep knocking? Energy and telecommunication companies and various religious callers usually moved on if you ignored them. Mum's friends knew she was at fellowship. Wait. Maybe something had happened to his mother. Despite the cotton wool in his head, he sprang out of bed and raced to the door.

"Megan!"

"Cam!"

It took a split second for him to see her standing on the doorstep holding a picnic hamper before he realized he was clothed only in his boxers. Thank goodness he had those on. It could have been worse.

"Sorry. I was asleep."

"Are you all right?" Megan asked, moving forward as if she was going to come inside. She *was* going to come inside. Should he stop her or go with it?

"I'm fine. I'd only just gone to bed."

"I heard about your heart attack. Should you be out of bed?"

What? Wait. Talk about crossed-wires. He couldn't have this discussion standing half-naked in the hallway.

"Go into the lounge and sit down. I'll go and put some clothes on."

"No. You should go back to bed. I don't want to go against doctor's orders."

"Megan. I'm fine! Go and sit down. I'll be two minutes."

She looked worried but eventually walked through to the lounge. He dashed back to his bedroom and found a pair of track pants and a t-shirt. His head was fuzzy at best. By the time he got back, he had to search for her, as she'd moved to the kitchen and was putting food containers from the hamper onto the kitchen bench.

"I brought you some soup and chocolate cake."

"If I'd really had a heart attack, should I be eating chocolate cake?"

She gave a strange look—alarm mixed with question.

"How did you hear about the heart attack?" he asked. "I haven't told anyone other than Joel."

"Chloe saw you when you came into A and E." The look of concern seemed to be etched into her face. She was really worried.

Cam frowned. This was ridiculous and he couldn't think clearly enough to form a sensible sentence.

"I know she wasn't supposed to say anything," Megan hurried on, "but when I hadn't heard anything from you, she let it slip you were probably unwell, following a heart attack."

"I didn't have a heart attack."

"But you were admitted to hospital?"

"I had a dizzy spell off the back of a hard training session, and the over-conscientious trainers felt it their duty to make sure it wasn't a heart attack."

"Are you all right?" Her tone of voice confirmed the concern he'd read in her expression.

"I'm fine. I suspect it was the shock of hearing about the end of the court case, and a combination of stress and stuff."

"So, you're all right?" She really wasn't hearing him.

"Megan, there's nothing wrong with me. I'm on night duty, so I sleep in the day. Well, I was trying to sleep."

Her expression changed. Now she looked embarrassed as she got up. "I'm so sorry. I shouldn't have come. I just thought you must have been—"

"Stop. Just sit down for a few minutes and let's make sure we're all on the same page." He was making a mess of this. If only he could gather his scattered thoughts.

Megan sat down again, but she looked uncomfortable.

"You brought me soup and a cake." He tried to smile. "I actually like cake."

"I'm glad."

Why had she gone all shy and reticent?

"Thank you for your concern. It was nice of you to think of me."

She had something ticking over in her brain. He could almost see the cogs turning.

"You want to say something else, don't you?"

She nodded.

"Shoot." That was smooth. His brain was fuzzy, and his brain was screaming for him to go back to sleep.

"I had thought there was something between us, you know, from before the incident. But when you didn't call, I got the feeling that whatever there had been was gone, and that you weren't interested in going any further. I've been trying to reconcile myself to that, and then Chloe told me about the … hospital visit."

"And you thought I hadn't called because I was sick."

She nodded. Were those tears gathering in her eyes?

"I can see now you're busy and … well, obviously we had a great time, but it's over now."

"Megan." He searched his foggy brain for something sensible to say. He was so tired he could hardly think straight. "I was facing a criminal charge with bail conditions that forbade me from coming near your place. Telford lives in your street, and I still want to kill him. I've just been demoted and I've been struggling with some personal issues. It's not you."

She nodded and pursed her lips. "That's OK. I'd better let you get back to sleep. I'm glad the court case is off, and that you're not sick."

She got up and took her picnic hamper from the kitchen bench. "I'll see you again sometime."

What had he just said? She was walking out and he couldn't figure out what he'd said wrong. He should call her back, but honestly, he'd really stuffed this up. He couldn't trust his brain to say anything sensible or sensitive and at a moment like this, he needed to be sensitive and alert. He watched sadly as she shut the front door after her. Good luck getting to sleep now.

* * *

'It's not you, it's me.' That was such a classic breakup line. Megan let the stupid tears stinging her eyes fall down her cheeks. Why had she let herself get so caught up in a faux relationship? Right from the very beginning, Cam had laughed with her about the game they were playing. It was a performance. He'd never meant it to be anything else.

She drove home caught up in a whirl of emotion and, by the time she got inside the house, she was a wreck.

She went inside and straight to her office. She would pull herself together. There was no way she was going to fall in a heap when her brother was relying on her to get his business functioning efficiently. And there was no way she was going to admit her embarrassment to Chloe. Seeing him standing there with just his boxers on, she knew why Chloe had checked him out at the hospital. But that was the end of it. She was like every other female who was attracted to a gorgeous looking man, and she would get over it.

"You keep telling yourself that," Chloe said later, after she got home. "You were not just attracted to him, you two were made to be together."

"That's nonsense," Megan said. "When did you ever see us together?"

"I saw how you were when you were hanging out with him. I've never seen you so happy in my life."

"Yes, but he doesn't feel the same way."

"Did he say that?"

Megan sorted through her memory to find the evidence Chloe asked for.

"Well did he? Because in all of the blah blah that you've just dumped on me, I don't recall hearing anything of the sort." Chloe had her in the cross hairs and wasn't about to let her off. "If he said he felt nothing for you, then by all means, get over him, but did he actually say it?"

"He didn't actually say it, in so many words." An arrow of hope shot through her chest, but she wasn't confident to grab hold of it.

"Well, what did he say?"

"He just listed all the reasons why he hadn't called."

"Which were?"

"The court case."

"That's gone. What else?"

"The demotion at work."

"And?"

"That Shane lived up the street from me and he wants to kill him."

"Didn't he say he was getting counseling, or something?"

Megan nodded.

"Well any counselor worth their salt will help him find a way to forgive Shane and cut him loose. That doesn't mean anything."

Megan did another scan for the evidence that supported her claim Cam wasn't interested, but came up short.

"He said he likes cake."

"There you go." Chloe slapped her knee and leaned back in her lounge chair.

"He likes cake. That doesn't mean he likes me."

"He does. Take it from me. He's just been sorting through stuff. Don't forget he's been under a cloud for the last month or so. It must have been awful feeling like a criminal and facing a possible jail sentence."

"I guess it would have been awful. I felt awful for him."

"If you ask me, all of his going on about having personal issues is really a cry for help."

"Chloe—"

"That's my opinion, and I'm sticking to it."

"Well, I've been sitting here all day full of misery."

"Why don't you tell him how you really feel? Tell him you're interested and that you won't take no for an answer."

"I don't think I could do that. I'm not that forward."

"Of course you are. Don't forget you are your mother's daughter."

Megan took a breath to speak, then shut her mouth.

"What?" Chloe asked.

"Actually, you're the one who's like Mum, with all her rush in and take-charge attitude. I'm not quite as bold." She got up from the couch and dropped her coffee cup in the dishwasher. "I need to think about it some more."

"You do that. I bet you don't sleep a wink tonight."

Megan went to her bedroom to get ready for bed. She needed to pray about it and think on it some more. She loved Cam, and she wanted him to know. But did she have the courage to risk it and tell him straight out?

Chapter Twenty-Six

Rosalie was miserable. Her father had brought her back from Italy and was once again plotting to find a suitable husband for her. The only silver lining to this state of affairs was that Lord Osmond was gone, suspected dead. But even this cloud had a dangerous storm behind it—Josiah was likely on the ocean bound for New South Wales, to a fate worse than death. If Osmond should turn up alive, as her aunt's investigator believed him to be, it would be the worst. Her true love was convicted for nothing and, in his place, the odious Lord Osmond. It was all too awful to think about.

"Excuse me, my lady?" Rosalie's maid curtsied just inside the door.

"What is it, Hannah?"

"Your Aunt Wordall has arrived and is waiting for you to greet her."

"I will be down directly," Rosalie said.

Aunt Wordall, bless her, was the only person who had taken steps to defend Josiah against the accusations. She had not heard of any new developments and had accepted the investigations had come to nothing. At least she had tried, despite Father's loud objections.

Rosalie checked her complexion in the mirror and pinched her cheeks. It wouldn't do for her aunt to suspect she was pining away in her room.

As Rosalie descended the large staircase to the ground floor, she heard her father's raised voice coming from his study. Who on earth was he lambasting this time? She walked past the door and into the *drawing room, feeling sorry for whoever was on the receiving end of his displeasure.*

"My dear girl," Lady Wordall stood up and crossed the room, her motherly arms outstretched to receive Rosalie in a warm hug. "It has taken me an age to get here, but at last I come with good news."

"Good news?" Rosalie stepped back and looked her aunt in the face.

"It is confirmed. Osmond is not dead. He is alive and well in France, hiding from the gaming debts he ran up here at home."

Rosalie felt her face pale. "Are you sure?"

"That he's hiding from his gaming debts?"

"That he's alive?"

"I have sworn statements from several reputable gentlemen who have seen him, and know of his whereabouts."

She was going to swoon. Rosalie stepped over to the chaise longue and sat down.

"He is unlikely to return to England, my dear," Aunt Wordall said. "He owes too much."

"But—"

"No buts. I will not allow your father to give you or your fortune to that man. I have too much proof that he would bring scandal and shame on your father's house. I'm sure you are safe from him."

Rosalie shook her head. "It's not that. Josiah is on his way to New South Wales. He might already be dead."

"Josiah is not dead, my dear—"

"Somebody called my name?"

Rosalie looked to the door at the sound of the beloved voice. Josiah. Standing in her drawing-room. Alive.

Should she faint? It was ridiculous, females fainting all over the place. But her corset was probably laced so tight she probably had to faint. And a good faint was of no use if the hero wasn't within catching distance. *Oh bother, I'm going to have to get him closer to her. She should still be standing up.* There were so many problems to sort out.

Louise closed her laptop. Sorting out Josiah and Rosalie had lost its charm. She wanted to sort out Cam and Megan. But she'd been given a cease and desist order in their case and Russell had backed it up.

She picked up her mobile phone. Nobody said anything about calling her daughter to see how she is going. It was a mother's job to be caring and concerned.

"Hi, it's me."

"Yes, Mum. It shows up on the caller ID."

"Just wanted to know how you're feeling."

"I'm all right."

Silence. What did that mean? The best guess was anything *but* all right.

"Are you going to elaborate?" Louise asked.

"Are you going to meddle?" Megan asked.

"I would never—"

Megan laughed outright. "You're classic, Mother. Your whole mission in life is to meddle."

"But I respect that you've asked me to leave you and Cam alone, so I'm just calling you, my daughter, to see if you're OK."

"I'm OK."

She could hear a 'but'. It was louder than any other word Megan had spoken. Louise waited for it to come, but it stalled.

"Anything else you wish to say?" Louise asked.

"Oh, all right," Megan gushed. "Should I let him know how I feel or just wait for him to contact me? And what if he doesn't contact me? Does that mean he doesn't care about me or does he think I don't care about him?"

"Are you sure you don't want me to meddle?"

"No. Yes. I'm sure! No meddling."

"Are you open to advice?"

"As long as I'm not obliged to take it."

"It's just advice."

"Go on, then."

"Let him know how you feel. Women have fought too hard and too long in the last two hundred years to emerge from a place of pathetic dependency for you to sit by the phone wondering. Communication is a two-way thing. You don't need to wait for him to call you."

"But what if I put myself out there and he rejects me?"

"That is usually the risk the man takes—historically and traditionally. If you're prepared to hear a 'thanks, but no thanks' and you think you can take it, let him know how you feel."

"I'm not sure if that's good advice or not."

"What did Chloe tell you?"

"To send him a text and not take no for an answer."

"Well, you could let the poor man have the option of saying no if he wants. It really depends on whether you're prepared to hear the answer."

"What if he says yes?"

"Are you prepared to hear *that* answer?"

"I think so."

"Well, I'm leaving it up to you."

"Seriously? You're not going to invite his mother over for a bogus book signing or something?"

"I'm cured. Your father has put his foot down."

Megan laughed again.

"I don't know why you find that funny," Louise said.

"I'll let you know if anything develops," Megan said. "But you better keep your focus on your novel. Don't get your hopes up. It may all come to nothing."

Louise hung up. Get her hopes up? As if. She went back to the computer. She had to get Rosalie standing up so she could faint properly, and needed to get Josiah positioned so that he could catch her in the nick of time.

* * *

Cam was working from his desk at the police station. He had paperwork to sort out and needed to schedule some interviews from certain witnesses. It wasn't his favorite job, but it had to be done. When his watched buzzed, alerting him to an incoming communication, he checked to see if it was important.

Megan.

Well *she* was important. He wondered if she'd responded to the text he'd sent following yesterday's disastrous meeting. He hoped she'd understood why he wasn't properly connected. He was a little disappointed she hadn't replied straight away, having sent the apology last night.

Whatever today's message was, he couldn't look at it now. She needed his full attention and right at this moment he had work obligations. He ignored the text and turned his concentration to the job at hand.

"Constable Fletcher, you up for a reprieve from desk-work?" Joel stopped by, his hat and keys in hand.

So much for paperwork. A chance to get out on the road was exactly what he wanted.

"What's the job?"

"Some information has come in from last week's break and enter and someone needs to follow it up."

Cam looked at his desk and the pile of unprocessed paper and stood up. He wasn't sleeping at night anyway. He may as well worry about unfinished filing as anything else.

Pulling his police-issue baseball cap on his head and shrugging into his jacket, Cam picked up his phone and followed Joel from the office.

"How are you coping back at work?" Joel asked as they got into the squad car.

Cam shrugged. "I'm glad to be back even if I'm spending more time in the office. It's a whole lot better than facing jail time."

They got in the car and fastened their seatbelts. Cam's phone buzzed with another message and he looked. It was his mother this time. He noticed Megan's message still sitting there unopened and couldn't resist reading it.

Hi Cam,

I'm sorry to bother you, but I need to get closure on our time together—or not. Personally, I'm not keen to call it quits and walk away. I know you're not feeling good about yourself, but I'm interested in seeing where a relationship could go. Chloe thinks I should bring more soup around to your place and not leave until we've had a chance to talk properly. What do you say? I could be around there in no time at all.

"What's wrong now?" Joel asked.

"Huh?" Cam had been caught up in reading the text and how it made him feel.

"The text. Who's it from?"

"Megan."

"I figured."

Cam closed his phone and looked straight ahead. She wanted to talk. He wanted to talk, but it needed time, not a quick call on the fly? And it wouldn't be any use her coming around to his place now while he was at work.

"Are you going to talk about it or just sit there stewing?" Joel asked.

"She wants to talk about our relationship, to see if it's going somewhere."

"And your problem?"

"I had a conversation with her yesterday and totally botched it up."

"What are you talking about?"

Cam shrugged. "Not worth going into. I do need to talk to her, but … work … my focus needs to be here."

"You've got five minutes. Text her back and tell her yes."

"I guess it can't hurt to talk."

"Exactly."

"She said she was going to bring soup around."

"Soup?"

"To help me recover from the heart attack."

"You moron. Did you tell her it was nothing?"

"Of course. I'm not sure if she meant it about the soup. She's probably just teasing."

"If I were you, I'd go and see her as soon as possible."

"Great idea. I wonder how the chief inspector will respond to me clocking off early?"

"We could swing by after this other visit. Given the trouble with the bloke living down the road from her, it doesn't hurt to run past every now and then."

Joel pulled the car over in front of a house. "Hurry up with that text. We're here."

"Hold on a sec." Cam opened the message icon and noticed the text he'd sent her last night had a 'failed to send' notice in red. A bolt of panic surged in his gut. No wonder she hadn't replied.

"She didn't get my apology I sent yesterday."

"Hurry up," Joel said.

He'd better put her off coming around in case she was serious about the soup. He quickly typed a reply.

Don't come …

"I'm moving," Joel called. "We don't want folks inside to get nervous and tear out the back door."

Cam needed to move as well. He'd sort this out later. Pressing send he pocketed his phone and put his mind back on the job.

* * *

Megan's heart sank. Don't come. Nothing could be plainer. He wasn't interested in pursuing anything. Mum had warned her if she was going to put her heart out there, she had to be prepared to hear the answer, even if it was no. He'd said no.

She went straight to the fridge and found a box of chocolates that had been hidden at the back for an emergency. This was an emergency. No matter what Chloe said in the future, she was never, ever going to put her feelings out again. She was done with men.

She'd only eaten three of her favorite chocolates when she decided that eating her misery away was not a sensible solution. She had work to do and she would do the job for Pete to such a high standard that he would become the city's most successful builder or she would die in the attempt. Stupid man. Faking a heart attack so she runs over there with chocolate cake and pumpkin soup, then pours her heart out and all he can say is "don't come". Fine, she wouldn't go.

Megan gritted her teeth and decided not to think about Cam. Which was a doomed decision from the start. Her mother had warned her she had to be prepared to hear the answer. But she had been so sure there was something between them. Why couldn't she have read the signs like a normal person?

This sort of stewing went on for an hour, and Megan achieved little by way of work for Pete. She was reprieved from her stewing emotions by a knock on the door.

Trigger.

She was much better than she'd been weeks ago, but was still cautious. There was no way she was going to open the door blind. Who would be coming by at this time of the day? Should she ignore them, especially if they were just trying to sell something? Another knock on the door. Megan went to the front window and peered out. There was a police car in the drive. She let out a sigh of relief. At least it wasn't Shane.

Carefully sliding back the safety chain and unlocking the dead-lock, Megan opened the door.

"Cam!" All the unkind things she'd been thinking about him flew right out the front door. He was dressed in his full uniform, police-issue handgun strapped to his utility belt. My goodness, this man looked good in uniform.

"Megan." He was looking at her, trying to get her attention. Should she lock onto his gaze? If she did, he would see how she really felt. Too late to decide. Her eyes found his like a homing beacon and held fast.

"I'm interested," Cam said.

Megan had to fight the tractor beam that was threatening to draw her in. She needed to concentrate.

"Wait. What? Really?" She blinked to get her focus. His face broke into a grin, the corners of his eyes creasing as his eyes sparked. "Really?" She asked the question again, her voice pitched a couple of tones higher. This was such a turnaround of emotion it was hard to recalibrate.

He nodded and his grin held.

"What about the text you just sent?"

"Can we just forget all texts and conversations that have passed in the last twenty-four hours. Sending text messages is no way to communicate—especially when it's something really important that needs saying."

"What's so important that you need to say?" She needed to hear him say it.

"Ever since we pretended to be engaged, I've wanted to talk about making it real."

"Me too."

"I'm so sorry all of that other stuff happened."

"Me too."

"So you're open …?"

"I'm open to it all. Love, marriage—"

"Really?" Cam looked surprised.

Megan closed the gap between them and threw her arms around his neck. "If I don't move this along, our mothers will do it for us. I'd like to ask you myself, and have the answer without any interference from them."

"Well, when you put it like that." He slid his arms around her waist and pulled her closer. "But I'd like to ask *you*," he said. "That's the traditional way."

"Could you hurry it up?"

Cam laughed. "What about the traditional going-out-together for a while?"

"We already did that."

Cam's forehead creased with frown lines, though his gaze still held hers. "But that was just pretend."

"For you, maybe," Megan said. "I was sold the day you walked into my mother's dining room."

"You don't want rose petals and candles and proposals written in the sand?" he asked.

"What is this, a Hallmark movie?"

Cam shrugged. "I'd like a little more time for a Hallmark proposal. Do you mind waiting a bit?"

"Of course I don't mind. Just so long as I can start seeing you again."

"That's what I'm here for. We need to make a time where we can spend loads of time talking and making sure we're all on the same page and getting to know each other."

"And no more texting important stuff?"

"No more texting important stuff."

Megan threw her arms around his neck again.

"Aren't you going to kiss me?" he asked.

"You've got to be in charge of something," she replied.

* * *

"Excellent." Cam closed the gap and caught her lips in a full and passionate kiss. This was right. This was how things should play out. Not what that fellow down the street …

"Don't think about him," Megan said, drawing back just a centimeter. "Just you and me. No one else."

"How did you know I *was* thinking about him?"

"I could feel you becoming tense and worried. It's going to be OK." She placed her hand against his heart, which he could feel beating at an accelerated pace. She seemed so sure it would work out. He was willing to believe her.

Megan closed the gap again, but this kiss was interrupted by the sound of the siren of the police car. Cam waved his hand behind his back. Joel could wait. He had business to finish here.

"YOU'RE ON THE CLOCK!"

Megan pulled back as the words came over the police car loud speaker. She laughed. "You've already got a demotion. I can't have you getting fired altogether. How would you save for the future?"

Chapter Twenty-Seven

Josiah's smile was so intense his cheeks hurt. Rosalie's father had been given no choice but to give his permission for Josiah to marry his daughter. Lady Wordall had added her influence to make sure her brother-in-law saw sense. Josiah may have been the second son of a baron, but his father had not squandered their inheritance. Even as the second son, he had an estate and a comfortable living. Lord Osmond might have outranked him, but the man was penniless. He was also a scoundrel, but it was the argument about his income that finally won Rosalie's father over.

Still, as the pair approached him, Rosalie on her father's arm, the man still had a scowl that would have inspired terror a few weeks ago. This day, Josiah easily dismissed his new father-in-law's mood. He should be thankful his daughter was marrying a man of integrity and honor.

The minister spoke the words of the marriage liturgy. Josiah was aware of the solemnity of the occasion, but he could not remain straight-faced. Especially when he was called upon to declare his vow of faithfulness to his bride. She was his heart and his joy.

Louise closed the book, looked up and smiled at her audience.

"Of course there is more, but I will leave that for you to read once you've purchased your copy."

The crowd of people gathered in the busy city bookstore broke into enthusiastic applause. It had taken another year to get rewrites, edits and designs done, but finally, Josiah and Rosalie were free to meet the reading world.

"And while I'm here, and before I make myself available to sign your books, I wish to introduce you to one of my inspirations." She looked across to her daughter and son-in-law and waved them across.

"This is my daughter, Megan, and her new husband, Senior Constable Cameron Fletcher. If you look very carefully, you will see Josiah in him."

Cameron blushed furiously and Megan laughed. She whispered something in his ear. Louise was irked that she couldn't hear it.

"But seriously, I would like to welcome Cameron to our family, and thank him for being a model of honesty and integrity in our community."

More applause. Then Pamela, the PR person from her publishing house, stepped forward and took the microphone.

"Luella Linley will be here for the next hour and looks forward to meeting you when you bring your copy of *Landown's Love* for her to sign. Thank you so much for coming today."

Louise stepped over to Megan and Cam. "Sorry about that."

"You are not," Megan replied. "You meant every word of it."

"The day you pulled me over for speeding," Louise looked at Cam, "I said to myself, that man looks like Josiah."

Megan laughed again and Cam gave a sheepish sort of grin.

"And I also said to myself, that man would be a great son-in-law."

"Now how could you have known that?" Megan said. "You were totally judging the book by its cover."

"True. But I was right, wasn't I?" She looked at Megan.

"I wouldn't know. He's *your* son-in-law. He's *my* husband."

"Do you need a rescue?" Russell came up to the group. "I'm off to the café for a coffee."

"Thanks, Russell," Cam said. "I'm tempted, but I'd best not desert my wife at the first sign of trouble."

"Suit yourself."

At that moment Pamela stepped over to the family group. "The table is set up for you to sign books now, Luella. Are you ready?"

"The fans await," she said. "Thank you for coming, Cam."

"It was my pleasure, Mother."

Louise felt a warm glow in her chest as she walked away from her family. She had organized this and it had taken some doing. They were still talking and she could hear what they were saying.

"She totally favors you," Megan said to Cam. "You can do no wrong."

"While I can trade on Josiah the hero, I may as well."

"Suit yourself," Russell said. "Coffee?"

Coming soon - 2021

Book 2 in the Luella Linley – License to Meddle series

In Want of a Wife

by Meredith Resce

The temptation to matchmake is too much to resist. Louise has one success already under her belt having introduced her other daughter, Megan, to her new husband. Now this handsome, successful lawyer has just admitted he isn't married. Single and in possession of a large fortune, Michael Sullivan must be in want of a wife. Louise's second daughter, Chloe, would be just the right sort of woman for him.

There is no way Chloe will let her mother organize a blind date for her like she'd done for her sister. Chloe has her principles—and she has a ridiculous, unjust speeding ticket. The person she needs is a lawyer to help argue her case in court. Is it dishonest, when her mother's lawyer calls and asks her on a date, to agree with ulterior motives?

Michael Sullivan has ulterior motives of his own. This all expenses paid trip to the sunny Gold Coast is merely a case of one person helping the other out—isn't it? Everyone else might think they're a couple, but it's just about winning a court case—isn't it?

Can Regency romance author, Luella Linley (AKA Louise Brooker) hit the target twice in a row? Meddling in her adult children's lives is almost as much fun as creating fiction characters, except her children have minds of their own and don't always cooperate.

Book 3 in the Luella Linley – License to Meddle series
All Arranged

by Meredith Resce

Mother of three adult children, and Regency romance author, Louise Brooker (AKA Luella Linley) should feel satisfied that she has been instrumental in getting her two daughters happily settled. Her meddling was successful but came at a price, and husband, Russell, has advised she leave the children to their own devices.

But her eldest, Pete, is thirty-five, living back at home and discouraged. His fiancée left him days before the planned wedding and six months on, Pete still hasn't recovered. Louise might be biased, but her responsible, hard-working and handsome son would make a good husband and father—but he's given up after three failed relationships. He is a good catch, but unlikely to be fooled by his mother's scheming and meddling as she did with his sisters.

This situation calls for something special. A direct approach. Just like in her novels. Let the parents do the arranging and sort out the wheat from the chaff. This method will take any risk of rejection out of the equation, and let's face it, a mother can tell what's needed for a successful long-term relationship.

Carrie Davis dedicated herself to her career long ago. Her one and only serious relationship was a disaster, put down mainly to her youthful naivety at the time. Up until the birth of her niece, Carrie had not considered she might even like a relationship, but now thoughts of loneliness are stalking her. Carrie's sister, Ellen, knows and when she sees an odd advert in the classified ads, she begins to wonder if this is a prank or an opportunity sent from heaven. "Wanted. For a social experiment. A family arranged marriage."

Also by Meredith Resce
The Heart of Green Valley series
(Period drama romance set in Colonial Australia)

Book 1 – The Manse
Book 2 – Green Valley
Book 3 – Through the Valley of Shadows
Book 4 – Wallace Hill
Book 5 – Beyond the Valley
Book 6 - Echoes in the Valley

The Schoolmaster's Bride (Period drama romance)
The Schoolmaster's Daughter (Period drama romance)

Mellington Hall (Murder mystery)
Cora Villa (Period drama romance)
For All Time (A time slip novel)
How Sweet the Sound (Fantasy Allegory)
The Greenfield Legacy (Contemporary romance)
Falling for Maddie Grace (Contemporary romance novella)
Where there's Smoke (Contemporary romance novella)
Four Short Stories (paperback of four novellas)
Mortal Insight (Contemporary political crime under pen-name E.B. James)

About the Author

South Australian Author, Meredith Resce, has been writing since 1991, and has had books in the Australian market since 1997.

Following the Australian success of her Heart of Green Valley series, they were released in the UK.

Organized Backup is Meredith's 20th published title.

Apart from writing, Meredith teaches drama to high school students. She is an avid reader, particularly Christian fiction. She is a fan of British costume-drama television series, and British murder mystery shows. Jane Austen, L.M. Montgomery and Charles Dickens are favorite classic authors. Meredith is a country-girl at heart, and takes every opportunity to visit the farm where she grew-up.

Aussie rules football and cricket are her choice when following televised sport. Come on Aussies!

Meredith often speaks to groups on issues relevant to relationships and emotional and spiritual growth.

Meredith has also been co-writer and co-producer in the 2007 feature film production, "Twin Rivers" now available on Amazon Prime.

With her husband, Nick, Meredith has worked in Christian ministry since 1983.

Meredith and Nick have three adult children.

www.meredithresce.com
www.facebook.com/MeredithResceAuthor

Lightning Source UK Ltd.
Milton Keynes UK
UKHW010630121120
373270UK00002B/308